LADY FROM
ST LOUIS

Joan Hessayon

CENTURY
LONDON SYDNEY AUCKLAND JOHANNESBURG

Copyright © Joan Hessayon 1989

All rights reserved
First published in Great Britain in 1989 by
Century Hutchinson Ltd
Brookmount House, 62–65 Chandos Place
London WC2N 4NW

Century Hutchinson South Africa (Pty) Ltd
PO Box 37737, Bergvlei, 2012 South Africa

Century Hutchinson Australia Pty Ltd
89–91 Albion Street, Surry Hills, New South Wales 2010
Australia

Century Hutchinson New Zealand Ltd
PO Box 40–086, Glenfield, Auckland 10
New Zealand

British Library Cataloguing in Publication Data

Hessayon, J. P. (Joan Parker)
    Lady from St. Louis.
    I. Title
    823'.914 [F]

ISBN 0 7126 2513 5

Printed in Great Britain by
Mackays of Chatham

This book is for my granddaughter, Georgia Kathleen Norris

Acknowledgements

I am indebted to Peter Walne, Hertfordshire
County Archivist, and Mett Curtis, Hertfordshire
Assistant County Librarian, for their highly
specialized reading list and good advice; to Dr John
Earle for his straightforward private lecture on
social diseases, and to my old friend, Dr John
Llewelyn, without whose advice I could not have
attempted to create a nineteenth-century surgeon.
I would like to thank Constance Barry for her
splendid manuscript preparation, as always.
Finally, I must thank my daughter, Angelina
Gibbs, for her thoughtful comments, and my father,
Tom Gray, for his fact-finding on the other side of
the Atlantic.

1

Halfway across Piccadilly, Marjory stopped to shake horse-dung off the skirt of her smart grey costume. She hadn't noticed the puddle in the middle of the road. Now her shoe was wet and the skirt would need some careful attention. It had been raining for days, not heavily but with a depressing persistence that she thought of as typically, maddeningly English.

Five o'clock on a wet day in March was a singularly bad time to pause in the middle of this fashionable street. She looked up, saw a brewer's dray bearing down on her and dashed for the safety of the broad pavement directly in front of the Burlington Arcade. As usual, the traffic came at her from an unexpected direction. She quitted the road just as an ancient bay horse pulling a shabby hansom swerved to avoid her. The horse rolled his eyes and whinnied in fright, while the driver swore furiously in an accent that mercifully made his words incomprehensible.

'I'm too old for this sort of thing,' she muttered, pressing a hand to her heart to slow its frantic beat. Marjory was fond of saying she was too old for whatever bored or irritated her. But she was in excellent health, and at forty her skin was smooth, her teeth straight, white and all present, and her hair a deep chestnut with just a few strands bleached by time.

As she stood by the curb, trying to catch her breath, a filthy woman of about her own age shuffled up to her, one hand clutching a tattered shawl around her head and bony shoulders, the other hand outstretched in the universal begging attitude.

Marjory considered the pockmarked skin, the sunken

lips over toothless gums, the look of total despair in the eyes, and reached into her purse for a few coins.

'Excuse me, ma'am,' drawled a masculine voice beside her.

She looked up into a pair of supercilious grey eyes, noticed the well-tailored black frockcoat, the highly polished shoes, the neatly trimmed beard and moustache. Altogether, the man was the perfect antithesis of the dirty beggar woman.

'Is this old crone pestering you, ma'am?'

'You can see she's not,' said Marjory, pressing coins into the woman's coarse hand. 'I guess I can give some money to a beggar lady if I want to.'

The man's eyebrows lifted slightly as a knowing smile disfigured his thin lips. 'I gather you are an American, and so perhaps are not accustomed to our ways. These people can be very cunning. They dress the part, you see, and prey on the sympathies of good-hearted ladies like yourself. Why, I daresay she is richer than you or I.'

'Maybe she's richer than you are, but she'd have to go a long way to be richer than I am. Now go on about your business, mister, I know what you're up to. It's five o'clock, Burlington Arcade's right behind you, and the fancy women are hanging around, just waiting for you to come up and make your choice.'

The man gasped and flushed all the way up to the brim of his top hat. 'Madam, I assure you I am not here for the purpose you suggest!'

'Oh, no?' asked Marjory belligerently. 'You must be the exception that proves the rule. I've lived in London for two whole months and I've got this town figured out. It's dirty, it's noisy, and it's full to overflowing with fallen women and lascivious men.'

'I wonder you wish to live among us.'

'It's my duty to stay and civilize you all.' Marjory turned to share the joke with the beggar, but the poor woman was shambling off, having spied another likely candidate for alms.

The gentleman also felt it was time to leave. He backed away a few paces and raised his hat before remembering that this rude woman did not deserve so much courtesy. Turning round, he made off down the street in such a hurry that he bumped into half a dozen people within ten yards.

Marjory watched with satisfaction until he was lost from view, swallowed up among the top hats and saucy little bonnets of the people she had learned to call the *haut ton*.

She turned her attention to the triple arches of the Burlington Arcade and entered its echoing depths. Small-paned shop windows crammed with expensive *bibelots* held no fascination for her, however.

She scanned the passers-by until she spied two young women of extravagant dress and bold eyes who were ambling down the length of the arcade. Marjory's earnest advice to them, to mend their ways and find proper employment, met with a stream of abuse spoken so loudly and clearly that she understood every word. Undeterred, she moved on, philosophically accepting three or four such rebuffs until she found herself at the other end of the Arcade, which opened onto Cork Street. Then, at last, she remembered she was late and must get home as quickly as possible.

She was giving a ball this evening: forty guests, a generous supper and a five-piece orchestra. And here she was in Cork Street without the slightest idea in which direction to walk. Mary Beth had commandeered the family carriage for the afternoon, but there was nothing to stop Marjory from hailing a hackney cab. She was determined not to do so, however. Cabbies spoke a jargon that left her mystified and, therefore, certain that she was being cheated.

Turning back into the arcade, she cheerfully

approached two prostitutes who eyed her with suspicion.

'Excuse me, ladies, can you tell me the way to Cavendish Place?'

2

It was obvious that Frederick Bennett was a gentleman of refinement. He was born of a good family and had been reared among cultured people, but he never gave his social background a moment's consideration. He preferred to think himself classless and worldly-wise, blasé and unshockable as a result of his calling. Anyone who had spent thirty years working in a London hospital had encountered every conceivable type of human activity. As befitted a man of his profession, the doctor prided himself on finding some saving grace to excuse even the most unseemly behaviour.

So it was not true, as his son had suggested, that he was prejudiced against the cousins across the water. He was sure the United States of America was a grand country, and that General Grant was as good a president as America deserved. All Bennett had ever said on the subject was that he wished American visitors would not draw attention to themselves by their loud loquacity.

He generally found Americans ignorant and staggeringly naive. Secretly, he thought this was due to their having missed the civilizing influence of the British Empire at such an early stage in their nation's development. But that was a thought he kept to himself. He had told Marcus that a single American, encountered under the right circumstances, could be an amusing companion. It was simply that one did not care for them in large numbers.

Tolerant though he knew himself to be, he found certain Americans insufferable, even when unaccompanied by their compatriots. For instance, he could not extend his well-known charitable feelings towards his hostess, an over-confident American who had the ebullience of twenty people, a voice that rasped like sandpaper and a laugh which set the crystal drops in the chandelier quivering.

Just two hours ago, he had met her for the first time as she greeted her guests at the top of the narrow staircase. She had taken his hand firmly, shaken it with vigour and said: 'How do you do?' in a strong voice. He had thought: *I don't like this woman*, and had been observing her closely all evening.

As widows of forty went, she was quite attractive. Some people, he conceded, would call her beautiful. Her dark brown hair was thick and lustrous, and her eyes glowed with happiness and high spirits in spite of the fact that she was (surely!) still in mourning. In the circumstances, her black gown was indecently well-cut. The fashion, in this year of 1875, was for tightly fitting dresses with low bustles. He had to admit the style suited the American very well. He thought she looked like a ship's figure-head sailing triumphantly into port.

She was plainly a selfish woman. Otherwise, why would she lace herself so tightly that she actually managed a smaller waist than that of her Junoesque daughter? A mother had no right to play so cruel a trick on a female child of marriageable age. There came a time when a woman should give up the struggle to look young and beautiful in order to make way for her offspring.

The doctor rested his shoulders against the wall in this very small ballroom and glanced round him critically. Cavendish Place was a good address, but these rented houses tended to be rather shabby. Pitted mirrors between the windows reflected thirty or forty slightly bored people apparently waiting for something interesting to happen. He hoped supper would soon be served, and assumed the food would be lavish and over-

14

decorated. He would have difficulty finding something plain to suit his uncertain digestion.

But he must not be churlish. Bennett had been invited to this party only because his godson, Jeremy Grimshaw, had requested an invitation for him. Despite his reservations about Americans, the doctor was happy to be present. His wife had died almost five years ago, and he thought he knew what was due to her memory, but five years is a long time. It was very agreeable to be in company once in a while, to forget medicine and the sick.

The American widow had apparently met only those people to whom Jeremy had introduced her in his capacity as lawyer and adviser. There were very few persons present the doctor didn't know. Bennett had greeted several old acquaintances warmly, assured Jeremy's (also widowed) mother that she was definitely not suffering either from the smallpox or a heart condition, and had even met two young men who would most probably be consulting him in the near future.

Throughout this pleasant time, his eyes had turned repeatedly to his hostess as she flitted here and there. Had she been from New York where the wealthier inhabitants seemed to have some town polish, he would not have troubled himself about her.

She hailed from the wild mid-west, however, from St Louis in Missouri on the Mississippi river, where the men probably ate peas from their knives when they were not fighting Indians. The widow could not be expected to understand the code, the rules of etiquette which governed the better classes and by which they recognized each other in this greatest of all cities. Polite Society was undoubtedly laughing at her. In spite of his dislike of this American, his prejudice as Marcus would say, her connections with Jeremy made it imperative for him to put her right on an important point. He was surprised no one had already done so.

At that moment, the American laughed again as she raised her pince-nez to give some gentleman the sort of frank look only a foreign widow would resort to in her own home. The doctor winced.

'Are you enjoying yourself, Uncle Frederick?'

Bennett was startled; he hadn't seen his godson approaching. 'Yes, I am, Jeremy. Has our hostess provided a card room, by any chance?'

'Yes, sir, I believe she has, although she doesn't approve of gambling.'

'Aha! Compromising her principles in order to further her social ambitions.'

Jeremy laughed. He was a small, neat man of twenty-nine, still struggling to establish himself as a solicitor. His personality had been formed by his misfortunes: five older sisters, an ineffectual, hypochondriac of a mother and a will left by his late father which put his meagre inheritance in the hands of three pettifogging relatives until he was thirty-five.

The doctor was extremely fond of his godson, and often wondered why it was he could feel so much more at ease with Jeremy than with his own son, Marcus, who was the same age.

'She won't allow bets to be made in the card room, so I doubt if many men will bother to play,' said Jeremy.

'So she's a puritan!' snorted the doctor. 'Directly descended from the Pilgrim Fathers. Isn't that what these Americans always claim?'

'I believe so. She also disapproves of dancing and the drinking of strong spirits, but feels that enforcing her views at parties like this would damage her daughter's chances of catching a husband.'

'You must find her an irritating client.'

'Not really,' said Jeremy. 'She is sharper-witted than my sisters and much less old-fashioned than my mother. No, it is the daughter, Miss Mary Beth

16

Hanson, who occasionally makes me contemplate taking up another profession.'

'You have business dealings with the daughter? Whatever for? She must be no more than twenty-four or five!'

'She wouldn't thank you for saying so. She is just twenty-one and has the sharpest mind for business I have ever encountered in a woman. Her mother gives her complete freedom to spend as she chooses. That young woman has been making a fortune, well, a modest fortune, on the stock exchange. Naturally, I make the transactions for her. It really would not do for a woman to deal directly with a broker. To my certain knowledge, she has made a profit of three hundred pounds on her dealings in the two months since she and her mother came to live in London.'

'By Jove!'

Bennett looked across the room to where Miss Hanson, head and shoulders above the other young girls, was apparently instructing the glum members of the small orchestra. She was expensively dressed. Her ball gown of pink tulle exposed a pair of creamy shoulders, and strong arms beneath the short puffed sleeves. Around her neck, she wore a black velvet ribbon tied in a bow at the back. It was a fashion that several of the young women had adopted with great success. Unfortunately, Miss Hanson's ribbon merely served to emphasize the strength of her neck.

'She looks remarkably strong-willed,' said the doctor.

'Oh, she is, sir! What disconcerts me is that she is not at all like my sisters. She never cries in order to get her own way. She argues her case like a man. Damned unnerving! Only yesterday – '

A man in his mid-thirties joined them at this point, causing Jeremy to break off his sentence with a guilty start.

'Uncle Frederick, may I introduce Mr Lucius

Falkner? He is a portrait painter who will one day be as famous as Mr Millais.'

'Don't believe it, sir,' said Falkner. 'Grimshaw is the best of friends which is why he is a poor judge of my talents.'

The doctor's eyes narrowed as he studied Falkner carefully: tall, exceedingly slim, his fair hair far too long and bushy at the back, his evening suit showing signs of wear, his linen wilting. The man's skin was pale, but without a blemish. Bennett had a low opinion of the sort of lives led by artists, with their fondness for painting the nude and their belief that chloral or opium could enhance their creative powers. He felt certain they always consorted with their models, thus spreading disease and threatening the very foundations of society.

Miss Mary Beth Hanson joined the three men, breaking into their conversation with staggering rudeness.

'Will you excuse me, Dr Bennett? Mr Grimshaw, I would like to see you tomorrow morning at nine o'clock, if you please. Now, come along, Lucius. This is our dance. You are the most aggravating man! Don't you ever look at your dance card?' Thrusting her arm in Falkner's, she guided him towards the centre of the floor. 'I don't know how many of my friends you have offended by your casual manners this evening. How do you expect to be commissioned to paint them when you don't show them the particular attentions that mean so much to a woman?'

'I'm not the sort of man to pay compliments to women who don't interest me,' Falkner was heard to say just before the music began and drowned his voice.

'Disgraceful!' said the doctor. 'I would never have believed it if I had not seen and heard it. She called him Lucius! He allowed her to scold him! Is there something going on here? You didn't say they were engaged. But then, how could they be? I distinctly remember your saying that mother and daughter have been in London for only two months. Even an American girl cannot have formed an attachment in so short a time.'

'I introduced them, of course, and you're right, they are not engaged. Miss Hanson is rather too forceful. Poor Falkner fell under her sway the first time she sat for him. She is determined that he will succeed as a portrait painter, and I must admit that she has brought him some valuable commissions. You have just seen the price she exacts for her patronage.'

'One hears tales of American girls. Too much money and too little breeding, but I had not appreciated how serious it is. Our young women will be corrupted. Miss Quinn seems to be on friendly terms with this Amazon. I do hope you are making it your business to see that she is not spoiled by her association with Miss Hanson.'

'I have no control over Miss Quinn's movements, Uncle Frederick. I cannot afford to marry, as you know.'

'Well, no you can't, but you could become engaged. It may be five years or more before you can marry, but you could propose to the poor girl. Stake your claim, as it were. She is a charming young lady and *could* set the American girl a fine example. I'm afraid it would be the other way around, however. Miss Quinn's great charm lies in the fact that she holds no strong opinions on any subject and can therefore be easily moulded. You should be the one to do the moulding, Jeremy. Excuse me. I must speak to our hostess. She is alone for once.'

'Uncle, don't say anything that would – ' Bennett was gone; Jeremy raised his eyes to heaven and shook his head. He hoped no feathers were about to be ruffled. Frederick Bennett was a humourless man of rigid standards and towering intellect who didn't suffer fools

19

gladly. Although the American mother and daughter were not fools by a long way, Jeremy had no doubt his godfather would speak to them as if they were.

Marjory saw Mr Grimshaw's godfather crossing the ballroom and knew at once that he was coming to join her. He was very impressive. His baldness did not in any way detract from his appearance, possibly because he had a very well-shaped head and a small neat beard and moustache. What hair there was circling his head was brown, but his beard was slightly ginger. A firm mouth, a straight nose, peaked eyebrows and intelligent eyes, combined with height and the sort of bulk that was entirely appropriate in a man in his fifties, made him just a trifle overwhelming. She smiled at him, raising her pince-nez as if to see him better, but actually to put two small panes of glass between herself and those penetrating eyes.

'Ma'am, may I have a word with you?'

'Dr Bennett, is it not?' She affected uncertainty. 'I believe young Mr Grimshaw said you are his godfather.'

'That is correct.'

'My daughter and I are greatly in his debt. I just don't know what we would have done if we had not had him to help us on our way. Why, do you know, he even rented this house for us before we ever arrived from Yorkshire! Servants employed, carriage and horses provided. And he and his mother have intro-duced us to so many people! But, I'm sorry. Here I am running on and you had something special you wanted to say to me.'

The doctor looked about him. 'Yes, somewhere private? I don't wish . . .'

Marjory arched an eyebrow, then silently led him to a small empty room which had two square tables laid out with cards. She closed the door behind them and, to Bennett's consternation, turned the key.

'That door doesn't fit properly,' she said. 'Everything needs repairing in this house. I've locked us in so we won't be disturbed. You look pretty serious.'

'Madam, that was hardly necessary, although what I have to say is not something I would wish to discuss before others. As a visitor to our shores – '

'Oh, I intend to stay.'

' – you may not understand certain matters. Certain delicate matters of form. What I mean is: you simply must *not* call yourself Lady Marjory.'

'Is that what all this secrecy is about? Well, I'll be darned! But then, I'm just an ignorant American. Let's sit down, my feet hurt.'

Bennett sighed heavily, but he took a chair opposite Marjory at one of the card tables.

'Perhaps I had better tell you a little about myself,' began Marjory, putting her elbows on the table and leaning towards him. 'I was born in St Louis, Missouri in 1835. There now, I've told you my age which I wouldn't do to anybody but a doctor. In fifty-three I married Jonathan Hanson. He was an attractive devil. Well, you'll know that as you've seen Mary Beth. She takes after him. Not in brains; she gets that from my side of the family. Jonathan was an amiable man, but he hadn't the brains to bait a fishhook. His parents died when he was twenty-four, leaving him without a single living relative. My daddy – he owned the largest chandlers and emporium in St Louis – he sort of took Jonathan in and trained him to run the store. I was only eighteen, too young to have any sense, but I thought Jonathan was beautiful. I knew several young men, but Daddy thought I was headstrong and should be married off to keep me from getting into trouble.'

'I don't see what this – '

'Jonathan did his best in that direction, making sure

21

I stayed at home, I mean. Mary Beth was born a year after we were married and Samuel the year after that. We rubbed along pretty well, I guess, but Jonathan took sick and died just ten years later. I took the children and went home to my folks.

'I'm getting to the point, doctor, so just bear with me. Have you ever noticed how death haunts some families? My daddy died eight years and two days after Jonathan, which was a real shock because it was Momma who had consumption. Very bad, she was and didn't have long to go. Naturally, she was worried about leaving me and the children all alone. We had no family living closer than a thousand miles away.

'Now, about this time an Englishman came into the store asking for Daddy, not knowing he was already dead, and saying he had a letter of introduction from someone he had met on his travels. I guess he was hoping for a job, or perhaps a loan. Because of the letter, the manager sent him over to our house. The Englishman had a fancy way of talking that I hadn't heard before and he was ever so gentlemanly. His hair was white, but I didn't think he was all that old. Said his name was Lord Manton, and how were we to know different?'

'By Jove!' said Bennett.

'Momma just loved him straight away, and she hung on until we were married in the spring of 1873, then died about a month later. She said I'd met my match in Gilbert and she was right. I couldn't make him do a thing I wanted. After about a year, he talked me into selling the store so that we could all take off for England.

'I always wanted to travel and I'm not saying that I don't like England. I do. But mostly I was pleased about coming to this country because I wanted the best for my children. I thought one day Samuel would inherit his step-father's title and Mary Beth might grow

22

up and marry a lord of her own. You'll say I was ignorant and so I was.'

'Yes, well . . .'

'When we got to Gilbert's home in Yorkshire, I soon found out the truth. First off, he wasn't a lord at all, he was just a baronet. Back here in England he was quick to call himself Sir Gilbert, but it was all right for me to carry on calling myself Lady Manton. Then I found out he'd got this son, Peregrine, who would get the title when Gilbert died.'

'I know Peregrine. Unfortunate disposition – '

'Those were my first two shocks. There was more to come. Peregrine was twenty-eight years old, which made me say right out to Gilbert: "How old are you?" And he said: "Sixty-four." I had thought he was in his fifties, which was enough of an age difference. But twenty-five years! I said to myself, "I'm going to be a widow again one of these days, and thousands of miles away from home, too. Let's just hope there's some money left when the time comes."

'In those days, my income was five thousand pounds a year, which you can live on in this country right nicely if you haven't got a husband dead set on improving his property. Well, Gilbert improved his property – which is now Peregrine's property – and I grew poorer in the meantime. Although in fairness, I should say Gilbert hardly had time to touch the principal before he died. Besides,' Marjory laughed, 'my lawyer in St Louis made sure Gilbert never knew the half of what I had.

'I soon learned a few things about the English, and one of them was that you can't catch a lord on what's left over from five thousand pounds a year, at least not if your grandfather was only the owner of an emporium. I began to fret what would happen to Mary Beth.'

'Very wise,' murmured the doctor.

'Gilbert was a bit of a rogue, but he was full of fight and I pretty well fell to pieces when he died. I was sick

23

in bed for months. The children and I just lived quietly after that. I hardly saw Peregrine at all. He had inherited some money from his grandmother – she wouldn't leave it to Gilbert because he had married an American – and he travelled all the time.

'Then four months ago Samuel and I fell out. He took off back to America without even saying goodbye. He's only twenty and I thought I'd go crazy with worry until I had the first letter from him. Now he's travelling everywhere, as far as I can tell. I wouldn't know where to find him even if I went back home to look.

'Then Peregrine started cutting up rough. He was to be married, you see, and wanted the house all to himself. He had been at school with your friend, Mr Grimshaw, and he said – Peregrine, that is – that Mary Beth and I should come to London and see if we could find her a husband, and Mr Grimshaw could handle our affairs, as we wouldn't know how to look after ourselves.

'To cut a long story short, a few weeks ago we took this house in Cavendish Place. It's a good address, I'm told, and a lot more lively than back in Yorkshire.'

'Yes, but . . .' said the doctor, 'this is beside the point, ma'am.'

Marjory ignored his interruption. 'And now we come to the heart of the matter, Dr Bennett. I don't think I owe all that much to Gilbert's memory, do you? I was tricked when he called himself Lord Manton and I don't want his name hanging around my neck like an albatross. I want to be Lady Marjory. Marjory's my name and no one else's. Mary Beth and I are going to enjoy life for a while. At least, I am. She's got herself tangled up with some degenerate artist, but I'm hoping she'll come to her senses before the matter goes too far. Luckily, she doesn't care for romancing and all that silly stuff. She's got her head screwed on, has that girl.

24

She knows what men are, knows she's smarter than most of them.

'So, there you are, doctor. I don't know why I've told you all this. I don't usually talk about my past. But what I want to know is this: are you going to call me Lady Marjory, or not?'

Bennett stroked his beard. His ears were ringing, but, as a doctor, he was not unfamiliar with the sudden urge to tell all. He had sat through far less intriguing personal histories than the one he had just heard.

'You have what seems to you to be valid reasons for choosing to call yourself Lady Marjory. I am a reasonable man. No one can say otherwise. I agree to address you as Lady Marjory when . . . *if* we should happen to meet. I feel strongly that you are mistaken in your decision. I suppose it hardly matters what *you* do. That is, you are an American and allowances will be made. It is your daughter I am thinking of. Form is important to the English. You are a fairly wealthy woman, although I must inform you that there are many Americans in London who would not know how to manage on so small a sum as you have at your disposal. You will find a husband for your daughter. Of course you will. But what sort of man? That is the question.'

'Well, that's plain speaking, I suppose.'

'However, I cannot promise to *refer* to you as Lady Marjory. My friends would think I had taken leave of my senses, and acquaintances would assume I was ignorant. You need someone to advise you, ma'am. You are in deep water. This is not the only solecism you have committed.'

'What do you mean?'

'I mean, *Lady Marjory*, that I am a surgeon and should, therefore, be addressed as *Mr* Bennett, not *Dr* Bennett.'

'Aren't you a doctor?'

25

'Yes. Well, I was. I am still a medical man, of course. I was apprenticed at eighteen to the resident apothecary at St Bartholomew's Hospital. When I had completed my five years, I excercised the right to call myself Dr Bennett.'

'Well, there you are!'

'Then I went to Paris for further study and returned to London four years later. When I was just twenty-seven,' he added with some pride, 'I became a member of the Royal College of Surgeons. Surgeons are addressed as mister. From that time on I became know as Mr Bennett.'

'Seems a silly way to do things, that's all I can say.'

'Two years later, following the publication of my treatise on – well, the subject is unimportant – I was elected a Fellow of the Royal College.'

'Then shouldn't you be called Fellow Bennett?'

'Mr Bennett will do.'

Marjory tapped one fingernail against her teeth, a gesture which Bennett had always found irritating.

'I think it's a shame. People ought to know you're a doctor when they meet you.'

'I can assure you I'm not the least bit interested in what *people* know. Besides, those who know that I am a medical man invariably expect free advice.'

'All this British title business is moonshine.'

'If you feel contemptuous of a system which has operated brilliantly for hundreds of years, then call yourself Mrs Manton,' snapped Bennett.

Marjory smile winningly. 'But that would also be wrong. You wouldn't want me to do anything wrong, now would you? You say I'm Lady Manton and must bear the burden of my proper title.'

It occurred to Bennett that the American was deliberately provoking him, but he could not resist replying waspishly. 'I did say you are Lady Manton, but I was wrong. As Peregrine has married, his wife is now to be called Lady Manton, and you are the *Dowager* Lady Manton.'

'Dowager? Isn't that what they call widowed old ladies? I won't have it. Besides, Cynthia and I can't both be called Lady Manton. It would be too confusing.'

Bennett bared his teeth in what was meant to be a superior smile. 'No confusion. She is Lady Manton. You are the Dowager Lady Manton.'

'You mean people will come up to me and say: "How do you do, Dowager Lady Manton"?'

'No, of course not.'

Marjory leaned back in her chair. 'That's what I said. Confusion.'

Bennett wished he could leave the room with a scathing remark on his lips, something that would bring a flush to those smooth cheeks. Regrettably, nothing vicious yet civilized occurred to him, so he bowed with extreme dignity.

'I must thank you for a charming evening enlivened by invigorating conversation. I'm sorry I cannot stay for supper, ma'am. The pressure of work, you know.'

'Somebody needing a leg cut off? Don't let me detain you, *Mr* Bennett.'

'Goodnight, madam.'

Bennett fumbled slightly when unlocking the door, heaved it open and shut it rather sharply behind him, almost stepping on Jeremy Grimshaw's toes as he re-entered the ballroom.

The young man had been hovering by the door and now looked pale and anxious. 'There is nothing wrong, I hope, Uncle Frederick?'

'Nothing whatsoever. I have had a most stimulating discussion with your client. It strikes me, Jeremy, that you work very hard for your living. I admire your fortitude, by God I do. Excuse me. I don't believe I will stay for supper. Goodnight, my boy.'

27

3

Marjory sat up in bed with a start. She had not slept one wink, a most unusual circumstance for her. But then she had never met a man quite like the doctor before. He had riled her with his imperious ways more than either of her husbands had ever been able to. Of course, the doctor was smarter than the two of them put together. And his voice! So deep and, therefore, so authoritative! Perhaps that was why his disapproval of her had been so unexpectedly painful. It was certainly the reason why she hadn't told him off the way she had despatched the stranger in front of the Burlington Arcade a few hours earlier. You didn't just tell Dr – *Mr* Bennett to go about his business. It wasn't that easy.

He was a good-looking man, no doubt about it: nice eyes, nice mouth. Yet it was his hands, not his face, which fascinated her. They were strong and well-shaped, the nails neatly pared. They were also the hands that regularly picked up a scalpel and sliced into people. A chilling thought. Did he ever amputate limbs? Most probably. Her mind raced ghoulishly on, out of control as she pictured the gory scene. It was this aspect of his life – the cutting – not his maleness, not the penetrating gaze nor the firmly worded rebukes that had hit her with such force in the pit of her stomach when she was alone with him. Marjory had never gone weak and fluttery at the sight of a man in all her forty years, and wasn't about to start at her time of life. She didn't like the thought of human flesh being violated by a knife, that was the trouble. She couldn't bear the image, yet couldn't banish it from her mind's eye.

Perks had answered the knock on the bedroom door. Any second now a maid would be placing Marjory's breakfast tray across her lap, and she didn't like the servants to see her in her nightcap. Quickly, she undid her plait and finger-combed her long dark hair, arranging it around her shoulders. It was not as dark as Mary Beth's, but had a quite dramatic white streak starting from above her left eye and going right down the back of her head. It was almost the only grey in her hair, the only sign, really, of the crowding years. She was rather proud of it.

Perks was a highly efficient servant, but she made Marjory uncomfortable. The woman had been chosen for her by Gilbert, and to Marjory's insensitive ear, Perks spoke just as fancy as Gilbert had. When the maid had let it be known that she was actually distantly related to Gilbert, Marjory had found it hard to assert her authority over such a superior woman.

Gilbert had died shortly after their arrival at his ancestral home, but those early days had set the tone for the relationship between Marjory and Perks: orders given by Marjory but amended if Perks could convince her that what she wanted was 'not the done thing'. It was not until Marjory was restored to health that she rediscovered her native pride and became determined, in spite of her very restricted social life, to do things her way.

'The post has come,' said Perks, watching critically as the maid settled the tray across Marjory's lap. 'There's a letter from Mr Samuel. At least, I presume it is. You don't receive letters from America these days except from Mr Samuel. Perhaps he's sorry he ran away and wants to come home.' She handed the letter to her mistress and began to pour a cup of coffee. 'If you hadn't pushed him so hard – '

'Hush and let me read,' said Marjory, frowning over the cramped hand. 'He's in San Francisco working for a builder.'

'*Labouring?*' said Perks. 'And to think you drove him away to that!'

'It will do him no harm. At least he won't go hungry. Got fifteen men working under him, he says, although what he knows about building you could put on a postage stamp. Doesn't know what he will do next nor where he'll go. Sends his love to Mary Beth and even remembered to send his regards to you. He always was a gentle boy.'

'And you were worried about him getting into trouble in this country,' said Perks. 'I've heard there are hundreds of harlots in San Francisco. It's said the place draws them like a magnet, and I daresay they are all diseased.'

'I won't listen to such talk, so you needn't try to worry me. How well do you think the party went last night? What did they have to say below stairs?'

Perks bent to nurture the new-born fire before facing her mistress. 'There were some very genteel people here last night. The food and wine held out well and nobody behaved badly. You can't ask for more than that. Sir Gilbert never liked grand affairs, but he would have had to say your first London party was a success. The young people enjoyed themselves and Miss Mary looked a picture.'

Perks opened the door to the bathroom and began to fill the tub. 'Nobody cares for Miss Mary's young man,' she called above the sound of running water. 'No, that's not quite true. The maids all think he's handsome and hope to catch his eye, but you needn't worry. If he does start paying them unwarranted attention, I'll be the first to hear and you will be the second. Mr Brogan and his wife think Miss Mary could do better for herself. You should be firm with her.'

Marjory set the tray aside. 'You talk as if I had any control over the girl, when you know I haven't. Besides, you said I was too hard on Samuel. I'm not going to push my daughter into running away. Mary Beth will do as she pleases. She's got spirit and intelligence. This infatuation won't last and then we can forget the whole business. But I know my daughter. One whiff of real opposition and she'll marry Falkner faster than you can blink an eye. Did you find out anything about that Mr Bennett? Sour-faced man. I'm not sure I want to see him again. Young Grimshaw says his father was the doctor's best friend.'

'You ought not to send out invitations willy-nilly, my lady. It could be a mistake,' said the maid as she came back into the bedroom.

'A mistake? To invite a friend of Mr Grimshaw's into my house? And a doctor, at that!'

'Ah, yes,' said Perks triumphantly. 'But what kind of doctor? That's the question. I daresay you didn't know Mr Bennett specializes in cases of, well you know, social disease.'

Marjory gasped and sat down on the edge of the bed. 'Then he doesn't cut off limbs, after all. But what does a surgeon do who specializes in – By the way, just how contagious *are* these diseases? Is it safe to shake hands with him? I hope all the china has been well washed. That scullery maid hasn't got much sense.'

'I asked Mr Brogan, my lady, you may be sure. 'How safe is it?' I said, and he said there couldn't be any danger from the doctor, who would know how to look after himself, after all. Only, my lady, a doctor who deals with that sort of thing can't add to your consequence.'

There she went again! Perks was always criticizing. Marjory went into the bathroom, climbed into the tub and splashed about, putting up a show of irritation to hide her uncertainty.

31

'There you go again, talking about my consequence. I keep telling you, Americans don't bother about things like that,' she called out through the closed bathroom door. 'The man behaves real gentlemanly. Besides, he's a friend of Mr Grimshaw's and that's enough for me. After all, I don't intend to discuss his work with him.' She wagged a wet finger. 'Although if I did, I might have some interesting things to say. Everyone knows of my interest in wayward girls. And they pose the major problem for people like the doctor, don't they? Prostitutes and their customers, that is.'

'That reminds me,' said Perks. Marjory came in to the bedroom wearing her undergarments, and the maid helped her into a cream satin negligée. 'There's a young maid downstairs in the kitchen, ma'am. She works for a Mrs Pringle, I believe. She's got herself into trouble and looks to you to save her.'

'What happened?' asked Marjory. 'Oh, never mind, I'll hear the girl's story from her own lips.'

Mary Beth Hanson knocked on the door, but didn't wait to be invited in before entering her mother's bedroom. Marjory was by this time seated at the dressing-table so that Perks could arrange her hair. On seeing Mary, however, Perks retired discreetly to her own quarters.

Mary Beth, handsomely dressed in a plum and white striped princess gown, looked around for a suitable chair. The gown fitted her like a second skin down to the hips. A deeply flounced bustle protruded at the back from hip level to the back of her knees, making it almost impossible for her to sit down gracefully. She finally perched on one hip on the edge of a straight chair, looking extremely uncomfortable.

'I think that dress goes too far for commonsense, Mary Beth,' said Marjory. 'You can't be comfortable in it.'

'Oh, don't be old-fashioned, Momma. I'm miserable,

32

but what does it matter? I must be fashionable and this is what is being worn. You wouldn't want me to be dowdy. Do you know, Mr Grimshaw was very unkind to me this morning. He said it was unladylike to take an interest in making money, and to be good at it is, he said, quite beyond anything. What am I going to do, Momma? You know I don't like sewing, and I can hardly present myself in the kitchen and say I wish to cook. When we were in Yorkshire, I could at least gather a few plants for the still room, but I can hardly do so in London. Yet I can't sit around doing nothing. I must take an interest in something and it may as well be an interest in making money.'

'I know. It is hard for you. I always had the store to keep me occupied, but you've been brought up to have fancier ways. You know a better class of person. At least, they think they're better. You have your friends.'

'Yes, I do,' agreed Mary. 'And I particularly like Susannah Quinn. I do hope Mr Grimshaw has not been so indiscreet as to discuss my business interests with her. I can't imagine what she would make of me if she knew. When we go shopping, Susannah can't reckon her own change and always says how remarkable I am because I do it for her. I do my best to be ladylike and helpless, but it can be inconvenient.'

'Well,' sighed Marjory. 'You've told me you plan to marry in the near future. I expect you will make new friends, artists and poets, people like that. Perhaps they won't mind about your secret talent. It sure comes in handy.'

'They will mind even more than Mr Grimshaw does. Sometimes I feel quite cross with Lucius. He has a contempt for money which I think is foolish. I may as well tell you: we quarrelled last night. He looked tired and – '

'I thought that. Dissipated, I'd have said,' interrupted Marjory.

'No! Just tired. And I asked him why he was tired and he snapped at me! He said he had been working long hours on *real* paintings, not the sort of thing I want him to do for money.'

'Well!'

'Yes, well! Oh, Momma, you know my temper. I gave him a dose.' Mary Beth stood up, rubbing her back. 'And then he just – you know what he's like – just went very quiet and apologized for speaking sharply to me. I wish he wouldn't give in to me so quickly. I don't want to be married to a mouse.'

Marjory looked away so that her daughter couldn't see the gleam of satisfaction in her eyes. 'I expect you'll be happiest with a weak man. You've got a very strong mind, Mary Beth.'

'I don't want a weak man, as you very well know. I despise men who can be ruled by their wives. I just want Lucius to be stronger.'

'You shouldn't call him Lucius. People in England don't take up first names like they do back home.'

'I never – oh, what's the use? You're no help to me.'

'Here now! What help do you want from me? If it's advice, I'll give you some. You make sure that artist of yours doesn't bring home loose women to pose for him. He might get more than he bargained for. *And* give it to you when you're married.'

'Oh, Momma, must you talk that way?' Mary Beth left the room and all but slammed the door.

Perks came back into the bedroom, having heard every word that passed between mother and daughter. 'I think Miss Mary may come to her senses, after all.'

'Yes,' said Marjory. 'See how smart I've been? I can never leave well alone. I shouldn't have made that remark about loose women.'

'Sometimes a mother must tell her daughter the ugly

34

truths of life even if the girl shows no sign of wishing to listen. Your warning did not fall on deaf ears, I'm sure.'

Marjory looked out of the tall window in time to see Mary Beth emerge from the house and climb into the family brougham.

'What's the world coming to, Perks? I feel frightened for my children every time they come near a strange man. I was always afraid Samuel would allow himself to be led into wicked ways by sophisticated men, and I know too many women whose health has been ruined by disease passed on to them by their husbands.'

Perks stared at her mistress's back with a frown. 'Yes,' she said slowly. 'One must feel sorry for innocent wives. Miss Mary could do much better than that artist, my lady. She should marry a gentleman of birth with a fortune to equal her own, or at any rate, a title to compensate for his having no money.'

'You English are the most money-minded people I ever met.'

Perks pressed a hand against her heart, deeply offended. 'I should say we aren't! For an American to speak so – '

'I'll have you know, Eliza Perks, that in America we believe in *working* for our money. We don't sell our daughters for it!'

'I know of several titles supported by American money – '

'Oh, yes, I've heard of those people too. Young girls sold by their rich mommas. It's disgraceful but they're all New York intellectuals, people who have made more money than is good for them on the railroads or something. I don't count them as Americans.'

'How convenient,' murmured Perks, turning her head away.

'And if you were thinking I married your relative for his so-called title, you can think again.'

'Madam, never! Shall I send up that maid?'

Marjory agreed, and within a few minutes the maid was seated on the edge of a straight chair, pulling her skirts over her cracked patent leather boots. In spite of the voluminous black skirt she wore, anyone looking closely could see the girl was pregnant. She twitched the threadbare velvet pelisse into place around her shoulders and straightened the old straw bonnet on the back of her head. Her curly, mouse-brown hair was probably her best feature, but she kept it rigorously pulled into a bun, leaving only the slightest frizzy fringe to soften the lines of her face. Small eyes, a largish nose and a slack full mouth gave the girl a rather stupid look. Marjory had no doubt that she *was* stupid. If not, how did she get herself into this fix?

'What's your name, young woman?'

'Betty Bridgeman, ma'am.'

'How old are you?'

'Twenty-seven next November.'

Marjory raised her eyebrows. 'You must have been in service for years! What position did you hold at Mrs Pringle's?'

'I've been in service for twelve years, my lady, and have always given satisfaction. I've been with Mrs Pringle for ten years and I'm head housemaid. Or I was until this morning.'

'And Mrs Pringle won't help you?'

'She says it would set a bad example for the other servants. Will you take me on, Lady Marjory?'

'I will not,' said Marjory, 'but I will help you. I know of a man who needs a wife. You can marry him.'

Marjory heard Perks give one of her disapproving sniffs, but the young maid was looking at her intently.

'Who is this man? Why should he want to marry me?'

'He's a coachman with a family I know in Green-wich,' said Marjory, and Perks clapped a hand over her mouth in horror. 'He was living with a woman he called his wife for five years. She died six weeks ago. The poor soul never recovered after giving birth to their second child, a girl who's about six months old now. And there's a boy of two. This coachman needs a mother for his children. You need a home and a husband. I'm betting the pair of your would be happy enough. I'll give you both a few pounds as a bride present. Now, wouldn't that be dandy?'

'I don't know . . .' began the girl.

'When is the baby due?'

'End of June.'

'Well, you will want some time to think about it. Has Mrs Pringle given you your notice?'

'Yes, ma'am. I've nowhere to stay tonight.'

'You may go down to the kitchen and tell them to feed you up and give you a bed for the night.'

When the maid had left the room, Perks turned to her mistress. 'Oh, my lady, what have you done? And what is Mrs Grimshaw going to say when you take that unprincipled girl down to marry her coachman?'

Marjory laughed. 'You knew straight away where I planned to take her, didn't you? The widow Grimshaw is afraid of me. Hadn't you noticed? Thinks I might turn Indian and scalp her. I'll just have to bully her a bit. As for Jabez Jackson, I was the one who found him the job of coachman when he and his woman were down on their luck. He owes me a favour in return.'

Perks fought to keep her thoughts to herself and lost. 'Lady Marjory, you can't act in this high-handed fashion.'

'Well, it's the way you want me to treat my own daughter. If the Bridgeman girl had worked for me for ten years, I wouldn't have thrown her out on the streets. That's high-handed. *And* unchristian. All I'm doing is trying to make the best of the tangle the girl has got herself into. The only alternatives, as you well know, are for her to starve, go to the workhouse or on the streets.'

'And what Mrs Pringle will say about your interference, I can't imagine.'

'She already thinks I'm an uncivilized American, so she won't be all that surprised. Now, go downstairs and see if you can get enough clothing together to give that girl some sort of trousseau. I want to write to Mrs Grimshaw.'

4

Marjory had put on her hat and gloves and was on the point of going out when Brogan brought a letter on a silver tray, saying that a young man was waiting in the hall to speak to her.

With a sigh, she read the two dozen words of introduction written in Mr Grimshaw's careful hand, and told the butler to show Mr Guy Dundalk into the room.

The man paused just inside the door, holding his top hat, grey chamois gloves and silver-headed stick in his right hand. He looked no more than twenty-five, but displayed the poise and self-confidence of someone much older as he gave her a chance to look him up and down, to assess his trustworthiness and, perhaps, to guess at his charm. He certainly had a winning smile.

'It is very kind of you to see me, Lady Marjory.'

'Come in, Mr Dundalk,' said Marjory. 'Mr Grimshaw says in his letter that you and he are old friends. Were you at Eton and Oxford together?'

A frown flicked across Guy Dundalk's handsome face. 'No, ma'am. I met Grimshaw in the way of business. I hope you will forgive the intrusion, but I believe what I have to say will be of interest to you.'

She indicated a straight chair and sat down beside him in the gloomy library. He couldn't resist those little tell-tale gestures of nervousness: a smoothing with thumb and forefinger of the waxed moustache and a reassuring touch to the short-cut crisp dark hair. Marjory knew then that he wanted something from her and wondered how much Mr Grimshaw's letter of recommendation was going to cost her.

Dundalk had an intriguing face: a long nose above that military moustache and eyebrows that seemed inches away from dreamy eyes. His frockcoat and checked trousers, his highly-starched collar and flamboyant tie completed the dress of a man Eliza Perks would undoubtedly call not-quite-a-gentleman. Marjory always had a soft spot for men whom Perks dismissed with that description, so she smiled warmly now.

'And why have you asked for this interview, sir?'

'Madam.' He leaned towards her, giving her a lopsided but engaging smile. Marjory sucked in her breath with pleasure. There was something about him . . . 'I have been hoping to meet the famous Lady Marjory for several weeks. Your good works are well-known, as is your compassion for women who have fallen from the paths of righteousness. Ladies in your position, of your intelligence, are desperately needed these days. I suppose you know the statistics? Eighty thousand prostitutes in London alone, disease-ridden, lost to all feelings of decency, preying on honourable men – '

' – too desperate for food to care what they do, with no hope of earning a decent living, there to be taken advantage of by men who ought to know better.'

His eyes opened wide, but his smile only broadened. 'Exactly, Lady Marjory. Did I not say that you are a lady of compassion? Something must be done for them.'

'I've heard,' said Marjory, 'that there are hundreds of charities in London. What have they achieved? All you people do is take in the most desperate women, feed them up, tell them they're the dregs of the earth and must repent, and expect them to love you for it. Which organization are you from, anyway?'

'Why, none! That is why I have come to you. Americans are well-known for their philanthropy, even, on occasion, for their generosity to this little island. The late Mr Peabody, for instance.'

'Who was Mr Peabody?' asked Marjory.

'You have not heard of Mr Peabody?' exclaimed Dundalk. 'Why, I am surprised! Ten or eleven years ago this gentleman, a City banker, I believe, decided to try to alleviate the suffering of the poor by building proper homes for them. The first Peabody Building is in Spitalfields: five stories high, three rooms and proper sanitation for five shillings a week. There are now two dozen such buildings in London, fitting monuments to the enlightenment and generosity of the American people.'

'And you think I could do something of the sort?'

Dundalk smiled regretfully. 'I believe Mr Peabody spent nearly five hundred thousand pounds on his buildings, whereas my scheme is for one rather modest establishment. You see, I have come to ask you to be the patron of a home for fallen women. I know your views on the subject of these wretched creatures which, I assure you, are exactly the same as my own. We could help these women, but not by forcing religion down their throats. We will leave the saving of souls to those whose profession it is. We will teach them a trade or prepare them for domestic service or, if they are too weakened by the ravages of their calling, we will humanely provide them with a refuge for their final days.'

'So you want money.'

'I cannot, unfortunately, do everything myself. I would, of course, do all the necessary work – find the site, buy or rent suitable premises, recruit the staff. A lady of tender sensibilities, like yourself, could not consider actually visiting such a place.'

'Well, I don't know . . .'

'I intend to name the establishment the Lady

41

Marjory Refuge for the Rehabilitation of Fallen Women.'

Dundalk's suggestion caught her completely by surprise, making it difficult to hide her pleasure. The title had a nice ring to it. It meant what it said, and Marjory suddenly knew that the foundation of this refuge was just what she had wanted to do for a long time.

She had been just a bit suspicious of this young man at first. She was no fool. She didn't come from the Show-Me state for nothing. She meant to be cautious, to take no chances of being tricked. She would keep the whole affair a secret, especially from Mary Beth, who was inclined to be sceptical of everything her mother did. Dundalk was a very charming man and might be dangerous. Marjory didn't think so, however, because she had noticed that he was a nail biter. Bless him! Rascals didn't bite their nails; they bit the hands that fed them. Guy Dundalk was just a boy, really, not puffed up with confidence at all. She felt quite motherly towards him, and with such feelings came a modicum of trust.

'Twenty-five or six in three dormitories, I thought,' Dundalk was saying. 'I will have some plans drawn up for your inspection and approval. We will need staff, of course, to teach the women needlework and household skills.'

Marjory laughed indulgently. 'You won't need to teach them how to sew. They'll have tried to stay respectable by sewing and found that they couldn't earn enough to keep away the hunger pangs.'

'Yes, that is probably quite true. In that case, what do you suggest we teach them, ma'am?'

'Teach them to be typewriters.'

'I beg your pardon?'

'You know, those new machines where you press a key and it comes up and prints a letter on the page.

An American invention, by the way. I wouldn't be surprised if that little machine doesn't prove to be as much of a benefit to the poor as Mr Peabody's buildings. What I thought is, we'll get some of those typewriters and teach the women how to use them. Then they will be able to find employment in offices that will pay enough to keep them decently.'

Dundalk took a deep breath and said rather shakily, 'What a splendid idea! However, many of these women can't read, you know.'

'Listen to me,' said Marjory earnestly. 'I know what I'm doing. You may think I'm hard or that I'm plain crazy. I'm neither. I'm just practical. You said there are eighty thousand prostitutes on the streets of London, all of them needing to be saved. Then you said that we will have no more than twenty-five or -six places at the Lady Marjory Refuge. Well, if I can't save them all, at least I can help those most likely to be able to help themselves in the future. Other agencies will do what they can. It will be your responsibility to offer places only to those women who can read and who are presentable enough to work in an office.'

Dundalk caressed his moustache to hide his quivering lips as he imagined himself going into the streets after dark to interview prostitutes. 'Yes, a capital scheme, Lady Marjory. A capital scheme, but expensive, I fear.'

'I will give you a hundred pounds to be going on with. But this business is to be our secret for the time being, do you hear? If I find out you have told anyone, I'll withdraw my support.'

That afternoon, Dundalk placed his feet on Jeremy Grimshaw's tidy desk and inhaled deeply on a small cigar.

'Sprightly old duck. Plucky. You know what I mean? You led me to expect an old harridan. Our Lady

Marjory is fair of face, Grimshaw. You should have told me.'

'She is forty years old, but well-preserved, I admit. However, she is not *your* Lady Marjory. Unless . . .' Grimshaw had a sudden dreadful thought. 'You're not planning to court her, are you?'

Dundalk took the cigar out of his mouth and looked at the lawyer with disgust. 'Understand me, old son. I'm not in the petticoat line. I'll leave marrying rich widows for their money to the aristocrats, if you don't mind. Anyway, I'm not fixing to get hitched. I have other plans. I'm a businessman.'

Dundalk's carefully enunciated vowel sounds had disappeared the minute he left Marjory's house. Instead, he spoke with an accent anyone with half an ear could place as common to dockland.

'Well, sir,' retorted Jeremy, nettled. 'Since you are a man of business, did the lady perform as you expected?'

Dundalk smilingly reached into his coat pocket and pulled out a wad of notes. 'One hundred pounds in cash. Here's your share: ten pounds.'

'Is that all? Just one hundred pounds? I would have thought she would be more anxious to – that is, less cautious. You are not concealing anything from me, are you?'

Dundalk removed his feet from the desk and leaned forward in his chair. 'You never will understand me, will you, old son? We're in business. Our bargain is for a ninety–ten split of the takings. My share is ninety per cent because it was my idea and my risk. Your share is ten for the introduction. That's the way it will always be, and I'll never cheat you and never split on you to the authorities. Now tell *me*. Are you behaving as you ought towards the daughter? Not letting any of her money stick to your fingers, are you?'

'Never! I wouldn't dare! She's too clever, so don't start thinking you might have a go at her. She employs me to buy and sell shares for her and, by God, she's brilliant at share dealing. When I buy for her, I buy for myself. When I sell for her, I sell my shares. I've made fifty pounds and could have made more if I had more capital at my disposal. But, please believe me, I've not touched a penny of hers. I leave the taking of money from unprotected women to the likes of you.'

'The perfect gentleman, that's what you are,' said Dundalk quietly. 'And getting rich with it. Perhaps the business with Lady Marjory sticks in your craw. Maybe it's beneath your touch. Give me back the ten pounds, and I'll never mention the business to you again.'

Grimsahw hesitated. Dundalk always unsettled him, and he knew he ought to back off and protect his good name. But, on the other hand, the money could be spent usefully. A gentleman had certain needs. Better in his own pocket than in Dundalk's.

'I'm staying in,' said Grimshaw, and bit his lip in vexation when Dundalk laughed softly.

The next morning, Mary Beth burst into Marjory's room even before the breakfast tray arrived.

'Momma, I've just heard about the maid you are proposing to marry off to Mrs Grimshaw's coachman. How could you do such a thing? Sometimes I think you are just plain heartless. Betty Bridgeman is a woman of some refinement. She is accustomed to living in a fine house. Jabez Jackson, on the other hand, is just a dirty feckless man! Why do you expect him to marry Betty Bridgeman when he wouldn't marry the mother of his children?'

'For money, that's why. I'll give them a dowry. What do you expect that poor woman to do?'

'Bring up her child alone, with dignity, not marry some dirty creature with whom she'll never be able to have a conversation. She could manage if you would take her on here.'

Marjory patted the covers around her legs irritably. 'Mary Beth, sometimes I get so aggravated with you. If she marries, the child will be born legitimate. That will count with a woman like Betty. And Jabez has got those two kids of his farmed out with some woman in the town. That's no way to bring up children. Martha Grimshaw said she didn't think much of the woman who has them. They deserve better. Let's think of the children in this business. If Jabez and Betty have any sense, they'll leap at the chance. Here's my breakfast. Go away and let me eat in peace. I'm taking Betty to Greenwich this morning and I want to be off early.'

Mary Beth left, but Marjory found she had exchanged one scold for another. Perks insisted on telling her mistress that Miss Mary was wrong about Betty Bridgeman. The woman was no better than she should be; Perks had heard talk.

Marjory endured the nagging largely in silence, because she had learned some time ago that it was futile to try to talk sense into Perks' head. But later she groaned out loud when she climbed into her carriage and found that Mary Beth was already inside, sitting opposite Betty Bridgeman. A look at the maid's pale face told Marjory that Mary Beth had been giving her own brand of advice.

Mrs Grimshaw's home in Greenwich was comfortable but modest by the standards of Sir Gilbert Manton's Yorkshire estate. The double wrought-iron entrance gates were handsome, though rusting in places, but the drive was so short that any passer-by could see quite clearly who was coming to call at Greenwich House if he cared to pause a moment on the opposite side of the road. Still, it had more privacy than Marjory's own house in Cavendish Place. Marjory sometimes thought she might like a nice house just like the one she was about to enter.

Martha Grimshaw's white cap was askew, as usual.

She greeted her guests at the door, all but elbowing her elderly manservant aside in her eagerness to invite Marjory and Mary Beth inside.

'Lady Manton, I didn't know what to think when I . . . and you've come all this way without waiting for an answer. I'm afraid your scheme won't prosper. Jabez Jackson is so . . . oh, you know.'

'I do know, but you know me. I can be pretty determined,' said Marjory, ushering her party inside.

'Oh, yes,' said Martha Grimshaw. 'I do know your little ways.'

Her black dress had been made for a slimmer widow Grimshaw, probably about five years ago when her husband had died. On this day it fitted too tightly under the arms and, in any case, had been made to be worn over a crinoline rather than a bustle – quite out of fashion. Young Grimshaw could certainly afford to purchase a few new gowns for his mother, therefore Marjory supposed that the widow had refused to wear new clothing in an attempt to convince the world that she still deeply mourned her husband. Perhaps Mr Grimshaw senior had been an exemplary man, worthy of such sacrifice. Marjory had yet to meet the man for whom it was worth wearing rags for five years, but she was willing to allow that there might be such a creature.

'Mrs Grimshaw, do you want to wait here in the house while Mary Beth, Betty and I go out to Jabez to conduct our business?'

'Oh, no, I wouldn't miss this for the world,' said Martha Grimshaw. 'I don't know how we managed our affairs before all you Americans came over to put us right.' When Marjory and Mary Beth laughed, she added, 'Not that I meant to be rude about Americans, it's just that . . . well, I believe I've forgotten what I was going to say. Shall we go out to see Jabez?'

The entire party was very soon trailing through the house and out of the back door. Mrs Grimshaw's property ran to about ten acres, including a few fields she rented to a neighbouring farmer. The ornamental garden was modest, to say the least, consisting almost entirely of laurels, straggling yews and rhododendrons. The pair of red brick cottages close to the stables was clearly visible through the naked trees, but would probably be almost hidden in the height of summer.

The Manton coachman had driven the brougham round to the stables and unhitched the horses. He was now lounging against a gatepost in solemn conversation with Jabez Jackson.

Jabez straightened his shoulders and scowled at the advancing party. He was thirty-five but looked rather older. Mrs Grimshaw didn't often send for her carriage, so he was accustomed to occupying his spare time with a little gardening. Growing vegetables was his special passion. Since a man didn't need to comb his hair just to hoe a few rows, Jabez often went for a week at a time without testing the tangles in his sandy hair.

Today, although he detested Marjory and was strongly opposed to the idea of marrying a perfect stranger, he had surprised himself by making a little extra effort over his dress. Pride had caused him to put on a fresh shirt in the middle of the week. His Sunday suit looked incongruous and very old, but he had actually tackled his unruly hair as well as trimming the narrow beard that traced his jaw-line from ear to ear. It was not until he had actually taken Betty's soft hand in his calloused one that everyone got the measure of the pair. Betty was a buxom woman, tall enough to look Jabez directly in the eyes.

Marjory noticed the profound disappointment in the faces of both maid and coachman when they met. What, in heaven's name, had each of them been expecting? They all walked the short distance to the cottage: Marjory, Mary Beth, Betty, Jabez and Martha

Grimshaw. Jabez opened the door and stood aside to allow the others to enter.

'Oh, Jabez, you are a fool,' said Marjory. 'It's just as well I've brought Betty down to you. Look at this mess.'

Mary Beth pushed her way inside the surprisingly spacious room as Betty sucked in her breath in horror. A flaxen-haired baby was seated on the brick floor, paddling in a puddle of her own making. She seemed to have been eating mud, but there were also streaks of white on her left cheek. Assorted lumps of lime marked the floor, a bucket of whitewash being just out of the baby's reach. A filthy boy of about two years had climbed on to the stout kitchen table and was attempting to paint one wall with a brush he could barely lift with both hands.

'I forgot I was whitewashing the walls,' said Jabez. 'I only left them alone for a moment.'

Betty rushed forward and lifted the boy from the table, setting him gently on the floor before picking up the baby at arm's length.

'Have you any fresh clothing for this child, Mr Jackson? This is dreadful. I am not accustomed to such filth as you choose to live in. You must mind your children or send them back to the person who has them in charge, although she seems incompetent to me.'

'There you are,' said Marjory. 'You are needed here.'

'Oh, Momma, how could you?' cried Mary Beth. 'A life of drudgery!'

'I don't care if I am needed,' said Betty. 'I have never been so disgusted in my life. How could you think I would live here? I am accustomed to a certain amount of refinement.'

'And I don't want another man's bastard in my house, neither,' said Jabez. 'I didn't ask you to come down here. It's hard for a man to manage two young 'uns and that's the truth, but I don't want a shameless woman looking after them and maybe leading them into bad ways.'

'Have you fresh clothing for this poor baby or not?' asked Betty in an icy voice.

'Upstairs.'

Betty took the baby to a small door by the side of the fireplace, correctly guessing that it hid the staircase. She disappeared and those left in the parlour could hear the outraged cries of the baby growing fainter.

'No use you pushing me, Lady Manton or Lady Marjory, or whatever you call yourself,' said Jabez. 'I just don't want her.'

'You don't deserve her,' said Mary Beth heatedly. 'She would be a wonderful mother for your children, but I think she would be sacrificing herself for nothing.'

'Oh, come now, Mary Beth,' said Marjory calmly. 'Jabez here is a hard-working man. I always thought well of him when we were up in Yorkshire. It would be good for the children's sakes, but what can we do? She doesn't want him and he doesn't want her.'

'I think you shouldn't allow it even if they do want to get married, Momma. Betty can do better elsewhere. Almost anywhere else but Jabez.'

'That's not true!' said Jabez. 'She would be very lucky to have me. I've got this cottage and a little money saved up. By and large, I'm a sober man and I can turn my hand to lots of things.'

Marjory turned away, hiding a slight triumphant smile, as Betty returned with the baby in her arms, cooing to it softly.

'Well, I think we had better be going,' said Marjory. 'I've tried my best for both of you. Heaven knows, you need each other. I don't know what's to become of either of you.'

Mary Beth had been watching Betty as she cuddled the two children. Grudgingly, she looked over at her mother. 'Perhaps if Mrs Grimshaw doesn't mind, Betty could sleep with the servants for a week or two, giving these two people time to sort out their feelings about the future. Betty, I'm certain you would prefer to leave these children in a cleaner condition than you have found them.'

'I'll do that,' said Betty. 'I'll turn out this pigsty of a cottage and clean up the children and their clothes. I will stay for two weeks and do what I can. I owe you that much, Lady Man . . . that is, Lady Marjory, for trying to help me and being so generous and all.'

'Do you mind?' asked Marjory, turning to Mrs Grimshaw.

'Why no, I suppose not. It is the quickest way to get rid of . . . that is, to sort out this affair. I don't suppose you will have time to stay for a cup of tea, Lady Manton?'

But Marjory said she would like a cup of tea very much, and she was sure Mary Beth would as well. The three ladies sat in the drawing-room, while Mrs Grimshaw went on at length about Jeremy and how well his practice was doing. 'You know,' she said suddenly, 'I just can't get over the way you are willing to spend so much time on the welfare of other people's servants. I'm sure I wouldn't . . . that is, I wouldn't know what to do for the best, quite apart from not wanting to . . .'

'Oh, Momma is always willing to help others,' said Mary Beth, unaware of any intended criticism of her mother. 'I'm not sure I always agree with her, but at least she does try. And Betty is being given time to think things out for herself. I wouldn't have wanted you to push her into anything she doesn't want to do, Momma.'

'Oh, no,' said Mrs Grimshaw drily. 'It is certainly wrong to force a servant to do something against her will. As for one's own children, well, sometimes a mother makes a few small sacrifices for the sake of peace.'

'You are quite right,' exclaimed Marjory, who was not thinking of Jeremy at this moment. 'I've stayed quiet many a time when Mary Beth has wanted to do something I didn't think well of. Just for the sake of peace.'

Mary Beth laughed affectionately. 'I've never known you to keep quiet on any subject, Momma. We've had some very good discussions.'

'How exhausting,' murmured Mrs Grimshaw. 'May I offer you some more tea, ladies?'

5

There was real warmth in the air for the first time since the previous autumn, a mild spring day that lifted the heart. Outside, the sun blazed down on the passing throng and the air was as clear and pure as it ever could be in a busy thoroughfare like the Strand. The rattle of coach wheels, the clop of horses' hooves and the cries of street sellers combined to make a fearful din which was clearly heard by the gentlemen on the second floor of Simpson's Tavern and Cigar Divan.

Indoors, the air was thick with tobacco smoke. The ponderous silence was broken occasionally by the crackle of a newspaper as its reader turned the page or by the occasional grunt of triumph as one player gained advantage over another in a friendly game of chess.

Jeremy Grimshaw and Frederick Bennett were seated side by side on a low divan facing Lucius Falkner, who was lounging in a leather chair.

Falkner smacked the palm of his hand down on the table, not loudly, but emphatically, to press home his words. 'Painting, indeed all the art forms, should reflect the chaos of life. We artists are not the keepers of the nation's morals.'

'I disagree,' said Bennett. 'You have a duty to the public. It lies within your powers to improve or corrupt those who look upon your work. A well-executed painting which tells an uplifting story is a force for good. Then again, a religious subject can be improving to all minds. On the other hand, certain classical studies involving the painting of the nude may stimulate susceptible persons to sexual excesses that destroy them.'

'Oh, yes!' said Jeremy.

'I must disagree, Mr Bennett. We artists are sensitive to the beauty of the human form. God's creation, after all. What we portray is not lascivious when properly executed. And the classics can also point a moral.'

'That's true,' said Jeremy.

'Certain classical themes are evil, and you know it, sir.'

'Oh?' queried Falkner. 'Which themes would you say have a corrupting influence?'

Bennett thought for a moment. 'The story of Leda who is approached by Zeus in the form of a swan. That's a legend that fits my argument. Zeus – in his animal form, mind you – seduces Leda. Then, the very same night, she has sexual congress with her husband. She has four children, two by her husband and two by Zeus. There is nothing morally uplifting in that sordid tale. Yet it is a popular artistic subject.'

'But swans are so attractive to paint, Mr Bennett, and quite intriguing when in close proximity to a naked woman in the throes of a strong emotion.'

'Leda might more properly be portrayed wearing some diaphanous article of clothing,' suggested Grimshaw.

'And what about the legend of Perseus and Andromeda,' pursued Bennett. 'An oracle tells the King of Ethiopia that his country can only be saved by sacrificing his daughter, Andromeda, to a monster. So, willy-nilly, she is chained to a rock to die.'

'A shocking circumstance,' agreed Falkner. 'But Andromeda is rescued by Perseus, who slays the monster. The couple marry and have many fine children. Surely, that is an allegory for our times: a noble woman in distress is rescued by a man who falls in love with her and marries her.'

Bennett puffed angrily on his cigar. 'What I want to know is: why do artists only portray that part of the story where Andromeda is chained to the rock? For that matter, why must Andromeda always be portrayed *naked* in her chains?'

Falkner grinned. 'Well, you may have a point, sir. There is something very powerful about the image of a naked woman bound in chains. You must admit, some of our finest artists have attempted the subject.'

'Admit?' cried Bennett, forgetting to keep his voice low. 'I proclaim it, sir. And it is a disgrace to the nation.'

'Well,' said Grimshaw nervously. 'Well, well.'

Falkner stood up, greatly amused. 'Gentlemen, I would love to continue this discussion longer, but I must be going. The light is fading fast and I have much work to do on the portrait of a certain – well-clothed – tallow merchant's daughter.'

The doctor waited until Falkner was out of earshot before speaking. 'As you know, I am engaged in the fight against the disease of the age, the scourge of our times, an epidemic which I don't hesitate to tell you could engulf us. And men like your friend are helping to spread it.'

'Oh, Uncle, you are too hard on him.'

'And what of Miss Quinn?' asked the doctor suddenly.

'You asked me about her just the other night.'

'Great scott, my boy, when are you going to stop this nonsense and ask the girl to marry you? You have said you love her and if you have told me once, you have told me a thousand times, you have kept yourself pure for her sake. Marry the girl and raise a family. I have been making enquiries. Her father says she will have a respectable dowry – ' Jeremy groaned loudly. 'Well, someone had to do it. Your father was my bosom friend. Now that he is dead, I feel I stand in the position of a parent to you. It was your father's dearest wish that you should take Miss Quinn as a wife.'

'There's time. I'm not ready for such a responsibility. I'm only twenty-nine.'

'You have been celibate too long. I have warned you in the past of the dangers of self-abuse.'

Jeremy looked round the room quickly, his ears reddening as he tried to read the expressions of the other men in Simpson's. Had they heard?

'I'm sure you don't talk to Marcus in this fashion, Uncle,' he whispered. '*He* is not married. He is also twenty-nine and, so far as I know, doesn't have a mistress.'

'My son can look after himself,' said Bennett complacently.

Enviously, Jeremy thought of the doctor's handsome son. Marcus Bennett had a self-contained manner that defied anyone to instruct him. Oh, to have such an air of reserve that even one's own father hesitated to give advice!

Falkner stopped on the pavement outside Simpson's, not certain what he wished to do next. Normally, the noise and push-and-shove of the Strand was sufficient to raise his spirits, but not today. He was depressed, but didn't know why. After a hair-raising scamper to avoid horses and carriages, he reached the north side of the Strand and walked past the Lyceum theatre without a glance. Crossing Wellington Street, he passed the Gaiety, for once not stopping to scan the advertisements for the evening's entertainment. Another five hundred yards brought him to Newcastle Street where he turned left just before the Globe theatre and the Opéra Comique. He lived and worked in Wych Street, a narrow road running behind these two shabby theatres. Being at their very doors, he naturally knew them well, knew the entertainers who performed in them. Theatres, or at least actresses, had once played an important part in his life. But his theatre-going, like so

56

much else, had undergone a radical change in the last few weeks.

He hadn't hesitated to take his dear wife to every show or play that attracted them. Barbara had loved the spectacle, even though she had not been able to appreciate his occasional desire to paint a pert-faced girl in a skimpy costume. Eventually, however, she had accepted that he couldn't restrict himself to using his own wife as a model on all occasions and had adopted a protective attitude towards the actresses and dancers who had come to his studio.

But Barbara had been dead for over a year, and Mary Beth Hanson had very different ideas. She was not sure she wished to visit any theatre except the Royal Opera House, and this despite the fact that he was almost certain she was tone deaf. Her conversation during the intervals tended to revolve around the cost of the costumes, the number of empty seats and the fees paid to the artistes. Very money-minded was Mary Beth, as was her mother.

Sometimes, he wondered if he and the American girl were best suited to one another. She was very different from Barbara with whom he had enjoyed five happy years. Barbara had hung on his every word, admired his every brushstroke and accepted their ever-present financial problems with dignified resignation.

He had met Mary Beth only a few weeks ago when she had come for her first sitting, accompanied by her mother. After half an hour, the restless Lady Marjory (as she chose to call herself) had remembered some shopping she wished to do, and had left the studio. Before Falkner could think of anything to say to the young woman posing for him, she had taken the lead in the conversation, showing the self-possession that was so remarkable in a woman of twenty-one.

'If you will take my advice, Mr Falkner, you will make a greater effort to flatter your subjects. You live by painting vain young women like myself and by pleasing doting mothers like my own. What difference does it make if you improve upon nature? And you really ought to move to more fashionable quarters and adopt a romantic style of dress. Your work is more concerned with the art of salesmanship than with the art of the brush, you know.'

This forthright speech had intrigued him. There was no point in arguing; what she had said was true. The novelty was in hearing the sentiment put into words. Accordingly, he had softened the strong line of Miss Hanson's chin, set the black eyes absurdly far apart and nipped a few inches off what was already an acceptably small waist.

Lady Manton, on seeing the finished portrait, had said her first kind words to him, telling him he had achieved a perfect likeness, which made him smile. Mary had invited him to call upon her, told him what to wear and how to behave. 'My protégé,' she had called him, and had taken great pride in the three commissions that came his way as a result of that one afternoon's visit.

For a great many years, Falkner had been comparatively poor and unrecognized as a serious artist, so his new though modest success tasted sweet indeed. Why not allow this shrewd young woman to help him to greater financial security? It had all been rather exiting during these last weeks. No wonder he had ended by thinking he could learn to love her. No wonder he had dared to say rather too much late one night when he had drunk deeply at a party given by her mother.

Wych Street was narrow and therefore dark and noisy. He lived in a plaster-and-tile Georgian building halfway down the street which was in urgent need of extensive repairs. The passageways and stairs were a disgrace, but his own set of rooms at the top was quite comfortable. His studio windows faced north and he

58

had recently purchased several chairs and a handsome turkey carpet. In the recent cold snap, he had kept the studio very warm by means of a stove, again at Mary's suggestion. He was always busy these days.

Calling a greeting to Mrs Strump who was leaning out of a first floor window in search of sun and a little fresh air, he took the internal stairs two at a time and opened his door on the fourth floor.

He had intended to work on a three-quarter portrait of Miss Annabelle Chalmers before the light faded. But now that the work was waiting for him, he found he didn't wish to paint. Memories of Barbara were everywhere. He had sketched and painted her dozens of times. Impressions of her, executed in many different styles, almost covered one wall. He still occasionally forgot that she had died. And the distant cry of a baby could make him feel physically sick. Barbara had died giving birth to the child she had longed for. He had been profoundly relieved when the infant had not outlived its mother. Now he was not so sure that he had been right to dread the responsibility of a motherless child. The infant's presence might have made his loss more bearable.

The stove was cold and he hadn't the energy to light a fire in the grate, although the landlady had laid it for him. He sat with his chin on his chest until the light was so dim there could be no hope of painting. Only then did he hold a match to the crumpled newspaper beneath the coals.

He stood up, stretched, scrubbed his face with his hands and then moved to the table to light the lamp. Gas had not been laid on in this old house, but he didn't mind, preferring the quality of the light from burning oil to the harsh glow of a gas lamp. He was just wondering where to go for supper, how to pass the hours until bedtime, when there was a knock on the door. He opened it to find Mary Beth Hanson smiling at him.

As always, she looked extremely smart, wearing a blue silk afternoon gown, fur stole and muff. A small hat, resembling nothing so much as a blue silk dinner plate, was tipped forward over her black hair. The draped apron-skirt clung to the front of her legs, while the underskirt touched the floor, hiding her feet completely. He knew she would be carrying an enormous bustle and a small train behind her.

'Mary, your gown will be filthy from the passageway.'

'Is that the way to greet your loved one?' she asked, holding out her gloved hand so that he could kiss her fingers. She seldom permitted his lips to touch her cheek.

'And you have come alone. What would your mother say? You shouldn't visit me without your maid, especially not at this time of the evening.'

'I was on my way home from visiting some friends. Is that the portrait of the tallow merchant's daughter? You have been lazy here, Lucius. Mr Chalmers will have paid a pretty price for the ruching, velvet trim and artificial flowers on his daughter's gown. You have merely suggested them. That won't suffice, you know. You must give the dressmaker her due.'

He put his hands in his pockets; the room was still cold and his fingers were beginning to feel numb. 'You surely have not flown in the face of convention to call upon an unmarried man merely in order to say that the dressmaker must be given her due.'

'You don't wish to starve for ever in an attic, do you? Not that I expect you to support me when we are married. But, nevertheless, Lucius, you will want to retain your self-respect, and you can only do that by working hard at your craft. Now stop pushing out your lower lip at me. You look like a sulking schoolboy.'

She wandered round the room, stopping now and then to inspect one of his many drawings of Barbara.

'So many lovely studies of your wife. She was very small, wasn't she?' Mary Beth turned suddenly to look at him. 'Why don't you ever sketch me?'

Falkner knew she was jealous of Barbara and understood why this should be so, but this evening he had very little patience with her.

'You have a Rossetti face and I no longer attempt the Pre-Raphaelite style.'

'Whatever do you mean? Who is Rossetti? Why should I have his sort of face? What is Pre-Raphaelite?'

'Oh, it is a style of painting, very tedious to execute. Gabriel Rossetti paints a particular sort of woman. Well, they all do. You remind me of Rossetti's *Proserpine*. I thought so the first time I met you. A very successful painting, by the way. The Pre-Raphaelite Brotherhood consists of a group of artists who believe certain, well, certain things about painting. I won't bore you with the details. You had better be on your way. You really ought not to have come.'

'I'm waiting for Momma. She is to meet me here.'

Her dark eyes surveyed him from head to toe, reminding him forcibly of his old headmaster. It was a relief to hear a bold knock on the door, although he was not so pleased to see Marjory.

'Oh, Momma, come in,' said Mary Beth. 'I want you to look at this painting of Miss Chalmers. What do you think? Will Mr Chalmers be pleased? Will he think his money was well spent?'

Marjory walked over to the easel, well aware of Falkner's fury. Mary Beth could be a trifle high-handed at times. Marjory didn't know where she got it from. Still, she couldn't like this artist, so it was hardly with an open mind that she viewed the painting.

'Seems all right to me, Mary Beth. Is it finished, Mr Falkner?'

61

'Can you not tell, ma'am? There is a good deal more work needed on it.'

'You ought not to spend too many more hours on this painting, Lucius. The price has been agreed. You will not receive a penny more no matter how much more painting you do on it. If I were you, I'd consider this one finished and go on to another.'

Marjory walked over to examine a small wooden dais which held a straight chair and shawl. Faulkner, it seemed to her, was having trouble keeping his temper. Well, so much the better. She didn't want these two to be tied for life. Mary Beth would be miserable within a year. Falkner would be miserable, too, but that was his look-out.

She poked her head behind a folding screen and smiled wryly when she heard Mary Beth explain her plan to open an art gallery.

'Mary Beth . . . that is, Miss Hanson, you do not know the first thing about paintings.' Falkner's voice was strained by the need for politeness. 'How can you possibly have a gallery?'

'I thought you would manage it for me, Lucius. I don't think it will work out, though. I've made enquiries and find that there is virtually no suitable building that I can purchase. I would be obliged to rent premises from one or other of the great land-owners. That makes me mad. I like to own property. You may think I know nothing about painting and art, but I know a great deal about business. And don't try to tell me that there is not money to be made dealing in paintings, my dear, because I have eyes to see with. And some of those engaged in the business are none too scrupulous. Why can you not understand that I love being around artists and studios and paintings. I think it's really fun, and if I had a gallery, I would be part of it all. I am still hoping you will introduce me to some of your models.'

'What a good idea,' said Marjory, coming from
behind the screen. 'You will do that, won't you, Mr
Falkner?'

'At the moment, all my time is spent painting
portraits on commission. I'm not using models. I have
no time for such work.'

Marjory turned to her daughter. 'What are you going
to do, honey? About the gallery, I mean.'

'Oh, well, I've had to abandon the idea for the time
being. I've bought some land in St John's Wood. I
plan to build some nice villas.'

'What a good idea!' Marjory had never heard of St
John's Wood. 'And so profitable. You must show me
the plans when we get home. Come along, dear. We
must not keep Mr Falkner from his work, although
how he can paint in this gloom is beyond me.'

Falkner did not enlighten her. He escorted the ladies
down to their carriage and waved them goodbye, before
wearily mounting the stairs again. If he were to marry
Miss Hanson, he would have an implacable enemy for
a mother-in-law. On the other hand, he would have a
wealthy wife, which might compensate for Mary Beth's
considerable shortcomings.

Morosely, he sat down before his stove and stared
into the flames for some time. After a while, he was
seized with a powerful hunger, fuelled not only by more
than four months of celibacy, but by a reprehensible
desire to spite Miss Mary Beth Hanson. And her
mother. It didn't matter that neither of them would
ever learn of his indiscretion. What mattered was the
restoration of his self-respect, which had nothing whatsoever to do with earning fat commissions by painting
plain girls.

In the end, he spent the early part of the evening at
the Gaiety Theatre, although his mind was not on the
performance. The entertainers seemed remote, not flesh
and blood at all.

63

As the evening wore on, he conceived the impression that he was viewing the stage as if through a kaleidoscope: two-dimensional forms making ever-changing patterns of colour. His argument with the doctor, his irritation with Mary Beth and her mother, the boredom of painting vacant-eyed girls all played their part in generating a rebellious mood within him. Seated alone in the darkened theatre he felt a growing excitement, an increasing certainty that, whatever others might think, he had the power to paint worthwhile pictures. All he needed was the right subject.

He was on his feet the moment the final curtain fell, impatient to leave the chattering crowd. Pushing his way out of the theatre, he walked to Jimmy's supper rooms where he ate voraciously, yet without tasting his food at all.

It was late when he reached Regent's Circus. Curved buildings at each corner gave the circus a pleasing appearance, a fine symmetry against the night sky. Even here, where gas lamps were lit in profusion, the light lay on the road and pavement in distinct discs, leaving much of the vast area in darkness. Falkner sought the shadows and took up his station by Swan and Edgar's, folding his arms and leaning against a half-pillar to wait.

Even at this hour, there was a considerable amount of traffic. No respectable woman was afoot, of course, but several well-dressed men strolled into view and out of it again as they headed for the porticoes that ran down both sides of Regent Street. By day, shoppers were protected from inclement weather as they looked into the fashionable shop windows. By night, prostitutes used the sheltering gloom to sell their own wares.

After a few minutes, he saw a very young prostitute emerge from the dark to be illumined briefly by a street lamp. She was small and excessively thin, her whole body hunched in an attitude of lost hope. Lifting his shoulders from the pillar, he walked briskly after her, his heels echoing in the sudden silence. When she heard his footsteps, she turned and, recognizing a potential customer, tilted her head provocatively and placed her hands on her hips.

Their bargaining was soon done; he was not in the mood to quibble. She wanted a shilling, because she wasn't one of those girls who did it in any old dark corner. She had a room to which she could take him, and that cost money. Just down Coventry Street, it was. Not far at all.

The room was extremely small and held only a narrow bed with a straw mattress and no bedding, a small table with an unlit candle on it, and a chamberpot. The candle was made of tallow and stank when lit, but even this strong odour could not disguise ranker smells of sweat, urine and previous customers.

He took her without a word, roughly and quickly, carrying out his intention of indulging in a degrading act, something so devoid of human emotion it would stir his creative imagination by its bestial nature. She endured it like a somnambulist, and was soon on her feet, anxious, now that she had her shilling, to return to the streets.

'I am an artist,' he said.

'Oh, yes?' Polite disbelief.

Her cynical response irritated him. 'It is true, I am an artist. I have a studio in Wych Street, off the Strand, and I would like to paint a picture of you.'

'How much?'

He removed a five pound note from his pocket and dramatically tore it in half as she gasped, horrified at such waste.

'Bring this half to my studio tomorrow evening and I will exchange it for two and sixpence when you have completed one posing session. Each time you sit for me, I will pay you another two and six until you have earned the whole five pounds.'

The girl approachd him and snatched the half note from his fingers, thrusting it safely away in her bodice. 'You just tell me how to get to your place, and I'll be there, sir.'

6

The day after the visit to Falkner's studio, Marjory stood before her mirror and made a face. She had dressed furtively, without Perks' help, and thought she looked a little ramshackle. She lifted her chin and moved her shoulders back. She had a good carriage. 'Slouching makes a woman look old,' her momma used to say, 'but you stand real good, Margie.' The gown was lavender with a cross-over bodice and only a modest bustle. Marjory thought it made her look rather short in the waist. The lavender silk had been a mistake and, anyway, the cut was not so smart as her London gowns. She had put it on this morning precisely because she didn't wish to look too fashionable. Besides, it wasn't so closely fitting as her London-made gowns which forced her to lace herself to the point of discomfort.

She might look like an old frump, but she felt like a giddy schoolgirl up to a prank, as she tiptoed down the stairs and slipped out of the front door. Walking as fast as the gown and six petticoats would allow, she rounded the corner of the road with a sigh of relief. She had an appointment with a gentleman and was about to have a great adventure, so naturally she didn't wish to be scolded by anyone, least of all her maid.

A passing hansom pulled up to the kerb in response to her signal. She called out: 'King's Cross!' and climbed inside, pulling the little doors closed in front of her knees.

She could do whatever she wished today, spend all her money if she chose. She could meet a man almost young enough to be her son in broad daylight outside

King's Cross station and go with him wherever the fancy took her. There was no husband to treat her like cattle, there were no parents to cancel her enjoyments without a word of explanation and no children to scoff at her attempts at self-improvement. She had been emancipated, like the slaves. She was going to kick up her heels and heaven help anyone who tried to stop her.

Naturally, being in London made all the difference. No one knew her here except Mary Beth. Marjory could commit any number of indiscretions, knowing that no one else from back home would ever come to hear of it.

She just loved the capital. It had many fine buildings, thousands of beautiful women and handsome men, and, of course, culture. She was doing her best to make the most of the culture and to be a match for the women. Handsome men did not interest her at all, except as possible husbands for Mary Beth.

For once in her life, Marjory had everything she wanted: the respectability of having been married without the inconvenience of a husband, as well as control over her own money. She frowned slightly, holding on to the strap as the hansom rattled over the cobblestones. She intended to *spend* her money, which did not mean letting any man trick her out of it. She had enough experience of the male sex to know that they were all born with cunning. She had to be cautious and clever, because she had no one to turn to for advice.

Marjory could never confide her deepest feelings to Mary Beth because the girl was inclined to say: 'Oh, Momma, *must* you?' A simple question which had the power to spoil all Marjory's pleasure. Mary Beth thought that women of forty in general, and her mother in particular, should stay at home and crochet or something. Therefore, Mary Beth must not be told what her mother was about to do.

'King's Cross!' shouted the cabman as the hansom shuddered to a halt.

Marjory paid the man his fare, gave a small tip and watched admiringly as the cabby skilfully turned the horse and carriage round in a small circle. The little transaction had been remarkably trouble-free and pleasurable, considering that this was the very first time she had travelled entirely alone since coming to England, and considering that she had difficulty understanding what was said to her by cabmen, streetsellers, road sweepers and even her own porter. They all spoke so fast! The smallest incident could be an adventure when one was entirely alone abroad.

'Lady Marjory!'

Marjory turned round and gave Mr Guy Dundalk a delighted smile as she offered her hand.

'Good morning, Mr Dundalk. Isn't it a beautiful day for an adventure? Shall we go?'

'Yes, ma'am. I have the tickets. I don't suppose you will enjoy riding on the underground, but if you must, I am very pleased that you have asked me to accompany you. I must warn you, the air is foul from here to Farringdon Road. The underground railway is a boon to the working man, but was never intended for use by ladies like yourself.'

'Maybe not, but they don't have an underground railroad in St Louis, so I intend to see this one for myself. In fact, I intend to see everything that's new and different. I can't be sitting at home all day. I want to be doing, and even if I hate the underground I'll be glad I rode on it, so don't try to talk me out of it!'

The adventure got off to a hair-raising start because the train stopped barely long enough for them to get on. Then there was an undignified scramble, with people pushing and shoving to find a place to sit. Marjory hated it when the train went into the long tunnels: the air was foul then, just as Mr Dundalk had said it would

be. She thought she would be very glad to reach street
level when – if – the narrow train arrived at the
Farringdon Road station.

'Are you courting, Mr Dundalk?'

'No, ma'am.'

Marjory nodded with approval. 'That's probably
wise. You're only young and you've got your way to
make in the world. What exactly is it that you do?'

'I?' said Dundalk in surprise. 'Why, this and that.'

'Uh-huh. Live on your wits, do you?'

Dundalk looked uncomfortable. 'Not exactly. I
wouldn't put it that way. I look for promising business
ventures. Then I invest a little money, hoping to make
more.'

'Do you have any sisters?'

'Half-sisters. Three of them, and two half-brothers.
My mother died when I was a lad. My dad re-married
a few months later.'

'What does your father do?'

'He manages . . . that is, he *owns* an inn.'

'Good business, innkeeping. You ought to take an
interest in your father's inn. It's most likely going to
come your way one day.'

'No chance. I'm out of favour. Whatever's going will
fall to his other children. I must make my own fortune.'

They fell silent for a minute or two. The journey was
very strange. One minute you were looking out of the
window at blue skies and the next, you were in a tunnel
staring at a blackened wall inches from your nose. The
carriage was dimly lit and when the train went into a
particularly long tunnel, Marjory saw Dundalk's face
reflected in the glass. He was watching her, and those
fly-away eyebrows and lazy eyes had a mocking look.
Marjory frowned. She could usually tame a man by
asking him a lot of personal questions. No man liked
it; Englishmen liked it least of all.

'I understand you aren't as fancy as you make out,'

70

she said, turning to him in time to see the faint smile disappear.

'I never pretended – '

'My maid heard you speak and she says you're putting on that gentrified accent. Although why *she* should feel so superior to you, I don't know.'

'Lady Marjory – '

'Still, you're probably the right man for the job. I'll bet you know more about prostitutes than you let on,' she added, well aware that the other passengers were listening to her every word.

Suddenly, Dundalk's gathering anger disappeared and he laughed out loud. When he winked at a navvy seated close by, Marjory regretted her unruly tongue. She had meant to let Dundalk know she could defend herself from clever young men, not give him the chance to laugh at her.

When they arrived at Farringdon Road, Dundalk hustled her out on to the platform just before the train started up again. Marjory had nothing to say until they were once more above ground.

'I hope you're not offended about what I said,' she shouted above the noise of passing traffic. 'I admire a man who pulls himself up by his own bootstraps. You should be proud.'

The dreamy eyes met Marjory's, and she wondered what thoughts were going on in that handsome head. She sensed the inner strength of the man, the determination to succeed. His quick temper and prickly pride were rigidly controlled, but not completely hidden. Charm was his ticket to a better life, but she thought he had to work at it. He was not by nature a charming man. For one thing, she noticed that he had two smiles: the one he forced upon his lips to get what he wanted, and the other one that lit up his face whenever she scored a direct hit, got inside the defences and hurt him. It seemed he laughed as a response to pain.

71

'I admit I have been trying to ape the gentleman, ma'am. But I will not apologize for it. In this country a man is judged by how he speaks and how he dresses. I play the game.'

'That's the spirit! You and I understand each other. I'm playing a game, too. When my stepson forced us out of the house and said we should come to London, I made up my mind I was going to get into London society. I'll make them accept me whether they want to or not. But isn't it all a lot of nonsense?'

'Without a doubt, but what are you referring to?'

'Oh, you know, all that business about calling cards. Exactly three and a half inches by two and a half with my address and the day of my *At Home* printed on it. I'm at home on Thursday afternoons. Do you want to call on me sometime. I could introduce you to my daughter. My son's in America. I wish you could meet him. Samuel's a good boy. What I said still applies, though. I don't want anybody to know about the Lady Marjory Refuge until it's finished.'

'Thank you for the invitation, ma'am, but I am usually working on Thursday afternoons. In the weeks since I last saw you, great progress has been made. Workmen are at this moment busy converting a large house in Seven Dials. I have an account of how much money I've spent if you would care to study it.' Dundalk reached into his coat pocket and pulled out a single sheet folded into three.

'I'll take it with me and read it some time. I suppose you will be needing some more money.'

When he readily agreed, Marjory opened her handbag to give him another hundred pounds, silently chiding herself for her foolishness. She had meant to make him ask, had meant to hesitate and then hand over the money in exchange for a promise that he would spend it wisely.

Not wanting to think about the money or the Refuge

any more, she changed the subject and told Dundalk about her good deed in introducing Betty Bridgeman to Mrs Grimshaw's coachman.

'Grimshaw told me you were attempting to get them married,' said Dundalk. 'Are they actually going to do so?'

'Oh, they're going to get married just like I thought they would. Betty Bridgeman held out for a while, but the baby she's carrying kicked some sense into her. She can't have the fine gentleman she likes to think she deserves, so she'll settle for what she can get.'

Something in Dundalk's expression caused Marjory to hurry into an explanation.

'You think I'm callous. Well, I don't mean to be. Some people may be able to have exactly what they want in this life, but Betty isn't one of them. And neither was I until these last few months. I did what I was told and made the best of it.'

'I'm sure you did, ma'am.'

'And you haven't had an easy time, I expect, although it's different for a man. If a man can stick to his work, he can make a place for himself. A woman can't do that. At least a young woman can't.'

There was that strange look on his face again! She sure couldn't figure out this young man. They talked about nothing in particular until he handed her into a hackney. As she moved off she saw he was wearing his I'll-have-my-own-way smile.

Marjory sat back in the cab and took a deep breath. It was exciting being in charge of one's own life and making important decisions, but she found it rather frightening, too.

Marjory had spent two lonely months in London. Now, all of a sudden, she had more company than she had time for. She needed to rest up a bit after the previous day's excitement on the underground, followed by an afternoon spent paying calls, which was in turn followed by a ball at the Pringles'.

Taking some needlework with her, she went into the conservatory, a narrow room which ran across the back of the first floor. Wicker chairs with faded chintz cushions abounded, but there were very few shade-giving plants, so that when the sun broke through the heavy clouds at last, the room quickly became very hot. The needlework was ignored. Marjory slipped down in one of the chairs so that she could rest her neck on the back. She put her feet on a nearby stool and closed her eyes.

It is possible that she fell asleep, because the next thing she knew, Brogan was announcing Mr Bennett, and the doctor was right on the butler's heels. The sound of Brogan's voice had brought her bolt upright and blinking in surprise. But it was only eleven o'clock (no time to be paying calls), and she felt a little wary of the doctor, anyway. So she lay back in her original position and closed her eyes again.

'Come in, Doctor, and sit awhile. Feel that glorious warmth! I miss the sun. Not the hot summers we used to have in St Louis. That's too much of a good thing. But I do long for a sight of the sun now and again. It's hot in here. Take off your coat if you want to. I won't tell on you.'

'No, thank you.'

Bennett took a chair and surveyed his hostess as she lay stretched out before him. The difference between Americans and Britons was exemplified by this woman's pose. Not one British lady of his acquaintance would display herself in this casual fashion. Not one. For the first time, it struck him that Americans were something other than minor irritations. They were exotic foreigners with strange ways. One was deceived into expecting the two nationalities to behave in a similar fashion, simply because they spoke the same language. Yet America was actually farther from Britain than was Russia. And no one judged the Russians by British standards!

Bennett studied Marjory's face. She had told him she had been 'sick in bed for months', by which he supposed she meant she had been ill. There was no sign of illness now. Her skin was creamy and glowing, virtually free of lines. Again, he marvelled that she was in every way so much smaller and more delicate than her daughter. It must be hard for a young girl of strong features to have so graceful and elegant a mother.

'What have you come to talk to me about, Doctor?'

'Must there be something in particular?'

'At eleven o'clock in the morning, yes there must,' said Marjory.

'Madam, will you sit up properly and look at me when I speak to you?'

'No, I won't. Say your piece.'

Bennett cleared his throat. 'I've come to tell you that I think . . . if you had a male relative, I wouldn't be here . . . that I think Mr Lucius Falkner is the wrong sort of man for your daughter to know.'

Marjory opened her eyes and looked levelly at him. 'Is Mr Falkner a patient of yours?'

'Certainly not! If he were, I would not be sitting in your conservatory discussing him.'

Marjory closed her eyes again. 'Then how do you know he's the wrong man for Mary Beth?'

The doctor wiped the perspiration from his bald head and carefully replaced the handkerchief in his pocket.

'As a doctor, I have had occasion to study men at close quarters. I have listened to their secrets and learned to read their minds to a certain extent. Your daughter is a commonsensical girl. Forthright. Down to earth. Falkner is a dreamer. I have not seen his work, but I suspect he is a man of little talent. His

75

friends will be of a Bohemian frame of mind. What will they make of your daughter?'

'They'll hate her. Do you think I don't know that?'

'You are a woman alone. A woman in need of advice. Forbid your daughter to see Falkner. I beg of you, be guided by me in this.'

Marjory laughed. 'I'm perfectly willing to be guided by you, my friend. I don't like Falkner. But Mary Beth wouldn't give two pins for your opinion.'

'She is out of hand.'

'Maybe she's had too many fathers.' Marjory opened her eyes and sat up. 'Her daddy thought she should have a carefree childhood, full of laughter and pretty clothes. If I ever tried to make her mind me, he'd take her side, and say what a pretty thing she was and how she was her daddy's sweetheart. Mary Beth took it hard when Jonathan died. We went to live with my parents, and *my* daddy saw Mary Beth differently. Oh, he petted and spoiled her, but he also spent a lot of time teaching her arithmetic and business ways and things that most girls don't learn about, because she was a quick student and showed an aptitude for those subjects. Samuel didn't show the same talent, so my daddy hardly took any notice of him at all. Naturally, I tried to make up to Sam for his grandfather's lack of attention.'

'One hears of favouritism shown to one child in a family, and it always causes trouble,' said the doctor sympathetically. 'You must have been sorely tried.'

'For years I struggled with three generations in one house, a house I wasn't even mistress of. I worked most days at the store, but Daddy never took my advice about anything. Then at home, Momma wouldn't so much as let me choose what to have for dinner. And they both criticized the way I brought up the children. No wonder I married Gilbert. I wanted a home of my own. I wanted to run my house my way. But of all the mistakes I've made, marrying Gilbert was the worst one. *He* wanted to turn Mary Beth and me into proper ladies. He called my daughter a great clumsy elephant.'

'But you could go home now,' suggested the doctor. 'You are your own mistress and you have enough money to live as comfortably as you choose. You could take your daughter away from a society she doesn't understand and also see your son.'

Brogan entered with a tray containing glasses and a jug of lemonade. Marjory sat pensively until the butler had served them and left the room. The sun went behind the clouds, causing her to look skywards with a frown.

'It's too late, you see. Samuel won't come to England and Mary Beth won't go back to Missouri. I'm bound to be separated from one of them. And anyway,' she smiled slightly, 'I kind of like it in England.'

Bennett was saddened by her story, which made his desire to help and advise her stronger than ever. 'Such a disastrous upbringing your daughter has had. Oh, no blame can be laid at your door! None at all. But surely now that you have her in your charge, you will want to guide her footsteps and set her on the right course for a happy life.'

'Like my parents guided my footsteps, you mean? Not once but twice! No, thank you, Mr Bennett. I made up my mind I would never bully Mary Beth into marrying anyone and never stop her from marrying the man of her choice, either.' Marjory finished her lemonade and set the glass on the tray. 'Have you any children?'

'Alas, only one of our children lived beyond the age of five. We lost two dear little boys. Marcus is twenty-nine. A fine young man who never gives his father a moment's disquiet.'

'You are very fortunate. Is he married?'

'Marcus doesn't see fit to rush into matrimony.'

'Is he a doctor like you?'

'No, he never showed any inclination to study medicine, but he is not idle. Marcus has political ambition. At the moment he is acting as a sort of agent for Mr Warren Wainwright, who is the Member of Parliament for a South Wales constituency. Wainwright has promised to do his best to find a seat in the House for Marcus in due course.'

'Member of Parliament,' mused Marjory. 'Does that pay well?'

The doctor was surprised by the question. 'Members do not receive any remuneration. A man serves his country out of a selfless sense of duty.'

'Our legislators receive five thousand dollars a year, as well as expenses.'

'Five thousand dollars?' exclaimed the doctor. 'Why, that's about a thousand pounds! A hard-working country doctor will be fortunate to earn more than one *hundred* pounds a year.'

'Just goes to show you who's the most important,' said Marjory. 'An English doctor or an American legislator. America's a big country. The men who make our laws have a heavy responsibility. Besides, a man has to have something to live on, or else he's going to get up to funny business.'

'There is no corruption in *British* politics, madam.'

To his annoyance, Marjory laughed loudly. 'You must have very strange politicians over here, that's all I can say. Very strange indeed.'

'Well,' he conceded, 'there are always a few rotten apples in the barrel.'

Marjory stood up and smoothed the creases from her gown. 'I'm glad you admitted that, Doctor, otherwise I might find it hard to think of you as a man of the world. You know, your idea of me as a green girl is wide of the mark. You must remember, I lived by the side of a mighty river for pretty near forty years. I was

78

just a girl when the steamer, the *White Cloud*, caught fire while it was tied up at the levee. Pretty soon, other boats nearby caught fire, too, and then it spread to buildings along the levee. I helped my parents when they tried to move some of the most valuable stock out of the store. We were too late; Daddy lost everything. We got into the buckboard and drove as fast as we could to our house which was on the waterfront. We'd hardly started moving the furniture when the fire caught up with us and we had to leave the house. My daddy had to start all over again. Fortunately, his gold was safe in the bank.'

'It must have been a terrifying experience for a young girl.'

'It was nothing compared to the war. Missouri was split, you see. Some people were for the South and others for the North. Oh, I didn't see any fighting; I only saw the tears of widows and mothers and sisters and children. Those were hard years. In the winter of sixty-five and six, ice floated down-river all winter long and crushed twenty-one steamboats altogether. Why, one day I saw six of them turned into matchwood in five minutes!

'The rivermen all came to my daddy's store. He sold manilla cotton and tarred rope and things like that. Rivermen are hard. The pilots made a lot of money before the war, and they used to spend it on gambling and drink and dancehall girls as soon as they got it. They lived dangerous lives, but they loved the river, and so do I.

'The railroads are taking all the business now. The great days of the river boats are pretty near gone. But when Gilbert and I decided to come to England, I said: "We'll go down-river and sail from New Orleans or I'm not going." So you see, Doctor, I'm not one of those delicate ladies you find sitting around on sofas

79

looking interesting. I can take care of myself, and so can Mary Beth. Don't you worry about us. We'll manage.'

'You should take her home to St Louis.'

'She won't go and neither will I. I made up my mind to get into London society and I'm going to do it. Now, don't aggravate me any more. I want to enjoy myself.'

'You speak of London society as if it were composed of objects to be collected, like butterflies.'

'Maybe,' said Marjory. 'When I was twelve, I decided to collect frogs. I made up my mind to catch one hundred of them, and I did it, too. Kept them in glass jars. When I had got a hundred, I let them all go free. Drove my momma to distraction there for a while.'

'Members of London society are not frogs, either.'

Marjory smiled at him. 'I'll have to take your word for that, as I haven't got near enough to one to find out for myself.'

'Madam . . .' The doctor shook his head, laughing.

'Don't imagine I'm not worried about Mary Beth, because I am. But what good will worrying do? You know, when I'm really worried about something that I can't do anything about, I take to collecting things. Not that I ever thought of it that way before.'

'What were you worried about when you collected frogs?'

'Momma had just had her seventh stillborn baby. She sort of cut herself off from Daddy and me for about six months.'

Bennett tried to imagine this delicate woman in the dove grey dress enduring all the trials and hardships she had just described. One thing was certain: Lady Marjory was a different breed from his own dear wife. Sophia had been a nervous woman who had suffered all her short life from poor health. Just listening to the American talking about her adventures would have exhausted Sophia.

80

Nevertheless, mother and daughter were mere women, in need of masculine guidance. Taking up his hat and cane, he urged Marjory to follow his advice and forbid the marriage. He ignored her smile, as he promised to come at a moment's notice if she sent for him for any reason. He ended by assuring her that he had no wish to pry or interfere in the lives of others. It was his custom to speak out only when he thought it was absolutely necessary.

She led him to the door, laughing all the way, but she did urge him to call again, as often as he could manage.

'You know,' she said with some surprise, 'I suppose it's because you are a doctor, but I feel I can really talk to you. I've told you things about my past I wouldn't mention to another person in this country, because I know they wouldn't understand.'

The doctor left, feeling unsure of his attitudes about several subjects. One thing did surprise him: how could an English baronet, no matter how impoverished, bring himself to marry the daughter of an American ships' chandler, no matter how rich and beautiful?

7

Marjory didn't see a great deal of Mary Beth during the next two weeks. The girl said she was engaged in getting her villas underway in St John's Wood, and left early each morning. As she invariably arrived home just in time to change for her evening engagements, the two women led rather separate lives.

So Marjory was pleasantly surprised when Mary Beth joined her in the drawing-room on a Thursday afternoon and said she would keep her mother company during the At Home.

'You've laced yourself too tight, Mary Beth,' said Marjory. 'You'll faint before the afternoon is over.'

'Don't you like the dress? I think it's very smart.'

The gown was of subtly-patterned tartan wool, cut in a princess line with tight sleeves and a high stiff collar. It buttoned all the way down the front and was relieved only by small white frills at the neck and wrists.

'Very smart,' said Marjory drily. 'You can't hardly turn your head. You can't bring your arms forward or lift them up to tidy your hair if it needs doing, and you've got to sit on one hip. I like your hair, though. I like to see a nice frizzy fringe on a young girl, and a neat bun at the back looks good when a woman's got thick hair like yours.'

Mary Bath smiled. 'And what have you done to your hair, Momma?'

Marjory quickly lifted a hand to her forehead. 'It's just a little fringe, just to soften the lines of my face, you know. You don't think I look like a poodle, do you?'

'Not in the slightest.'

They lapsed into silence after that, expecting any minute to hear the doorbell ring.

'If anybody's coming, they're leaving it late,' said Marjory finally. 'Tell me about your villas.'

'Oh I've sold the whole thing, all the land. A gentleman who lives in the area was worried that my villas would spoil his view, so he bought the land from me.'

'You didn't lose money, did you?'

'Of course not, Momma. I made one hundred per cent profit. It's not clever to make a loss, so I never do it.'

Another pause, as the two ladies strained their ears for the sound of the bell.

'I went to Lucius' studio yesterday, and met one of his models,' said Mary Beth. 'It was very interesting.

'Was she dressed? What was the model wearing? I thought he said he didn't have time for that sort of thing.'

'She was wearing a black skirt, a white chemise and a shawl. She was barefooted, and Lucius had posed her sitting on the edge of a table. You know, one hip on the table and one leg off the ground.'

'Well, I suppose it could be worse.'

'Yes,' said Mary Beth. She had knocked on the door in her usual way, but instead of opening the door immediately, Falkner had asked who was calling, then kept her waiting a minute or two during which she had heard the sounds of frantic movement.

Mary Beth had entered swiftly as soon as the door was opened, but she hadn't found anything suspicious. There was a charming charcoal sketch of the girl on Falkner's easel. The model was dreadfully thin, but had smiled in a friendly way and said: 'How do you do?' and 'Pleased to meet you,' rather shyly. Her name, she told Mary Beth, was Josie Smiff. It was several

83

seconds before it occurred to Mary Beth that the surname was actually Smith.

'She was a respectable girl, Momma. Nothing to worry about.'

Mary Beth had insisted that Falkner send out immediately for a hot pie for the girl, and had poured a glass of red wine with her own hands. Josie Smith had been very surprised to be asked if she were warm enough and did she wish to have the fire lit. The girl had looked anxiously at Falkner and then said no, she wasn't cold at all.

Just to keep him on his toes, Mary Beth had told Falkner that she intended to call often. The artist had not looked pleased, and the girl had looked positively frightened.

Mary Beth was not at all happy about the model, although she had no intention of letting her mother know it. Mary Beth's attitude to Falkner and his work confused even her, because although she hated his having models, she couldn't help but be dazzled by the apparent ease with which he drew and painted.

Having no creative talent herself, she was awed by even the most minimal signs of creativity in others. Not that Falkner's talent was slight. She knew he was clever. It was this cleverness which explained the awkward silences that often fell between them, and the sudden sharp disagreements. Sometimes she wondered why he courted her at all. Of all the men she knew, he seemed to have the least regard for her intelligence, personality and appearance. Paradoxically, it was this withholding of his respect and praise that intrigued her and kept her knocking at his door. She sometimes wondered if she would be so interested in becoming Mrs Falkner, if Lucius were to fall to his knees at her feet.

'It doesn't look as if anyone is coming,' said Marjory. 'I don't know what I'm doing wrong.'

84

'You should take Perks' advice about social matters, Momma.'

'If you mean about calling myself Lady Marjory, it's too late. How could I change now?'

'I don't suppose you could. You will just have to brazen it out. I hate their silly titles, anyway.'

'Well, they are kind of funny and it wouldn't do for America, but the titled people are top of the totem pole here. My aim is to be accepted, to have a few of them in my house and to get into some of theirs. It's just a game and I intend to win. After all, you don't play poker, or any other game, if you don't want to win.'

'If you want to impress these people,' laughed Mary Beth, 'you shouldn't let on you know how to play poker. It isn't ladylike.'

'There are lots of things I don't let on about, Mary Beth. But I'll tell you a funny thing. I went to Mrs Pringle's the other night and they all wanted to play a card game called Brag, because they seemed to think I would be good at it, being an American. And do you know what? You play it a lot like poker. I did win, too.'

'Serve them right. I thought you disapproved of gambling.'

'We played for counters. I'll bet they were glad . . .' Marjory sighed suddenly. 'Honey, would you like to go back to St Louis?'

'No I'm going to get married one day and live in London. I know you don't approve of Lucius, Momma, but I'm old enough to know my own mind.'

'Then you are very much older than I ever expect to be. I don't see what the attraction is in getting married so soon. Why not have some fun first? You're only twenty-one.'

'You were only eighteen when you were married.'

'Yes, I was,' said Marjory. 'Why do you think I want you to wait? Because I know what marriage is like, that's why. I know what it's like to be bossed about by some pig-headed man who thinks he knows what's best. You think you can do what you please with Mr Falkner, but you just wait.Once you're married and he has all sorts of legal rights over you and your money, he won't be willing to say "How high?" when you say "Jump".'

'You think he's not good enough for me. But, Momma, I'm never going to catch a duke.'

'Mary Beth, you mustn't take seriously what I say about English titles. I don't want you to marry a titled man. I married one myself and look where it got me. All I ask is that you don't hurry into marriage.'

'No, I won't. Lucius doesn't wish to marry just yet. Momma, like you said, titled people are top of the totem pole in this country, and I'd like to be a Lady like you are, I admit it. And it's still possible, even if I marry Lucius. Artists are very highly thought of in England. I want to help Lucius to be a famous painter, then one day if he becomes Sir Lucius, I'll know I've earned it. I mean, I'll know Lucius has earned it. That's the American way, isn't it?'

'I guess,' said Marjory. She walked idly round the room straightening cushions and kicking footstools into place, although she knew the maid would do these things as soon as she and Mary Beth left the room. 'Are you planning to live among the English or wage war with them? Yes, I suppose it's challenging to live among these people and try to make them accept us. Maybe one day Sam will come over for a visit and we can all be together again.'

'I know you miss Sam,' said Mary Beth, 'but perhaps after Lucius and I are married, you could go back to America for a visit by yourself.'

'Yes,' said Marjory drily. 'That would be real nice.'

Shortly afterwards, Mary Beth went to her room to change for dinner. Marjory was left to her thoughts as she sat in the drawing-room, wondering whether to order her tea now or not.

The door opened, and Marjory jumped. 'The Countess of Dumfries!' cried Brogan. Marjory rose to her feet with a smile, wishing with all her heart that Mary Beth were here to see her triumph.

The countess glided into the room wearing a superb walking dress of maroon silk. She was slightly taller than Marjory and slender to the point of emaciation. She had protuberant blue eyes that swivelled slowly about the room, a hawk nose and thin wide mouth. When she smiled, lines radiated from the corners of those eyes, and she was transformed from an ugly dragon into the sort of woman who could be counted on to enjoy a joke, probably at someone else's expense. In fairness, Marjory imagined that the countess was perfectly capable of laughing at herself when she was in the mood.

The two women were about the same age. Both knew at once that the differences in their background were less important to their future friendship than the similarities in their robust personalities.

'I was acquainted with your late husband, and decided that I really must call upon his widow while I am in town.'

'You were a friend of Gilbert?'

'I was *acquainted* with him,' repeated the countess. 'Do you mind if I smoke a cigarette?'

'Why no.' Marjory watched in silence as the lady, having fished a cigarette from her handbag, attempted to light it with a match.

'Would you care for one?' asked the countess, having failed to get the third match to light the end of the cigarette.

'No, thank you,' said Marjory. 'There's no point now that Gilbert's passed away.' The countess removed the dead cigarette from her lips in surprise and trained her

87

large eyes on Marjory. 'What I mean is,' Marjory explained, 'the only reason why a lady should have anything to do with tobacco is to annoy her husband. I haven't got one, but if you have, do carry on.'

'Yes, it does infuriate Dumfries, but as he isn't here, I suppose it really is too much trouble.'

'And a terrible taste,' said Marjory. 'My mother dipped snuff. Used to make Daddy awful mad.'

'*Take* snuff, do you mean?'

'Not like you do here, sniffing it up your nose. You put some in your mouth between the gum and the cheek.'

'But . . . for what purpose?'

'I just told you,' laughed Marjory. 'You do it because your husband doesn't want you to.'

'I do so admire American women. They know how to keep their men in check. We have not the knack of it here.'

Marjory smiled, but made no comment. Brogan and a maid entered with the tea tray and a cake stand. Marjory prepared to pour, apologizing as she did so for the fact that no one else had decided to call on her this Thursday.

'I don't know many people yet,' she explained.

'But that's why I am here. I intend to introduce you to scores of the very best people.'

'That would be lovely,' said Marjory, 'but I think I should tell you that although I call myself Lady Marjory, I have no right to the title. I'm just Lady Manton.'

'I know, but it doesn't matter. I love an eccentric!'

'So do I,' said Marjory, smiling sweetly.

The countess was as good as her word. Marjory, Mary Beth and Lucius were invited to a small soirée at Dumfries House in Hanover Square. Mary Beth and the countess's elder daughter Lady Fenella, became friends almost immediately. Lucius was made much of by the other guests, to Marjory's surprise.

While Marjory could not complain about her own reception at Dumfries House – the earl was particularly attentive – there was no doubt that the assembled members of the *haut ton* were prepared to treat Lucius as something of a pet.

After that night, the friendship progressed to first names. They became Marjory and Caroline. The two women went shopping together, paid calls together and sat gossiping for hours. Someone named them the Deadly Duo, which pleased them both very much. Marjory had not been so happy since she had first come to England. She was particularly pleased that Mary Beth had a new friend. Fenella was twenty-five, with a strong mind of her own. Over the next few weeks, as Lucius became ever more involved in his work, Mary Beth failed to feel neglected, because Fenella more than filled the hiatus in her social life.

One hot afternoon, the countess sent in her card and immediately followed it into the drawing-room.

'Marjory! So much excitement! There is to be a protest meeting of concerned women about the Contagious Diseases Act. Do say you will come. Mrs Josephine Butler is expected to put in an appearance. It is a very serious matter. I need hardly tell you that we must find a way of preventing Mary and Fenella from discovering where we are going. This is far too delicate a subject for their ears.'

8

The plainness of the Friends' Meeting Hall in Westminster, together with its atmosphere of scrubbed divinity, did not help the occupants to feel cheerful and at their ease. The mood was serious; Majory and Caroline were not alone in deciding that the occasion required yards of heavy veiling.

Marjory sat on the hard chair with her eyes downcast, waiting to be electrified by the speakers. Caroline had explained the Contagious Diseases Act very succinctly. Any woman who was deemed, for whatever reason, to be a prostitute could be brought before a magistrate. He might then order her to be examined by a surgeon who was in the employ of the State. If she refused, she was considered to have committed a crime. She could then be forced to submit to the examination and, if found to be diseased, locked away in a special hospital until such time as the authorities thought she was cured.

Any woman of the lower orders, going about her business, might find herself brought to court as a prostitute, and the burden of proving that she was *not* a prostitute was on her. Thus, perfectly decent women could be, and often were, 'raped' by the doctors' instruments.

Marjory had been deeply shocked. She hadn't needed to ask if men could be picked up on the street and subjected to examination in the same way. Parliament would not have permitted such an Act to be passed if it could have been enforced against men.

'Caroline, I hate to ask,' said Marjory suddenly, 'but

just what sort of instrument do doctors use to violate these women?'

'I haven't the faintest idea,' said Caroline frankly. 'It is enough that the doctors *look*, don't you think? I have no idea how these things are managed in America, but when I had my children, one end of a sheet was tied around my neck and the other end tied around the doctor's neck so that he could not see any part of my body under any circumstances.'

'What does a woman need a man for when she's having a baby? My two were brought into this world by a midwife, the same as everybody else's.'

The two women were silent for a moment. The hall was filling up rapidly, but neither Marjory nor Caroline cared to turn round to see if any of their friends were present.

'Caroline, you remember when you said you could tell everything you needed to know about a woman by the way she laughs?'

'Yes, the laugh is a test of good breeding and cultivation.'

'Well, listen a minute.'

A peel of laughter came to them from several rows back, girlish with a hint of a bray and very distinctive.

'What do you make of that laugh?'

The countess gripped her hands together. 'She is young, stupid, spoiled, an abominable seamstress, sits a horse badly and can do no wrong in her grand-mother's eyes. Her mother is a poor fool who has done her best.'

'Do you know the girl?'

'My younger daughter, Marianne, whom I had thought until this minute was staying with my mother-in-law in the country.' Caroline turned her head to glare at her daughter. 'And she is sitting with Fenella and *your* Mary Beth. Don't turn round! We mustn't make a scene.'

91

A stout woman in a black costume came to the rostrum. Speaking in a voice that easily penetrated the hubbub, she said: 'It has come to our attention that about a dozen young, unmarried women are present in the hall. It would be most unsuitable for them to remain. We will, therefore, not proceed with the meeting until they have left. Would these young women please leave *now*.'

An excited buzz echoed round the room, but there was no scraping of chairs, no trample of retreating feet.

'I said: Will you young women on the left side of the hall *please leave*.'

Marjory could stand it no more. She turned her head, met Mary Beth's eyes and mouthed the word: 'Go.' Mary Beth looked away. Marjory turned back to her friend. 'I'll skin her alive when I get her home.'

'What if we had not come? We would not have known what our daughters were up to.'

'We still don't know what they've *been* up to. How many other meetings about ... things ... do you suppose they have attended?'

'I would never have dared to defy my mother as our girls are defying us, would you? Where have we gone wrong, Marjory?'

Marjory didn't answer, because the woman in the black costume was being supplanted by a rather grand lady in a very smart gown of lavender silk.

'She's the wife of a bishop,' murmured Caroline. 'But I can't remember which one.'

'This is disgraceful!' said the bishop's wife to vigorous nods of agreement from the woman in black. 'The young girls must leave the hall this minute. I wonder at your boldness in daring to come here at all. I don't know what the bishop would say if he knew. Will you leave now, please?' A hush of sorts descended on the occupants of the hall. Heads were turned to look at the girls. Only Marjory and Caroline were silent as the other women called out 'Brazen!' and 'Disgraceful!' and 'Go home to your mothers!' which made Marjory suppress an hysterical giggle.

'*Well!*' said the bishop's wife finally. 'I think it's blasphemous.'

'Oh, now that's coming it a bit too strong,' exclaimed the countess under her breath. 'I'm ready to sink with shame, but I wouldn't call their being here "blasphemous". Will this evening never end?'

Eventually, the organizers saw that they were faced with two ugly alternatives: to cancel the meeting, or press on regardless.

The first speaker came to the rostrum, introduced herself as Mrs Slocumb, apologized for the unavoidable absence of Mrs Butler to loud mutterings of disappointment, and announced that she would be reading from pamphlets written by the great lady. The meeting was underway, and no one had left the hall.

'Politically speaking, the Act is without precedent in the history of our country, in its tyranny and its defiance of all which has ever been considered by Englishmen as justice,' read Mrs Slocumb. 'In its system of paid spies, and the admission of anonymous whispers as evidence not to be rebutted, it is contrary to the entire spirit of English Law. The whole burden of proof is thrown not upon the accuser, but upon the accused; there is a complete absence of all fair and open court – to say nothing of jury. It may be objected that the ordeal of examination is imposed without the assumption of criminality, prostitution not being a crime against the State. But disobedience of a law *is* a crime, and this ordeal being, in fact, as great a punishment as any criminal could be subjected to, a woman will naturally, if possible, refuse to obey it. She is thus forced to become a criminal, and may be imprisoned.

'What can we think of a government which brings in a system for wholesale and legalized indecent assaults upon women? Truly, if we are driven to our last resources, we shall not despair; for then we women of England shall be found to be the representatives of truth and morality when we rise up in open rebellion and declare that we will not be so outraged, that we will not endure to see women deprived of jury trials. Nor will we consent that they shall be indecently assaulted by government officials, any more than by some obscure son of Belial.'

The audience applauded loudly, and under cover of the noise, Marjory leaned towards her friend to say: 'You know, I'm kind of glad Mary Beth has come to hear this. There are some things all women should know.'

'Perhaps no one here present,' continued the speaker, 'has ever experienced the pain of hunger – I mean starvation hunger. That gnawing and faintness increasing through weeks of fasting which becomes a raging instinct and drowns all other feeling. A girl I saw lately had lived, motherless, in a wretched home with her father who, in a fit of intoxication, violated her. She fled in horror. She found a shelter where she slept for many nights on a bare hard floor. Hunger increased. She was young, not more than sixteen. She lighted by chance on a low house, where the woman said: "I'll take you in; here are soldiers every evening." The way seemed easy. I asked how much she earned, how much a soldier paid. She said: "Sixpence, and out of that I have to pay fourpence to the woman of the house." Twopence, ladies, is the price in England of a poor girl's honour!'

Marjory felt tears pricking her eyes. *I must do something*, she thought. *But what?*

'You know,' continued Mrs Slocumb, 'in a recent speech, Mr Gladstone said there was a tendency in the country to look to the legislature for the solution of every social question, and to make laws for the govern-

94

ment of persons who ought to govern themselves. Mrs Butler has written: We might answer Mr Gladstone with the information that there is in the country a very strong disapproval of this tendency, a growing disgust felt against a legislature which is a "busybody" in the worst sense, showing a disposition, as unreasonable as it is eager, to touch every question which concerns domestic life. Such action on the part of the legislature, if it be permitted by the people to continue its present course, will succeed very rapidly in depriving us of the power of self-government and will weaken the benevolent instinct and the sense of social responsibility.'

Mrs Slocumb sat down to tumultuous applause. 'These laws are just made to protect men from getting diseased, aren't they?' said Marjory. 'Men should have to take the consequences of their actions.'

'And what of their wives who become diseased from their husbands and are never even told of it?'

'Ah, well,' said Marjory wryly. 'There should be a law protecting them.'

'A law which would keep the men healthy and so protect their innocent wives,' said the countess with a laugh. 'Like the Contagious Diseases Act.'

'Don't confuse me, my friend,' said Marjory, as the lady in the black costume rose to speak.

Mrs Barber was a powerful speaker, and she knew just whom to blame for the troubles of the century. 'It is a lie which is at the foundation of the whole of the mistaken treatment of this question. Legal language, and the corresponding action of men, expresses the idea, *false as hell*, that women are an aggressive army of malignant persons, of unclean harpies, bent on the corruption of the male sex. And that men are a class at the worst guilty of weakness, and liable to fall into the snares of the other sex; that, when they do so fall, it is an accident to be regretted, to be silent about as much as possible. While at the same time the most

95

strict and tender precautions must be adopted to prevent the multiplying of such sad accidents. From the beginning of the world it appears that men, acting alone in this matter, have acted a lie in dealing with women, as if *they* were the sole cause of the existence of immorality in society.

'The world is sick of disease – sick to death, bodily and morally, of self-inflicted diseases. The world needs to be undone in order to be renewed again; but in its wild endeavours to cure itself, mad with its own folly, it only presses the chains of slavery closer, and crushes itself more and more under the super-added mountains of its own regulations.'

When every other women present rose to her feet to applaud these stirring words, Marjory sat quite still, shaken by the feelings of man-hatred Mrs Barber had awakened in her. *Not all men are bad*, she told herself firmly. *I've just been unlucky.*

Caroline sat down and studied her friend's troubled face. 'Has the meeting upset you, my dear?'

'It was intended to and it did. I'm glad I came. Caroline, not all men are bad. Some are good; some are doctors trying to stem this tide of disease.'

'Yes, but don't you go discussing this evening's meeting with Benny. He would be furious if he knew I had brought you here.'

'Benny?'

'My cousin, Frederick Bennett. My dear Marjory, how did you suppose I heard about you? And it is the kindest thing Benny has ever done for me, because, you know, I value your friendship very highly.'

For several seconds, Marjory was too surprised to speak. Then she smiled broadly. 'Like I said. Not all men are bad.'

9

Bennett saw almost all his female patients at St Bartho-lomews, but had made an exception of his patient this afternoon. She had arrived at his home in Harley Street in a state of great agitation. He had, therefore, taken pity on her and agreed to examine her in his consulting room.

The young woman had tears standing in her eyes as she rose from the examinatiion table and adjusted her clothing. Bennett indicated a chair on the far side of his desk, and she sat down obediently.

'I'm sorry, Mrs Drew, if my examination distressed you, but it was the only way to make sure that you are healthy.'

The girl knuckled her tears away, sniffing loudly. 'You was . . . *were* . . . very gentle, sir, and I appreciate it. I had to know if I was all right. You understand. You will help me, won't you?'

Bennett picked up a pen and studied the nib as if he had never seen one before. The girl was breath-takingly beautiful: the bloom of youth was on her cheeks; thick golden hair fell into unruly curls beneath her garish bonnet. She was a healthy girl with full lips and excellent teeth, a young woman who could command the lustful attentions of men.

'I will help you all I can, but you must tell me the truth. You have lied to me, have you not? A respectable wife would not know what branch of medicine I specialize in, nor where I live, nor at what times I am available for consultation. So, the decision is yours, young miss. Tell me the truth, or leave my rooms.'

The girl bent her head and began to cry quietly but

so hopelessly that Bennett, moved in spite of himself, whipped out his own linen handkerchief and thrust it at her.

'You have guessed correctly,' said the girl in a voice hardly above a whisper. 'What can I say? I am so ashamed, yet relieved. I am, sir, truly grateful to have this opportunity to unburden my soul, to tell someone what has become of me. I know you despise me and I don't blame you. But you will help me, won't you? You said if I tell the truth . . .

'My name really is Florence Drew, but not Mrs, just Miss. I was an upstairs maid in the home of a banker in Portsmouth. I was twenty years old last Friday and I first went into service after my father died when I was sixteen. There were four young ones at home and my mother was in poor health. I had to go to work. My father had been a guard on the railway and I was brought up proper . . . properly. I hated being a maid, but I had to earn money so that I could send something home. Those first months, I was so lonely I just cried all the time.

'Last November, a gentleman came to stay with my employer. He was about thirty-five years of age and ever so handsome. Right away, he noticed me. I did some trifling service for him, and he gave me half a sovereign! He spoke to me as if I was a proper lady. I did visit him in his room just once, but we didn't do nothing, that is, nothing wrong, just a few kisses. He asked me to marry him, you see.'

'They usually do,' said the doctor drily.

'I packed my bags. I didn't give notice because Robert (that was his name) said I wouldn't need the sort of piffling money Mrs Baker owed me, and it would be best for us just to leave one night after everyone was in bed.'

'You must have known you were doing wrong.'

'Yes, sir, but I thought it would come right. We went

98

to Paris and I kept asking him when we would be married and he kept saying soon. I lived as his wife, I admit it, but I truly loved him and I believed what he told me. He was so handsome. He bought some pretty clothes for me, and we dined out ever such a lot and went to the theatre and the circus. I was very happy. Then one morning I woke up and he was gone. He left me fifteen pounds and a note saying I could keep the clothes. But there wasn't no . . . any explanation.

'I didn't know what to do. It still makes me shake when I think about it. I don't speak French, but somehow I managed to make the Frenchies understand that I wanted to return to England. Eventually, I boarded a train for Boulogne and was in Folkestone a few hours after the steam-packet set sail. I spent one night at a respectable inn and the next day I travelled on to Portsmouth.

'I was that confused, I didn't know what to do for the best nor where to turn. I took lodgings in the town, five shillings the week. I knew, of course, that I would probably never get another place in service, because I had left Mrs Baker without notice and I didn't have a reference. I did think some of the girls I knew at the Bakers' house might help me. I had scarcely any money left, what with the fare and all. Can you understand what desperation I felt, sir? I suppose not. You're a man and men always manage somehow. And being a man, you think I'm wicked, and I daresay you don't blame Robert at all.'

'You're wrong, Florence. I blame him very much. Your story is all too common. Had you no one to turn to?'

'I thought I did. I was out walking on the second day and who should I see but Mary Marsden, Mrs Baker's maid? I called out to her. She had always been kind to me, but she just gave me an evil look and walked right past me! So I knew there was no hope of help from anyone at the Baker house, and I knew it was no use going home. I'm too ashamed, and besides, my brothers have started working. I stopped sending money home two years ago and never seemed to find the time to write a letter. The boys wouldn't have me in the house.

'I wanted to cry, but that wouldn't have done no good. It was beginning to get dark. I bought a baked potato from a street seller and while I was eating it, a man come up . . . that is, *came* up to me.

' "May I walk you home?" he says. "There are many soldiers in Portsmouth, it being a garrison town. A young lady on her own might be insulted by a drunken soldier."

'I thanked the man for his thoughtfulness and we walked down the street to my lodgings, talking pleasantly and politely all the way. When we got to the door, I held out my hand in a friendly way to say thank you and goodbye. Do you know what he said?'

The doctor could have made an intelligent guess, but he shook his head and told the girl to continue.

' "I am a policeman," he says, "and you are a prostitute."

'I said I wasn't. He said I must be, else why had I let a perfect stranger walk with me?

'I suppose you know what happened next,' said Florence. 'Well, of course you do. It's your line of work, isn't it? But I'll tell you what it was like for me, just the same. You may know all about the Contagious Diseases Act, but I had never heard of it. They took me before a magistrate and said I might be diseased and a threat to all them . . . those fine soldiers. They said I had to be examined and I could have the examination voluntary – or not. And if I was diseased, they would force me to stay in a lock hospital until I was cured.'

'I'm very sorry this had to happen to you, my dear,

100

but the Contagious Diseases Act is vital if we are to stamp out this terrible scourge.'

'They fill you full of mercury.'

'It is the only – '

'And sometimes the mercury kills you and it's terribly painful.'

'Yes, well, heroic doses are no longer – '

'*Heroic?*' cried the girl. 'Is that what you call it? Anyway, the doctor was pleased with himself because he could examine so many women in one hour. Forty, he said he could do. You have to get up on this table and put your feet in little pockets to keep your legs apart – ' She stopped to blow her nose. 'And then he shoves that metal thing – '

'The speculum.'

' – right into your private parts, and it hurts something terrible. And the doctor says you're all clear, and you get down and you feel dirty, and they don't care at all. Some of the women who were examined at the same time as me were respectable married women what . . . who had just happened to be out on the streets late at night.'

'But *most* of them were prostitutes,' said the doctor quietly. 'Why did you come to London?'

'I couldn't stay in Portsmouth. Not after being arrested and called a prostitute. I thought I might have a better life in London.'

'If only you young girls would not come crowding into the capital! There is much viciousness and depravity in London. Tell me the truth, Florence. How many men have you been with since you came to town?'

'Just one, as God is my witness. He was a well-dressed gentleman. I asked ten shillings and he agreed. He treated me decent, I must say. Afterwards, when he was gone, I just cried and cried. But I'll get used to it, you see if I don't. They want to treat me like a prostitute, well then I'll *be* one and live well and not

101

have to work as hard as I did when I was a maid. I don't care no . . . any more, what becomes of me.'

'Now, Florence, degrading yourself won't punish those who misunderstood your situation. Don't you see? You are confirming their opinion of you. Won't you try to find some decent work?'

'My mind's made up,' said Florence, meeting Bennett's eyes squarely for the first time.

Bennett sighed. 'Then, if you would avoid becoming infected, be sure to look at your customer's member to see if there is a sore on it.'

'*I couldn't!*'

'And press your hand into his crotch to see if he has swollen glands.'

'No!' Florence covered her face with her hands. 'Don't say anything more.'

'He may have a blotchy rash on the palms of his hands, forearms, ankles, or perhaps the soles of his feet. I am telling you this for your own preservation, so pay attention to me. If you go wtih a man who is infected, you will develop sores within about twenty-four hours. But whereas a man will see straightaway if he has contracted the disease, you will not be so fortunate. You will not be able to see the sores and they are often painless.'

The doctor had done his best to shock the girl. He watched impassively as Florence sobbed into the handkerchief he had just given her. It was several minutes before she recovered her composure.

'You mustn't speak so,' she whispered.

'If he is diseased, you must send him away. Of course, he may become angry. He may strike you, but you will get used to ill-treatment.'

Florence stood up. 'That will do, Mr Bennett. I don't want to hear any more. Just tell me your fee.'

Bennett was suddenly angry. 'Do you think I would charge you, knowing how you have earned the money?

102

Consider my words. Save yourself while there is still time. Money is not everything.'

'It is to them what hasn't got it,' said Florence. She walked to the door, turning towards him with her hand on the doorknob.

'That was a very kind thing you did, doctor. Not to ask for your fee. I was told you'd want half a crown. I want you to know I appreciate your generosity. I'm going to save my money, I am. And one day I'll be able to live like a lady.'

Bennett watched her go. 'No, you won't,' he said to himself. 'You will contract gonorrhoea or syphilis or both. You will lose your looks and your health. You will probably become sterile, old before your time, and end in the gutter.'

The door opened and Marcus entered the room. 'I beg your pardon, Father, were you speaking to someone?'

'I was talking to myself, I'm afraid. Did you see that pretty young girl who just left here?'

'The whore, you mean? Yes, I saw her.'

'She is a whore,' sighed the doctor, 'but one who is just starting out on her despicable career. I tried to frighten her into abandoning her way of life, but it was no use. She was a maid, seduced by a guest in her employer's home, then abandoned in Paris. Inevitably, she was arrested on her return to this country and charged under the Contagious Diseases Act. Our laws, though often just and necessary, are sometimes improperly applied.'

Marcus picked up the half-dozen books which were scattered across his father's desk and replaced them in the bookcase. He often tidied the doctor's consulting rooms and filed away the correspondence which would otherwise lie for ever on the mahogany top. Marcus could never be still in the presence of disorder.

'You say the law is *often* just, Father. I would have

103

said it is always just and certainly necessary. If the girl was improperly arrested, it is the fault of the police, who often allow their sense of power to run away with them. But she need not have turned to prositution because of one unfortunate experience. The seeds of depravity were there. Otherwise, she would not have allowed herself to be seduced in the first place.'

'It is too bad. The police occasionally arrest respectable married women who are not prostitutes at all. I have heard of several cases.'

'But then – ' Marcus sat down in the chair so often used by his father's patients. 'But then, if these women are disease-free, they are released.'

'With their reputations in tatters and their lives effectively ruined.'

Marcus smiled. 'You talk as if they lived in our milieu, in which case they would certainly suffer. The labouring classes are not like us, Father. They don't have the same set of values and should not be compared to us.' He removed a small pocket diary and consulted it. 'I shall be dining out for the next six evenings. Will you inform Mrs Davis, or shall I?'

'I will tell her. You would do well to tell me only the dates on which you will be dining at home. You are so often out.'

'I must be at the House in the evenings, Father. You know that.'

'Surely, you hear more debates than Mr Wainwright does.'

'He has certain business matters to attend to, but wants a detailed report from me. Besides, he already has his seat and need not work too hard, whereas I must be diligent in learning all I can.'

'You do the work which that man was elected to perform. He imposes on your good nature, or rather, he takes advantage of your ambition.'

Marcus Bennett was a handsome man; tall like his

father, but slimmer, with a full head of sandy hair and the peaked Bennett eyebrows. Like his parent, he kept his emotions on a very tight rein, indeed. Only the flush on his lean cheeks and the slight frown indicated his annoyance. 'It is not a sin to be ambitious, nor is it a crime. Warren Wainwright does make me work hard. It is good training. I'm learning a trade, as it were, with no cost to myself.'

'You should be paid a salary. American legislators receive one thousand pounds a year. Did you know that?'

Marcus's blue eyes met his father's brown ones. 'I know I am a financial burden to you – '

'That isn't true and it isn't what I meant.'

'I promise you that the very generous allowance you give me is greatly appreciated. And not a penny of it is misspent.'

The doctor sighed loudly. This was old ground, frequently trampled to no purpose by father and son.

Apparently anxious to change the subject, Marcus said: 'If you were not satisfied with the Contagious Diseases Act in all its details, Father, you should have argued with your mentor eleven years ago.'

'Mr Acton is not my mentor! He is my colleague, the leading authority in my field. It is just that he has the gift of being able to put his theories on paper, whereas I have not.'

'You have lived in his shadow for twenty years,' said Marcus. 'If there is some way in which you think the Contagious Diseases Act is unjust, you should say so.'

'In order to win some notoriety for myself, you mean. That is the way your politicians behave. They talk *for* something when the general view is against it, and *against* something when the general view is for it, and so draw attention to themselves and further their ambitions. Well, I am not a politician, and, besides, if I were to oppose the Act, I would be accused of

105

following in the shadow of that Josephine Butler woman. I'd rather be called Acton's shadow. At least, I respect him.'

'Yes, that would be a great embarrassment to me. Mrs Butler opposes the Act on the grounds that prostitutes are just like other women and would be just as horrified by an internal examination as a pure woman would be.'

Bennett shook his head slowly. 'Will I never convince you that prostitutes are, or were at some time in their lives, just like other women of their class?'

'Even your Mr Action says that some women are just naturally depraved. I find his book on prostitution disgusting and riddled with inconsistencies, by the way. *Someone* should speak up in opposition to him. Why should it not be you?'

'Because I am not ambitious for fame and fortune. Acton has scarcely any time to give to his patients, because so many hours of his days are spent in politicking and writing. I prefer to spend my time with my patients, and in some research.'

'Yet, you have always shown a great interest in the law as it affects your work. You could do so much good.'

'Yes, I admit I am interested in politicians and the laws they make. But a man may enjoy cock-fighting without wishing to be a chicken.'

Marcus smiled. 'So you will continue to treat diseased little trollops like the one who just left here. Measuring out your professional life in half crowns from the ill-gotten earnings of – '

'That is enough, sir!' said Bennett. 'The child who just left here is not diseased, merely desperate. And I did not charge her. You and I would be in a pretty fix if I depended upon the fees of prostitutes to keep us in comfort. Remember, I earn *guineas*, not *shillings* by treating diseased men, and hundreds of pounds from

106

my post as Surgeon to the Islington Dispensary. I earn four thousand pounds a year, my boy, by doing what I can for profligate men and the women who are their victims! More even than an American congressman.'

'Oh, Father, really! Those women carry within them the disease which can drive men to madness and death. I see Acton's influence over you, with his belief that prostitution is inevitable. And worse, his insistence that these women are often healthier and live longer than respectable, child-bearing women!'

'I know that my profession is an embarrassment to you, Marcus.' Marcus, tight-lipped, looked away. 'I'm sorry for your sake that my interests led me to this specialization, but it is too late now. As for the relative health of prostitutes, some live longer, healthier lives than respectable women and some are themselves cut down by syphilis. It is a question, to some extent, of the woman's own moral fibre. If she is of strong character, she will survive her pathetic life, she will eat well and probably avoid the dangers of childbirth, which still kills more women than syphilis does. I wish I had your absolute moral convictions, my lad. You are so *certain* that the views you hold are the right ones. While I . . . every time I see a patient or prescribe a certain treatment, I wonder if I have made the right decision. My calling breeds a certain humility.'

'I am not ashamed of the work you do.' Marcus stood up and pulled his waistcoat into place, stretching out his arms to expose his shirt cuffs and putting on his hat and gloves in quick neat movements. 'Your profession has bred humility in you, because you are a decent man. I have to tell you that I find many medical men insufferably pompous and superior.'

'We should not quarrel, Marcus. We have only each other left now that your mother has gone.'

'No, indeed we shouldn't. I beg your pardon, sir.' Marcus approached Bennett and briefly kissed him on

107

the cheek, as he had done on parting ever since he was old enough to feel loved and safe in the presence of his quiet parent.

'Goodbye, Papa, and try to forgive me for provoking you. Don't wait up for me. I shall be in very late this evening.'

10

With downcast eyes, Florence slipped past a grand-looking gentleman in the hallway and left the doctor's house.

The last day of April was cold and wet. The fine rain insinuated itself into the fibres of her black felt hat, leeching the cherry-red dye from the ribbons so that coloured water dripped from the bow like blood. Florence lifted her face to the bleak sky to let the rain cool her flaming cheeks, hoping that the sick dread of the future, which had turned her legs to India rubber, would fade in a minute or two so that she could walk away. How she hated the house, Harley Street, the doctor, all men!

Mr Bennett had tried to scare her away from prostitution. She knew what he was up to; she wasn't a fool. Only, scaring someone wasn't good enough, was it? It wasn't good enough for him to tell her she must lead a respectable life, if he didn't also show her how she might find work that would put food in her belly and keep her warm and dry. *And* without leaving her bone weary at the end of every day!

Besides, her weeks with Robert in Paris had given her a taste for an easier life. That wasn't too much to ask, was it? Girls like her, who had been born poor and had bad luck, always paid for whatever good things they got, one way or another. She hadn't liked being a servant. All that humility; all that curtseying; all that bullying by the housekeeper. She would never do that again. In future, she would have her own servants to wait on her, and there was only one way the Florence Drews of this world could afford servants. She would have to find some rich man who was willing to keep her.

Finding the right man would be difficult. You couldn't stand around the Haymarket after the theatres closed, or drift from one coffee shop to another in the hope of finding the perfect gentleman. And you couldn't get the best of everything by promenading the Burlington Arcade at five o'clock of an evening, for all it was well known that gentlemen went there expressly to meet girls like her.

She had a room in St Giles near Drury Lane for which she paid half a crown each week. A whole week's rent, that's what the doctor could have cost her. She had reason to feel grateful to him, but just thinking about the embarrassing visit made her feel physically sick.

There was a small, rather dirty coffee shop in Drury Lane, in which Florence could see several unattached women gossiping over their cups. She went inside, but walked straight to a table already occupied by a single woman who was unmistakably a prostitute of long experience. The woman was middle-aged and bent pathetically over a dirty scrap of a handkerchief as she gave in to an incapacitating, dry cough.

'Do you mind?' asked Florence, with her hand on the back of the chair.

The woman hadn't the strength to speak, but nodded as she continued to cough. Her hair was mousy and thin, and she hadn't combed it for some time. All of her front teeth were missing. In response to Florence's shy smile, she grinned weakly when the spasm had passed.

'Are you gay, dear?'

Florence flushed. 'I suppose so. I'm just starting out, you see. I want to get me a rich man and live in style, but I don't know how to find one.'

'Then you're wasting your time sitting round in here.

Ain't no man as comes in here what has any tin, I can tell you. They's all poor as church mice. And even them no-good men don't want the likes of me.'

'I'm ever so sorry. Here, let me buy you another cup of coffee and a pie. I'll bet you could eat a pie, couldn't you?'

'Well, I ain't had nothing all day, but to tell you the truth, I'm not so hungry. Anyways, I'll have the pie, if you don't mind.'

The woman studied Florence carefully, looking her up and down with a professional eye, feeling the cloth of her gown, noting the softness of her hands.

'I could help you. I could, really. You don't think I'm much to look at now, but I was all the rage in my youth. I lived real well. I could help you to get just what you want. My name's Lil Crane, by the way. What's yours?'

'Florence Drew. I tell you what. If you and me become pals, I'll give you some money when I get it. How's that?'

'It's a bargain. You're pretty, Florence, but you've looked in your mirror, so I don't have to tell you that. The proper place to find a rich man is an introducing house and I can write to the lady what owns the best one. But you got to have fine clothes.'

'I've got them. They were given to me by the gentleman I thought was going to marry me, and I've taken ever such good care of them.'

'Well, that's just fine. Never go near them madams who lend you clothes to wear on the streets, then send some old crone to follow you so that you don't run off. But, what am I saying? You must never go on the streets. Once you do, your value will drop and you won't never recover. You go to the introducing house I'm going to tell you about. And don't get mixed up with any bullies who tell you they'll find men for you. You act like a lady, do you hear?'

111

'Oh, yes, Lil, I'll do just what you say. I'm ever so grateful.'

'Don't go rushing off! I've got something else to tell you. Lord, you are green, girl! I got to tell you how to keep from having babies. You takes a piece of sponge, or maybe two or three, and you ties a long double twist of cotton on each piece. Then you put them in (you know where, I suppose – you can't be *that* green) before your man comes to you. Best dampen the sponges, it's easier to get them in. Then after your man has gone to sleep or left you, you takes them out and give them a real good wash, ready for the next time. Be sure to put a long enough thread on them or you won't be able to get them out. And don't you never forget!'

'And does it work? Really keep you from getting pregnant?'

'Of course it does!' said Lil. 'And if it don't, you come to old Lil and I'll give you the name of a woman what'll get rid of it for you.'

They talked for another twenty minutes, but Lil was very tired. The two women parted, agreeing to meet again in a few days' time.

'I'm always here,' said Lil. 'They lets me sit here in the warm, because I brought them good money in the old days.'

Florence focused her thoughts on the evening ahead, planning what she would wear, how she would arrange her hair. She indulged in a little daydream about a handsome young man who would be bowled over by her beauty, offer her four thousand pounds a year and install her in a house overlooking Regent's Park. Lil said it had happened to a few lucky women. Why shouldn't it happen to her?

The dream carried her all the way from the doctor's house to the Strand. She had just got to the part where, enslaved by her charms, the rich gentleman was begging her to marry him, when she reached the door of her humble room in a large but respectable lodging house. The drab chamber, with its lumpy bed and peeling, mould-scarred wallpaper, banished the rosy dream. It was then she remembered the doctor's warning, with a shudder.

That night she put on her best linen and several dabs of what was almost surely the finest perfume Paris had to offer. Robert had been surprisingly generous at times. Fortunately, just a little of the potent fragrance went a long way. Her supply, carefully managed, should last for many weeks.

She wore her dinner dress of sky blue satin, lavishly decorated with blond lace on the corsage and cuffs. The small train, also of blue satin, was deeply scalloped and trimmed with more lace, and there were tufts of apple blossom on the corsage, cuffs and skirt. Robert had paid a fortune for this gown, and she had looked after it well. There was only one small stain on the front of the skirt which hardly showed at all.

Later, as she sat proudly in the hansom, she was anxious not to allow the satin train to touch the dirty floor of the cab. She must be extremely careful. If she found the right man this evening, she would be laughing. If not, she would soon have to sell something – a lace-edged petticoat, perhaps, or two or three pairs of kid gloves – in order to keep herself in funds. Wearing fine clothes, it seemed, was her best hope of finding someone to pay for more fine clothes. Lil had been most emphatic on that point. She would go hungry before she parted with one item, but the rent would have to be paid somehow.

The owner of the Pimlico introducing house greeted Florence in the hall. A large woman in her late forties, she had painted cheeks, bad teeth, dyed orange hair and a knowing look. Florence was instantly afraid of her and wanted to run away from the feral welcoming smile that dared you even to think of cheating her.

113

'How nice of you to come this evening,' said the woman, just as if Florence had been invited. 'I am Mrs Morgan, and I assure you my dear, that you will meet some very charming gentlemen in my house. I see this note of introduction is from Lil Crane. Well, well. I must find some way to thank Lil. How is she? Still feeling poorly? I really must send her something. So kind of her to have remembered me. Of course, Lil did very well in this house in her younger days. And who else but Mrs Morgan should have the privilege of introducing so pretty a young girl to just the right gentleman?

'Now, do try to compose yourself, my dear. You're shaking like a leaf. Gentlemen don't like frightened bunnies. You must look them in the eye and give them an inviting smile. Show them you think they are charming. Talk amusingly on unimportant subjects, but not for too long. Gentlemen like to hear their own voices. Besides, they have been listening to serious conversations all day. Gentlemen come to Mrs Morgan's for dalliance and to forget their cares.

'Here's Aspasia. I think you two should sit together on this brown settee. How charming you look! What a picture! Aspasia's black hair and white dress don't clash at all with your blue gown and beautiful blonde curls. Natural, are they? My word! You are a fortunate girl. Oh, there's another new arrival. Now, who could have sent her? Never seen her before. Hardly up to Mrs Morgan's standards. Look at that gown! I must send her away. Excuse me, girls. Do get acquainted.'

When Mrs Morgan had gone away to deal with the new arrival, Aspasia, a plump girl of no more than sixteen, said she was the daughter of a curate who had been seduced twelve months ago by a boy in her Surrey village. Florence said she had been seduced by a guest in her employer's home and had gone to live in Paris. Aspasia pouted, never having been to Paris. With ill-concealed envy, she praised the Parisian gown, which helped Florence's confidence no end. On Mrs Morgan's orders, everyone was given a single glass of champagne to put them more at their ease. When she had drunk the contents of her glass, Florence began to study her surroundings.

The large room was ever so fine, far grander than any room Mrs Baker had possessed in Portsmouth. There were crystal chandeliers and thick carpets and two male servants in brown livery. Around the room were seated or standing about twenty-five very young women. They were all tastefully dressed and had arranged themselves in small groups, nervously holding their poses as if expecting to have their pictures taken. There was a suppressed air of excitement, a low-voiced hum of feminine conversation that was broken only occasionally by raucous laughter quickly silenced.

The huge mantel clock was about to strike ten when the mahogany doors opened and several men in evening dress ambled in. No one announced their names, understandably enough. To Florence, they all appeared to be old, perhaps even forty or fifty. Not one of their rapidly swelling number could be described as handsome. None, that is, until a solitary sullen gentleman marched purposefully through the doorway. His eyes scanned the girls as if he were looking for someone in particular and had not come to enjoy himself at all.

Several of the other gentlemen spoke to him politely. He would nod in acknowledgement of their greeting, perhaps murmur a few words before moving on. Mrs Morgan approached him; he said something; she shrugged and walked away. His hair was sandy, his clean-shaven jaw square and uncompromising. Angry he undoubtedly was, and probably the rudest person in the room, but also undeniably the handsomest man she had ever seen.

Aspasia was speaking with great animation into her

right ear. Florence made no reply. Aspasia flicked open her fan with an angry click and raised it to hide her lips. 'You are a bitch, Florence. Answer me when I speak to you. It's all part of the game. Smile and don't stare at the men. You can't hope to win a rich beau if you look as if you've just swallowed vinegar.'

It was then Florence noticed for the first time that she had forgotten to bring a fan. Now she had nothing with which to busy her hands, nothing to cool her burning face, nothing to hide behind as the man, having seen her at last, approached the settee. He bowed slightly, his peaked eyebrows, so pale yet so expressive, giving him the look of the devil come to take her to hell.

'May I have a word with you, ma'am?'

'Yes, sir.' Florence stood up, aware of Aspasia's surprise, and walked a few paces to an unoccupied part of the huge room. She turned, meeting his eyes squarely but with great difficulty.

He couldn't keep his lips from curling contemptuously. Or perhaps he wasn't trying. 'Have you been with anyone this afternoon?'

'I beg your pardon, sir?'

'Have you had sexual congress with any man since you left the doctor's home?' he said through gritted teeth.

'No, I haven't.'

'Then I will make you an offer you will find it hard to refuse: an elegant apartment, fine new gowns within reason and the opportunity to attend many balls and eat lavishly. I suggest you come with me now.'

Tears filled her eyes, but she blinked them into submission. 'You're pretty saucy, ain't you? That's no way to speak to a girl. You ain't said one polite thing to me. Besides, I'm hungry. I ain't had nothing to eat since breakfast. They serve supper here at eleven o'clock and I was counting on it.'

116

The man drew in his breath irritably. 'Very well. We will have supper here, because I certainly don't intend to parade you in some public supper bar. In the meantime, that harpy will be wanting her *douceur*. What is the rate for an introduction? Don't you know? Probably about fifty pounds. You may have a glass or two of champagne if you wish, but mind you don't become intoxicated. And you may speak to as many people as you please so long as you do not discuss me with any man present. And wait until I am ready to take you down to supper!'

He went in search of Mrs Morgan, leaving Florence in the middle of the floor feeling like a fool. So it had actually happened: a handsome gentleman with an offer of an elegant apartment and beautiful clothes. But it was not at all like her dream. For one thing, she wondered if the gentleman was as free of disease as she was herself. Why had he been visiting Mr Bennett? Should she have said no to him? But then, perhaps he was a friend of the doctor's. Perhaps the doctor had actually sent him in search of her!

Florence's gentleman did not come near her for the next hour. Not that she ever lost sight of him. She knew just where he was, whom he was with. She saw him speak with great seriousness to several men until they managed to move away, visibly bored. To her intense relief, he never so much as smiled at any of the girls in the room, although they did their best to catch his eye.

Mrs Morgan joined her just before eleven. 'You lucky puss! Such a handsome man! You allowed your heart to make your choice for you, didn't you?'

'Who is he?' asked Florence. 'What's his name?'

'Well now, he wouldn't give his name. He's only a commoner and not particularly wealthy, of that I'm sure. But don't despair, my dear. He's only your first. When he tires of you or you of him, come back to Mrs

Morgan and we'll see what we can do. I should have advised you not to accept an offer so early in the evening. But there! You are inexperienced, as I pointed out to your gentleman. Men like innocence, although why they should do so, I'll never know. It's too late for regrets. You will have to go with him, because I've given my word. A bargain has been struck.'

Florence's gentleman took her by the elbow when it was time to go downstairs for supper. All around them couples were laughing and talking. There was a fair amount of hand-kissing, too, and gallant remarks from the gentlemen that made the girls' eyes sparkle.

Her gentleman didn't speak at all, except to tell her to please keep her mouth closed when eating. She told him right out what she thought about that kind of remark, dropping her aitches at every opportunity. She knew all her carefully learned speech was eluding her, but she couldn't help it. He was so rude!

Some gentleman sitting two tables away, called out: 'I say, old chap, don't be miserable. If you don't like your choice, change partners. I'll have her!'

Everyone laughed except Florence and her gentleman. For several minutes the two of them ate in silence, and Florence was very careful about her table manners. Then the talk got kind of raw, what with the gentlemen saying all manner of rude things and the girls being just as coarse.

Florence couldn't help being embarrassed. 'Please, can we go now? People is . . . *are* getting rather drunk.'

He gave her a funny look, as if surprised that she should mind what was said. Then he almost smiled as he stood up to lead her away.

The set of rooms, where she was to live, was close to Paddington station. The building was old, but the rooms were ever so nice. Florence thought the red velvet curtains and bright turkey carpet were just beautiful. The brass bedstead was new, and there were plenty of wardrobes in which to place all the clothes she was ever likely to own. Best of all, there was a bathroom with a real bath you could run water into.

Florence exclaimed over everything, hurrying from one room to the other while the gentleman put her things away in drawers. After that, he stood by the plush-clothed table and dropped his gloves into his upturned hat, before placing his evening cape neatly over the back of a straight chair.

It was one o'clock in the morning, and Florence felt so tired she just wanted to drop down on the bed and sleep. They had gone first to her own lodging house and packed up everything she possessed. The gentleman had given her an angry talking to when he saw what a state her chamber was in. He'd gone on for so long about the need to be neat and tidy that she wondered if he was going to change his mind about taking her away.

But here they were, and the time had come for Florence to pay for what she was being given.

'I see there's a nightgown and wrapper on the bed,' she said in her best voice. 'Shall I get ready for bed now?'

'Good Lord, no!' said the gentleman. 'Stay as you are.'

Just then there was a knocking at the door. Her gentleman opened it and talked quietly for several seconds, then opened the door wide so that an elderly man with a fat belly, a grey moustache and Dundreary whiskers could enter the room. His mouth seemed small beneath the neatly clipped moustache. His dark eyes were small, too, hidden in folds of flesh, but they told her he found her attractive.

'By God, you're uncommonly pretty, my dear. What's your name?'

Florence looked questioningly at her gentleman, and when he nodded, said: 'Florence Drew, sir.'

'You've done well, my lad, as I knew you would,' said the older man. His diamond shirt studs winked in the light. 'You may call me Warren, my dear, and if you are a good girl, I'll buy you some pretty little things. You would like that, wouldn't you?'

Florence felt as if someone had hit her in the stomach. She looked at her gentleman and saw by his expression that he wasn't *her* gentleman at all. He was just someone who found girls for other men.

The man called Warren looked suddenly serious. 'You're sure your father said this girl is healthy, Bennett? When did you say he examined her?'

'This afternoon, Mr Wainwright. The girl tells me she has not been active today, and I believe her.'

'You've done well, by George, you have. I have the highest respect for your father's skills. If he says she's healthy, then I can feel perfectly safe. It's extraordinary that you were able to find her.'

'I have a fair idea where her sort might be found, sir. I tried three other introducing houses before I saw her at Mrs Morgan's.'

Mr Warren Wainwright dropped his hat and cane on a chair. His gloves and cape soon followed. Meanwhile, the doctor's son, her betrayer, was putting on his cape and gloves, taking up his hat, preparing to leave her alone with this fat old man.

She thought about saying she wouldn't stay. She wished she had the courage to demand that the doctor's son, *her* gentleman, should take her away. But in the end, she said nothing. It was such a nice set of rooms, and what did it matter who paid for them? She just wished she dare cry or scream or throw something, just to relieve her feelings a bit, because it was hard being tricked in such a cruel fashion.

'My dear Marcus,' Mr Wainwright was saying. 'I am most grateful to you. I am amazed by your ingenuity in finding just what I wanted. That shows initiative, my lad. A necessary quality in your chosen profession. I've put in a good word about you at the House. Old Smithers can't stand again. Indeed, I doubt if he will be able to last out the year. His heart, you know. And when he goes, that seat could be yours. If you continue to work hard, that is. You must be guided by me.'

Now, at last, he smiled: her gentleman, the son of Mr Bennett, whose name was Marcus and who was still the handsomest man she had ever seen. If that smile had been directed at her, she would have been happy for a week.

'We mustn't keep you from your own affairs,' said Mr Wainwright. 'Continue to take notes at the debates for me, there's a good fellow. And I'll see you on the fourth at the Summer Exhibition.'

'Yes, sir,' said Marcus Bennett. 'And will you be taking – ' He nodded in the direction of Florence.

Mr Wainwright laughed heartily. 'Good Lord, no! Horses for courses, dear boy. I shall be accompanied by my wife, unless she has one of her headaches.'

Warren Wainwright didn't leave the Paddington apartment until after ten o'clock the next morning. Florence's face ached from keeping a smile upon it. Her head ached from the effort of hiding her disgust.

She removed the sponges and washed them, feeling sick as she did so. She bathed and put on a street gown, then took one of her plainer lace-trimmed petticoats and stuffed it inside the large muff Robert had given her. She was in an agony of doubt, but finally decided to spend some of her money on a hackney cab.

Lil Crane was in the coffee shop looking, if possible, dirtier and weaker than she had the day before. She was surprised to see Florence.

'I've got me a man,' said Florence without preamble. 'He's a Member of Parliament. He's old and hairy and I hate him, but I've been given some nice rooms over by Paddington station.'

'Oh, I'm so pleased for you. You'll be all right now. We could have a pie to celebrate, if you don't mind paying for it. He's only your first. You'll meet others. Get what you can from this old geezer, but always keep your eyes open for somebody better.'

'Lil, I can't bear it. I don't want this life. I'm going to quit. When I've left you, I'm going back to pack my things. I don't care where I go. I'll find work.'

Lil was so stunned that she began to cough, and nothing more could be said until the spasm had passed and Lil recovered her breath.

'Don't ever say that again, my girl. Whatever would you do? No use both of us starving. Forget your grand ideas. You're a fallen woman. You've lost your honour and there's no way back. Everybody despises you now, except your own sort. Not only would you be so poor your belly ached all day, but respectable people would never let you forget what you had been. The likes of us can't afford to have pride. Make the best of it, that's my advice.'

'Oh, Lil, what have I done? If I could go back to Mrs Baker's and start over, I'd scrub floors for the rest of my life, and be glad to do it.'

'You'll get used to your new life. In another month, you won't think that way. You'll be proud of your nice rooms and fine clothes. You'll be used to eating good food and all. I have high hopes for you, Flo.'

Florence bowed her head. A cup of weak coffee sat before her on the rickety table, quaking greasily. 'I suppose you're right. At least I can keep us both from starving.'

'I didn't expect – ' began Lil, but shut her lips on so obvious a lie.

Florence leaned close to her new friend so that other customers couldn't hear. 'In my muff, I've got a petticoat. You can have it to sell.'

122

'Cor! I could get two shillings for it down Petticoat Lane.'

Florence was horrified. 'Don't you sell it for less than five. I haven't much more to sell, and I don't know if the old man will give me any *money*.'

She gave Lil half a crown, warning her to keep it safe and spend it carefully, before giving the older woman a friendly pat on the back. No question of taking a cab home. She would walk. Lil had meant well, but her words had destroyed what was left of Florence's self-respect. By the time she had reached the sanctuary of her new home, she was convinced of her own worthlessness and had lost the will to leave Wainwright in search of a respectable life.

11

In recent years, Burlington House, Piccadilly, had suffered two architectural assaults. The first was by a Mr Smirke who had added a second storey and built large exhibition rooms behind the old house. More recently, Mr Banks and Mr Barry had removed the old colonnade and gateway and replaced them with an Italianate entrance. Opinions varied as to the success of these improvements. Some people felt very strongly on the subject, but as Marjory had never looked carefully at the building before, she thought it looked just grand. Mary Beth had been right when she said the English thought highly of artists. They must do, since they regularly held an exhibition for living British artists in such a magnificent building. And the elegantly printed programme told her this was the one-hundred-and-seventh such annual event!

The women had been warned that the opening of the Summer Exhibition was an important social occasion and had, therefore, taken great care with their choice of dress. Mary Beth was wearing her favourite bright blue, and Marjory looked ethereal in grey.

Lucius Falkner, for once dressed very smartly, met them at the top of the stairs and began to complain about the difficulties he had encountered on varnishing day, about where his painting had been hung, about the fact that only one of his entries had been accepted. Nevertheless, he was clearly pleased and excited to be among the chosen artists. He led the two women through the galleries, the wood-strip flooring springing beneath their feet like the deck of a ship. The paintings, which began below eye level, covered the walls, on and on up to the ceiling. Although it was early in the day, the rooms were crowded with London's fashionable few hundred and the would-be-fashionable few thousand. Everywhere braying voices were raised in greeting as the tail-coated men sweated in the growing heat, and the women – hatted, gloved, whaleboned and shod to suffocation – paraded for the benefit of each other.

Falkner's painting was in Gallery Ten, and Marjory's hat had been knocked askew more times than she could count by the time they reached the room.

'There it is!' said Falkner proudly from the doorway. He pointed to the far wall.

Marjory was almost speechless. 'Why . . . why, Mr Falkner, that's just wonderful!'

'Lucius, I'm so proud of you!' cried Mary Beth. 'I knew you would do well one day. Momma, don't you just love the black dress? If only the model didn't have her back turned. You should have painted the face of the lady in black, Lucius. The woman playing the violin does not have nearly so pretty a gown.'

Falkner glowered as they crossed the floor. 'You are looking at a painting called *Hush* by Mr Tissot, which is obviously just the thing to appeal to unformed tastes. Agnew's have already purchased it for twelve hundred guineas.'

'Good heavens! Do you mean to say people are willing to pay that amount of money just for a painting?' asked Marjory.

'The *nouveau riche*, who recognize their own sort in his paintings, will certainly pay handsomely for Tissot's work. I'm afraid I do not care for his style, nor do many authoritative figures in the art world. Unfortunately, the great public disagrees. My painting hangs directly above Mr Tissot's, too high to be properly appreciated. It's been skyed, but I must not complain.

It is very important for my future that I have had a painting accepted.'

Marjory and Mary Beth looked upwards and gasped in unison at the painting of a young woman whom Marjory would later refer to as 'naked as a jay bird'.

'*Slave Maiden*, I've called it, but it really needs no explanation.' Falkner was pleased to see mother and daughter so disconcerted. It was a fine, even erotic picture, and their dislike only confirmed his belief that he had succeeded in bringing to the canvas the passionate nature of the girl.

'I don't see anything clever in painting a young woman wearing nothing but a pair of manacles,' said Marjory at last.

Mary Beth's face was flushed to the roots of her hair. 'It's Josie Smith! How could you have done this to me? I'll be a laughing stock. Come to that, how could you have shamed that poor girl? Oh, Lucius, why could you not have exhibited a painting of a well-bred girl wearing something fetching, like Mr Tissot has? You said yourself he gets a lot of money for his paintings.'

'And I said I do not admire Mr Tissot's work. Although there is nothing shameful about the human form, no so-called well-bred woman would have posed for me. I would not have wanted one in any case. You women of the better classes allow your mothers to lace you into corsets when your young bones are still forming, with the result that by the time you are fully-grown, your ribcages are distorted and grotesque. Girls of the labouring classes are at least spared such deformities.'

Marjory glared at Falkner. 'I've heard that some women do begin to train their daughters' bodies when they are no more than twelve, Mr Falkner, but I never did such a thing to Mary Beth. She is not deformed. But I'd better never hear of you painting her any way but fully dressed!'

126

Mary Beth snorted. 'Lucius does not wish to paint me at all. He says I have a Rossetti face, which is no compliment. I've seen a painting Mr Rossetti executed last year, of a woman with crinkly hair, a thick neck and the thickest lips I've ever seen on a woman. It's not surprising Lucius doesn't want to paint me if he thinks I look like that!'

'I'm sorry if I annoyed you, Mary Beth. It was a painterly remark. No offence was intended.'

Falkner saw three men approaching. One, he recognized as Mr Bennett. With him was a young man who bore a striking resemblance to the doctor; a younger, slimmer, handsomer version. The third man was at least as old as the doctor, but had run to fat. Side whiskers hid most of his face, but what could be seen of his cheeks was livid with broken veins. His clothes were very fine, expensive and flashy, in strong contrast to the understated elegance of the Bennetts.

'Good morning' said Frederick Bennett. 'I thought we might see you here, Lady Manton. Allow me to introduce Mr Warren Wainwright, a Member of Parliament, and my son, Marcus. Lady Manton, Miss Hanson and Mr Falkner, whose painting is . . .' the doctor looked along the wall.

'There,' said Falkner with a smile. The three men silently studied the *Slave Maiden*. Marcus Bennett smiled slightly; the doctor's face showed shock and anger; Mr Wainwright could not hide his pleasure.

'Damned fine painting, Falkner,' said Wainwright. 'I beg your pardon, ladies, but I was quite carried away. You paint uncommonly well, sir. I consider myself something of a connoisseur. My collection is recognized as being worth consideration by the most discerning people. And it is my belief, Mr Falkner, that you will be famous one of these days. Yes, sir. I've made the reputations of several painters in my time.'

'Mr Wainwright, the Member of Parliament?' asked

Falkner. 'Why, sir, you represent my old home, Monmouth. I haven't been there for many years, but I hear you are very well regarded by the citizens of that town.'

Wainwright beamed. Marcus Bennett, smiling slightly, looked down at his shoes. The quiet young man seemed not at all surprised when the MP said he would buy the painting. Wainwright asked the price.

'I believe you said you wouldn't take less than two hundred and fifty guineas, Mr Falkner,' said Mary Beth.

'Why . . . yes, that was the price I had in mind.' Falkner had expected to earn fifty guineas, if he were lucky. He smiled at Mary Beth, grateful for her intervention.

'Bennett.' Wainwright turned slightly towards Marcus. 'Give Mr Falkner a cheque and tell him where the painting must be delivered. A word with you, Mr Falkner.' The painter walked with Wainwright a few paces away from the others. 'I want *hair*,' murmured the MP. 'Do you understand me? Hair, sir. Don't deliver the painting until the model is restored to her natural state.'

'I do so agree, Mr Wainwright. The hypocrisy, the false modesty of our times prevents me from painting the female form as it really is. At least, The Royal Academy would not have accepted the painting if I had.'

Meanwhile, Marcus, who had made out a cheque and written an address on a sheet of notepaper, was now solemnly making a notation in his small notebook. His father and Marjory were talking about mutual acquaintances, which gave him the opportunity to covertly assess the charms of the sulky daughter. He thought she looked displeased about the picture her fiancé had chosen to exhibit, which didn't surprise Marcus. Quite apart from the fact that the painting

128

was of a standing nude, the girl in the picture was ten times more beautiful than Miss Hanson. Marcus was surprised that Falkner, who clearly had an eye for beauty, could be romantically interested in so plain a woman. Perhaps the artist *wasn't* interested in her. Marcus had learned not to put too much trust in his father's gossip.

'Mr Falkner's success is assured, now that Mr Wainwright has taken an interest in him,' said Marcus.

'Is that so?' Mary Beth looked over to where Falkner and Wainwright were deep in conversation.

'I am sure the subject matter is embarrassing to a well-bred lady like yourself, but artists are a breed apart. Not like other men at all.'

Mary Beth gazed coolly at Marcus. 'Do you think so? I think artists are exactly like other men. What distresses me is that some women are forced to behave in a manner they must loathe in order to earn enough money to eat.' She glanced up at the painting. 'I have met the model and had thought she was quite a respectable young woman. Obviously, I was mistaken.'

Wainwright was ready to move on. Marcus handed the cheque and address to Falkner, then he and Wainwright said their farewells and were soon swallowed up in the crowd.

'It's a disgraceful picture, but I guess you've done very well for yourself,' said Marjory. 'I wouldn't give you a wooden nickel for that painting, but men are bound to see things differently. Two hundred and fifty guineas! I'll be darned.'

'Lady Manton, Miss Hanson, may I accompany you round the rest of the exhibition?' asked Bennett. 'Will you join us, Mr Falkner?'

Falkner said he preferred to stay close to his painting as he wanted the opinion of fellow artists, so Marjory and Mary Beth agreed to go off with Bennett. But first, the doctor said he wished to have a word in private

129

with Falkner. He suggested that the ladies study the excellent painting by Mr Frith on the far wall, where he would join them in a moment.

'I must tell you,' said Bennett when he was alone with the artist, 'that I think you have behaved most improperly by embarrassing Lady Manton and her daughter in this fashion.'

'There are many nude paintings in the galleries, Doctor. My nude is no more erotic than any other.' Falkner paused for thought. 'No, that's not true. It *is* erotic, isn't it? It is that element which appealed to Mr Wainwright, I'm sure. I have made a valuable contact today. You know, I have been meaning to tell you that I owe you a debt of gratitude, sir. After our friendly discussion, I took stock of my work and my attitude towards it. I began to cultivate the inner eye. I had become stale. Now my enthusiasm is renewed.'

'And this is the result of your renewed enthusiasm? The girl looks terrified.'

'But a woman about to be sold in a slave market would be in great distress, don't you think? My model had no idea how to feign such an emotion, so I was forced to be very harsh with her, to make her frightened of me.'

'My God!'

'Of course, as soon as I had completed the face, got the expression as I wanted it to be, I told her why I had been so sharp. She understood, I promise you. Besides, I paid her very well.'

'Will you stop at nothing?'

'My talent drives me, Doctor.'

'You would have done better to paint something more uplifting.'

'Come, Mr Bennett, now that the ladies have gone, can you not admit that the *Slave Maiden* is a damned fine painting that stirs the blood?'

'Certainly not! I see nothing erotic in the high flush,

reddened lips and liquid eye of the consumptive. Poor thin thing.'

'Forget you are a doctor. Look at the painting from an artistic point of view. Consumptives often show a fevered passion. They want to experience everything before the flame of life flickers out. I have captured that. It is a good painting. A moving one. I know it is.'

Bennett took a deep breath. 'Everything you see is fodder for the nightmare of your imagination, isn't it? But just as you can't forget you are an artist, so I can't forget that I am a doctor. Consumption robs us daily of our young. I see them everywhere I look. Beautiful young men and women doomed to early graves. You have stripped a dying girl of her last shred of dignity. I hope you are satisfied.'

'I have immortalized her,' said Falkner, but he was talking to Bennett's back, as the older man walked away. 'When she is dead, her image will live on. I have done something for her that you, with all your scientific skill, cannot do.'

Bennett had composed himself by the time he reached Marjory and Mary Beth. The three of them pushed their way through the crowds to see those paintings that Bennett thought would please the women: Elmore's *Mary, Queen of Scots;* Millais' portrait of Miss EveleenTennant; Frederick Leighton's *Grand Mosque of Damascus, Little Fatima* and *Venetian Girl.* Those paintings which the women liked best were sweet and sentimental to a degree. Frederick Bennett approved their taste and said so frequently. The image of the slave maiden haunted him. He could not shake off the memory of the petrified look in the girl's eyes. He had an uncomfortable feeling that the painting really was something out of the ordinary. The realization disturbed him considerably. He had always thought that people who had great creative talents were

131

thoroughly selfish. Bennett feared for the happiness of Miss Hanson.

After about an hour, they came upon Jeremy Grimshaw and Miss Quinn as the young couple were admiring one of Mr Millais' comforting contributions. Grimshaw, who had just moments before told Falkner privately that the *Slave Maiden* was a magnificent painting, now quite happily assured the ladies that he was shocked by it. He wished his dear friend had not embarrassed Lady Manton and Miss Hanson by exhibiting it. Miss Quinn squeezed Mary Beth's arm sympathetically and invited her to come with herself and Jeremy for the rest of the day. Mary Beth was heartily sick of following in the wake of her mother and the doctor, so the three young people went off together.

'You do see why I am anxious for you to bring your daughter's association with Falkner to an end, don't you?' said Bennett when he and Marjory were alone.

'I wish you wouldn't be on at me for ever,' responded Marjory. 'Mary Beth knows her own mind. I've talked to her. She says she intends to marry him. Although, I must say today's affair was very upsetting. He downright insulted the girl before you arrived, yet she's still loyal to him.'

'I repeat: you should take her home to St Louis.'

'You can forget about our going home to St Louis. You know, I just can't get it into my head that anyone would pay twelve hundred guineas for one painting. And I'll bet that Tissot man paints more than one picture a year. Say, how much is twelve hundred guineas in American money?'

The doctor began making complicated mental calculations, but Marjory beat him to the answer. 'That's about six thousand dollars!'

'More than is paid to an American legislator,' said Bennett, and Marjory laughed delightedly.

'Some of our legislators would do the country a

service if they stopped meddling in what they don't
understand and took up painting.'

The day turned out to be quite a pleasant one, after
all. Marjory dined with the doctor at Brown's Hotel in
Dover Street, returning home about half past ten, with
the intention of going to bed early. In her customary
way, Perks had heard all about the painting at the
Summer Exhibition, and was ready to be scandalized
at length the moment Marjory entered the bedroom.
Marjory asked if she had her own personal telegraph
wire, and what business was it of Perks', anyway? She
told the maid to be quiet, to mind her own business,
to find another position if she couldn't hold her tongue.
But she didn't mean any of it. Perks was given considerable latitude, because it was obvious to Marjory that
the maid was genuinely fond of Mary Beth (by no
means a universal feeling below stairs) and totally loyal
to Marjory herself. After all, Perks was only echoing
the doctor, and putting into words Marjory's own
unspoken worries.

Although she got straight into bed, she had no intention of going to sleep. Instead, she sat up reading,
hoping to have a word with Mary Beth when the girl
came back from supper at the Quinns'. At about twelve
o'clock Marjory fell asleep, however, and didn't waken
until one in the morning, far too late to speak to anyone.

The following day was a Sunday. Marjory attended
two services in two different churches, and didn't think
much of the sermons in either church. She liked to be
threatened with hell-fire on a Sunday, and found these
English vicars too genteel for her liking. She would
have enjoyed telling Mary Beth what she thought about
the ministers, but Mary Beth managed to keep out of
her mother's way, so Marjory told Perks instead.

On Monday, Marjory met Guy Dundalk for a quiet
stroll round the zoological gardens, where she heard

133

about the progess of her refuge. Dundalk brought along a photograph of a large tumbledown brick building with a small sign that clearly said: *Lady Marjory Refuge for Fallen Women*. A small boy, considerably blurred, occupied the doorway. Marjory was greatly cheered by this proof that Dundalk was making headway. She allowed herself to be dissuaded from visiting Seven Dials to see the building for herself and gave the young man another one hundred pounds in cash.

Dundalk was an interesting companion, and since she had no intention of telling him of her private troubles with Mary Beth, she was able to put the subject from her mind for half a day.

On the Tuesday she went shopping. In an attack of absentmindedness at Swan and Edgars, she bought two dozen pairs of stockings and half a dozen pairs of kid gloves. She was about to climb into her carriage when she remembered she had bought a dozen pairs of gloves just two weeks ago.

'Maybe I'm collecting gloves,' she said, and John the footman said: 'Yes, ma'am,' just as if he knew what she was talking about.

On Wednesday it rained heavily all day, but it didn't stop Mary Beth from going out to the British Museum with friends. She left just after Marjory had finally managed to have her little talk with the girl.

'Mary Beth, I think you ought to tell young Falkner that you're not interested in marrying him.'

'But I am, Momma.'

'I don't know why. He would understand why you had changed your mind after he exhibited that painting.'

'I'll have you know, that painting was considered a great success. Mr Ruskin, whoever he is, didn't like it, but everybody else says Lucius is a rare painter with great talent who was discovered at the Summer Exhibition. Lucius is going to be rich and famous.'

'So that's it,' said Marjory. 'Well, that's just fine and dandy, but does he have to paint naked women in order to be rich and famous? Does that fellow Millais paint naked women?'

'I don't know and it doesn't matter, Momma. Let me be. Don't you want me to be happy?'

'How can you be happy when the man you're going to marry insults your face and figure in front of your own mother?'

Mary Beth could not give a satisfactory answer to that question. She left the house in a huff, and Marjory was free to ask herself some painful questions. Where had she failed in bringing the girl up, for instance? And why did a fine-looking young woman hang on to a man who plainly didn't give two pins for her?

Marjory was defeated. She had done her best. You couldn't tell a clever, independent young woman that she must not marry the man of her choice. Nor could you slip off and give money to a man like Falkner to persuade him to jilt your daughter. Falkner would be richer than Marjory was in a month or two, if he kept painting lewd women! At least she could be reasonably sure that he *wasn't* after Mary Beth's money . . .

12

Lucius Falkner was fond of Jeremy Grimshaw and acknowledged a debt of gratitude. The young solicitor led a quiet, even constrained life. Yet this same man was continually busy introducing his acquaintances to one another, seeing if this friend's need could be met by that friend's talents. Because of Grimshaw's thoughtfulness, Falkner had met Mary Beth Hanson, her mother, Mr Bennett and Mr Warren Wainwright. All of them had one way or another, furthered his career or expanded his ideas about his work.

Falkner, in mellow mood, thought he should do something in return for Grimshaw. And given his new-found obsession, what more suitable favour than to 'make a man' of Jeremy before he was one day older?

When the matter was put to him, Grimshaw jumped at the opportunity. He was certain he could summon more passion for an unknown prostitute than he had ever felt for the persistent Miss Quinn. So the two men set out one warm June night to visit the notorious Cremorne Gardens. Grimshaw brought with him his sweating palms and thudding heart; Falkner had a small sketchpad and half a dozen pencils.

A thousand gaslights turned night into day at the gardens. The men paid a shilling each for the privilege of walking the tree-lined avenues, past brightly lit kiosks and pagodas as they headed towards the sound of dancing music.

All innocent visitors had left the gardens by ten o'clock and were on their way home, leaving the alleys to adventurous shop girls and seamstresses, and to the professional prostitutes in their silks and satins. No man brought his womenfolk to Cremorne Gardens after dark. The men came singly or in noisy parties of ten or twelve to dance and drink and find the very women who were parading the grounds looking for *them*.

Grimshaw noticed that most of the women, those who had not yet found gentlemen, were walking alone, lonely but dignified. He knew they must be prostitutes, because the shop girls tended to huddle together in giggling groups, taking courage from one another. The professional women were amazingly well dressed and clean, and surprisingly indifferent to the strolling men. Not one of them gave Grimshaw an inviting smile, not one turned to speak when he passed so close that her skirts brushed his legs. Almost at once, he was in despair. He would never find the courage to engage one of these haughty creatures in conversation. And if he did, to be rebuffed by a common prostitute would be the ultimate humiliation!

Falkner found a large elm not too far from the well-lit dancing area and pulled out his sketchpad and pencils. With quick, assured strokes, he drew the dancers as they circled the floor. Looking over Falkner's shoulder at the sketches, Grimshaw felt several conflicting emotions: how clever his friend was to capture a fleeting moment on paper with such apparent ease, and how attractive the drawings were, a pleasure to the eye. But above all, how subtly these tawdry, awkward people had been transformed by Falkner into works of art. In real life, Grimshaw found the dancers rather repugnant. On paper, they were quite beautiful.

'This place bores me,' said Falkner suddenly. 'I will take you somewhere else.'

'But, are we not to – ?'

'No, my friend. These whores are trying to be ladies, aping their betters.'

'Well,' said Grimshaw doubtfully, 'is that not desirable?'

'Certainly not. Why should a woman *try* to be cold, unfeeling and scornful of men, when she has not been brought up to it by her mother? What do I want with a woman who adopts all the failings of respectable women, while suppressing her own natural eroticism? I will take you to places where the women of the night are proud of their calling and need no airs and graces.'

In spite of Grimshaw's protests, he was carried off to Deptford, long associated with royal dockyards. There, the two men (one of them very nervous about being in so rough an area) walked the dark streets, following the crowd until they entered a large yard brightly lit by naphtha lamps. Their noses told them they were close to the foreign cattle market. There were no silks and satins here. The people were meanly dressed and noisy, many the worse for drink, all intent on having a good time. Bare-footed, light-fingered children ran among the crowd, and jeered at the two swells in fine clothing. Grimshaw placed his hand on his wallet and looked about him fearfully. He had never been to such a low place in his life and saw nothing amusing about it.

'Come on, old chap! It's a fair! Let us enjoy ourselves as the common people do,' Falkner rallied him. 'See that stand? Look what a fine, trustworthy man is in charge! Three shies-a-penny. Toss these three rings on to the handle of that knife and you will win a prize.'

With a heavy sigh, Grimshaw took the wooden rings and tossed them half-heartedly at the knife which had been stuck into a plank. It was more difficult than he imagined; he had to try once more, and then again. After he had spent a shilling, he finally managed it and won a cigar worth far less than twelve pence.

No matter; it is always exciting to win a prize. In better mood now, Grimshaw followed his friend to the Penny Gaff, a small travelling theatre which this night was offering dedicated theatregoers a tragedy entitled *Murder Most Foul, or The Wronged Woman.*

The play was acted with great gusto by players who were seen from such a short distance to be distinctly dirty. The audience loved it all, hissing the villain, applauding the hero, shedding a tear when the pure maiden died with great energy and suddenness. All around them, members of the audience were eating fried fish, baked potatoes or anything else that took their fancy. Grimshaw felt quite queasy and tried unsuccessfully to concentrate on the play. It was the audience, not the actors, which held Falkner's interest. Even in the dim light, he managed to make several drawings.

A farce followed the tragedy, for they were entitled to two plays for the price of their penny seats, and after five minutes Grimshaw whispered that the tragedy had been the funnier of the two. Falkner nodded absently, now drawing the actors with the same intense concentration that he had shown when drawing the audience earlier.

By the time they left the theatre, Grimshaw was thoroughly bored and ready for his bed. He should not have said so.

'Bed?' said Falkner. 'I know just the place,' and took him to an opium den.

The 'den' was no more than the small front room of a terraced house in Bluegate Fields which was owned by a Chinese. Six metal beds with thin mattresses and greasy pillows filled the small room. Chinese men occupying two of the beds were lost in their dreams and paid no attention to the new arrivals. Falkner paid for two pipes and they lay down to experience the ultimate wickedness of smoking opium in the company of heathen Chinese.

Grimshaw had some initial difficulty in getting his pipe to stay alight, but eventually managed to puff away quite strongly. As a result, he fell asleep for an hour, and could not get fully awake even when Falkner dragged him to a low brothel where the pathetic inmates were all so plain and dirty that Grimshaw abandoned any idea of experiencing the manly pleasures. With a mumbled 'I'll await you here,' he lay down on a horsehair-upholstered settee in the main room, drew up his knees and fell asleep, while Falkner went to the back with an emaciated girl of fifteen or sixteen.

'What is the pleasure in it all?' Grimshaw asked Falkner the next day. 'Why do you do it?'

'Because those people are free of cant and humbug, because Polite Society says I must not, because the girls inspire me to my best work.'

'Your best work makes ugliness attractive. Your best work fails to convey the smell, the noise, the low greed,' said Jeremy, who really wished he had not accompanied his friend to the East End.

'The meanest imagination is capable of discovering filth, noise and greed. I am trying to record the despair, to make others see that those women are human beings, earning our pity occasionally, sometimes deserving our admiration for their free and defiant spirits. Don't be downhearted, Grimshaw. You have lost nothing by your night's adventures.'

'I lost my wallet.'

'Ah, well,' laughed Falkner. 'That was only to be expected.'

A few days later, when Falkner discovered that he had brought an unwelcome souvenir away with him, he did not inform Grimshaw, but sent immediately for Frederick Bennett.

The fact that Falkner needed a doctor specializing in certain diseases didn't surprise Bennett at all. He read the note requesting his attendance and immediately sent for his carriage.

Falkner had apparently moved. His new address was that of a smart town house in Doughty Street. Bennett was surprised by the spaciousness and comfort of the house. The rent could surely not be less than one hundred pounds a year. A smart male servant opened the door, indicating to the doctor that Falkner must have a substantial staff: probably a valet, cook and housemaid, as well as the butler. Perhaps there was a coachman, too, although Bennett doubted it. Could the man really afford so large an establishment, or was he counting on Miss Hanson's money to pay the bills when they came due?

Bennett was shown directly to Falkner's bedroom, where he found his new patient looking very sorry for himself in dressing-gown and slippers. He put on his wash leather gloves, sat down on a straight chair and requested his patient to stand before him. The artist presented all the usual symptoms, and Bennett spent very little time examining him. A sore on Falkner's thumb, which the artist had thought was a whitlow, was merely a further indication to Bennett that he was dealing with a case of syphilis.

'I have a sore throat,' said Falkner. 'I don't feel at all well.'

Bennett removed his gloves and went to the wash-stand. 'I will just wash my hands before having a look at your throat.' He found that Falkner was, as he had suspected, suffering from tonsillitis and a swelling of the sub-maxillary gland on the right side. 'There is no doubt of it. You have syphilis.'

'Well,' said Falkner jauntily. 'I'm certainly not the first to do so.'

'No, nor will you be the last. You have behaved with so little regard for your health recently, I'm surprised you have reached the age of thirty-five before contracting the disease. You have lived your life to suit yourself, which is as it should be, but now you must think of others. You must not even consider marrying again for five years.'

'What? Don't be ridiculous. I shall marry when I choose. You have never approved of my liaison with Miss Hanson, but it has nothing to do with you. If you will just give me the proper treatment – '

Bennett went to the window and looked down on the passing traffic. Falkner, despite his bravado, was feeling rather queasy and sat down in a nearby chair.

'Whatever you may think, Falkner, I am not here to criticize your behaviour, nor to interfere in your private affairs for reasons of my own. It is just that I know what the consequences of your marrying would be. It is my duty to explain certain matters to you, and I am determined that you should heed my words.'

'Five years is too long. I know of many men who have married within months.'

'So do I, unfortunately. You will probably not, to your knowledge, have met a syphilitic married woman. But perhaps if I describe the history of a typical one, you will recall some woman of your acquaintance who has been so unfortunate. She will have endured a number of miscarriages. Then, perhaps, one or two stillbirths. Later still, she might have had a child which lived for a few months or years. If her strength allowed it, she may have continued in this sorry way until she actually managed to produce a healthy infant. By that time, she will have suffered such heartache and such a drain on her physical resources that she is unable to take pleasure in her healthy child, and will certainly, every waking moment, be fearful for the child's well-being. Have you ever met a woman like that, sir? Women are capable of passing on the disease to their unborn children for years after they have ceased to be sexually contagious. Can you truly say that you would willingly put Miss Hanson through so dreadful a cycle of pregnancy and infant death?'

Falkner passed a hand across his eyes. 'I thought women did not suffer from syphilis as men do.'

'With them the disease is milder, which is just as well. Respectable women are never informed of the possibility of their being infected. Those with delicate constitutions and tender sensibilities would not be able to endure the treatment, anyway.'

'Good God! Of what does the treatment consist? I had thought the Blue Pill – '

'The Blue Pill causes digestive problems and for that reason I do not favour it. No, I prefer inunctions of mercurial ointment on successive days. I will send a rubber to rub in the ointment on your thighs, calves, arms and chest. He will come every day, and the rubbing session lasts for twenty minutes, so arrange your social life to allow time for his visits.'

'Why won't *you* come to give me the treatment? You are the doctor, after all.'

'I do not have time to treat all my patients personally. The rubber I have in mind is excellent.' Besides, thought Bennett, wash leather gloves were insuffícent protection against prolonged exposure to the mercurial ointment. It was possible for the rubber who treated several men to suffer more seriously from mercury poisoning than the patients did. Bennett had experienced the symptoms in his youth; nowadays he left others to the task.

'My God, what is to become of me? I am a busy man. I must paint, must finish several portraits if I am to maintain this house.'

'We will start with a course of sixty days if your health holds up. If not, we may have to suspend the treatment until you feel better. Mercury can cause stomatitis, that is, problems with your gums. I hope your teeth are in good order. I will visit you each week

143

to see how you are progressing.' Bennett turned away from the window to confront his patient. 'Did you suppose that having syphilis was a jolly jape? I assure you it is not. I know I sound puritanical, perhaps unsophisticated. Some of my colleagues have accused me of it. But I must tell you, I have seen so much suffering that I cannot regard the marriage of a young girl to a man in your condition with anything but horror.'

'I should have done as other men do, and confined myself to virgins. But what can I do? I don't care for girls as young as twelve, and even then one may be deceived. I could kill the bitch who gave me this.'

'But had every intention of passing it on to an innocent young woman. Cheer up, Falkner. You have a strong constitution, and I will monitor the treatment very carefully. Mercurial inunctions are unpleasant, but not nearly so unpleasant as the later stages of syphilis.'

'It is not so simple as you imagine. I have no real desire to marry Miss Hanson. I changed my mind some time ago. But I have said certain things . . . I have no wish to find myself in court facing a suit for breach of promise, if you must know.'

'Perhaps she will also change her mind. Nothing has been made public, I gather.'

Falkner laughed harshly. 'Since she regards me as her only chance of marriage, I have no hope that she will cry off.'

'It would be despicable of you to go through with this. Something must be done.'

'Don't lecture me, Bennett. You have no right to instruct me in proper behaviour when you have misused your position as a *confidant* of prostitutes. You pronounced a poor young girl to be clean, and your son then procured her for Wainwright. *I* have never sunk so low.'

144

Shock momentarily took Bennett's breath away. 'I don't understand you.'

'Where do you think my painting of the *Slave Maiden* is hanging? Not in Wainwright's home. I delivered it to an address in Paddington given me by your son. A most fascinating yellow-haired young woman lives there. It is no secret how Wainwright came by her. He told me about it himself when I sold him a few pen-and-ink sketches last week. You had examined her and said she was clean. Wainwright needed a safe outlet for his manly urges, so your son, Marcus, tracked the girl down to an introducing house.'

'I swear I know nothing of this,' said Bennett. But he thought he knew which prostitute Falkner was referring to. The girl did not even have gonorrhoea, which was most unusual. Of course, women were never treated for that disease, but they passed it on to their customers in whom it caused some nasty problems.

Falkner lifted a hand wearily, his anger suddenly gone. 'Forgive me. I am tired and understandably concerned about my health. I should not have spoken so freely. Of course I believe you, when you say you had no part in the matter. I hope this will not cause a rift between you and your son.'

'It cannot cause a rift between us, because I don't intend to mention it to him. And you must never speak of this to anyone. I warn you, I will not be slandered.'

'No, no, of course not,' said Falkner. 'The girl seems happy enough. She shares your view of my painting, by the way. She is well-fed and housed and seems excessively proud of her new clothes. Wainwright will treat her decently.'

'Mr Wainwright is not my patient, but I know him to be a man obsessed by matters of health. At least, while she is with him, she will be spared *your* misfortune. By the way, do you want me to continue treating you, or would you rather find another doctor?'

'Yes, yes, of course I want you to continue treating me. I have every confidence in your skill. I would not be happy with a stranger. Forgive me for my intemperate speech. Blame it on anxiety about my health. You won't give a hint to Miss Hanson about this, will you?' said Falkner, indicating his groin.

'How could I do such a thing? You are my patient. Our dealings are confidential. I will return tomorrow to introduce you to the rubber and discuss the treatment.' Bennett rested a hand briefly on the artist's shoulder. 'Sit down, sit down. I can find my own way out.'

13

The doctor was in the habit of travelling to visit his patients in a hooded phaeton, a neat, easily manoeuvred carriage. He disliked driving himself, however, and so rode beside his coachman, attempting, in spite of the rough roads, to make notes about his visits.

'Do you wish to go home now, Mr Bennett?' asked the coachman.

'What's that? No, no. Drive me to Lady Manton's house in Cavendish Place. I do hope she is at home.'

Marjory was in the library and greeted him with undisguised pleasure and surprise. She had been feeling rather homesick, she said, and had come into the library to look through her many photograph albums. She invited him to sit beside her on the chesterfield so that she could show him pictures of the family back home.

Pensively, Bennett sat down, refused the tea which Brogan proposed to bring and surprised his hostess by asking for a large port instead.

Marjory was determined to share her memories of another life. She turned the pages of the albums, explaining each photograph at length, gently touching the images of every departed relative as she did so, as if trying to restore them to life. Bennett said very little, confining himself to a sympathetic comment now and again or a muted exclamation of surprise.

'You seem very tired,' said Marjory when they had looked at every picture in six albums. 'Is there anything wrong? Have you had bad news?'

'No, nothing of that sort.' Bennett stood up, put on

a bright smile and rubbed his hands together. 'What a pleasant room this is! Do you spend much time here? I prefer to sit in my library most evenings. I like to – '

'What's the matter with you, Mr Bennett? What's happened?'

'Marjory . . . that is, Lady Marjory, I – '

'Oh, you can call me Marjory. Why not?'

'May I? Splendid! Just between ourselves, of course.'

'It's Lucius, isn't it? You've come to talk to me about Lucius. Tell me the worst. What's happened?'

'Nothing at all. It is just that I feel you should be taking steps to break up this alliance. I am convinced Falkner does not wish to marry your daughter, but fears an action for breach of promise.'

'There's more to your visit than that. Is it . . .' She mouthed the word 'pox'.

'Madam! I never expected to hear that word on the lips of a lady. I cannot believe such language is common in the drawing-rooms of America.'

Marjory blushed. 'I'm sorry if I offended you. Where I come from, there are times when only plain speaking will do. People have to know about diseases and how to treat themselves. I've got a book and I've studied all about . . . things. That book was a real help when I was bringing up my children.'

'A book?' said Bennett faintly. 'A medical book?'

Marjory went to the bookshelves and drew out a well-worn volume which she handed to Bennett.

'*Gunn's Domestic Medicine*,' he read aloud, flipping through the pages. 'You say you have studied this book?'

'Read every page. Turned to it in time of need. There wasn't always a doctor around when we needed one, especially when I was younger. Besides, Gunn can tell a sensible woman everything she needs to know.'

'Yes, I suppose so.'

'You haven't answered my question. Does Lucius . . . you know?'

'Whatever is the norm in the state of Missouri, this is England, ma'am. You cannot expect me to discuss . . .' Seeing her distress, he sighed. 'You may speak freely to me. Indeed, I hope you will.'

'I've shocked you, and now you think less of me.'

'No, no. You must not think that. I have the highest regard for you. America, especially that part of America where you were born, is undoubtedly very different from London. What would be acceptable, indeed necessary there, would *here* be, what should I say, remarkable.' He paused. 'Marjory, this book is of great interest to me. Do you mind if I borrow it, as well as the last album of photographs we looked at? I would like to study them, if you can trust me with your precious mementoes. Do you mind?'

'No, I don't mind.' Marjory stared hard at him. 'Have you nothing further to say to me?'

'Nothing, beyond telling you that you must speak firmly to your daughter. I believe in vigorous action where our children are concerned. And plain speaking. They are never too old to learn from their parents. I will say no more on that topic. I believe we are all going to the theatre on Saturday: Caroline and Dumfries and four of their friends. I'm glad you now know that Caroline is my cousin. When you made some remark about polite society and frogs, I naturally thought of her at once.'

'You're being unkind. The countess doesn't look like a frog.'

'Not even slightly?'

'Well . . .' Marjory smiled in spite of herself. 'Never mind frogs. I've got myself a whole menagerie with Caroline's help: a jackass, several peacocks and a parcel of vultures.'

'Now who's being unkind? I'm glad to have been of

149

service to you in your collection, but please excuse me. My patients await.'

Marjory nodded glumly. 'Thank you for the warning.'

Bennett didn't know what to say. He took up his hat and cane rather awkwardly, because he still had a finger firmly stuck in the pages of *Gunn's Domestic Medicine*, and left Marjory to her thoughts.

Marjory paced the floor for several minutes after Bennett had left. What on earth could she do now? Not tell Mary Beth about Falkner, that was certain. Heaven only knew what the girl might do. She was as likely to marry him in spite of everything as run away back to America. Mary Beth was capable of any extreme action, and Marjory had never been able to guess which way she would jump. Having lost one child to the New World, she was not prepared to do anything that would cause the other one to leave home.

She just wished the girl was not so headstrong. Take the meeting about the Contagious Diseases Act, for instance. Marjory and Mary Beth had travelled home separately. Mary Beth had arrived first and was waiting in her mother's bedroom, having already sent Perks to her bed.

'I don't want to hear a word of censure, Momma,' Mary Beth had said as Marjory walked through the door. 'I am a woman from the New World. I will not conform to the petty social strictures of the European middle classes.'

Marjory had said of course not. Really, it was a good thing Mary Beth had heard the speakers, because these were the important issues that her generation would have to deal with.

Mary Beth had come off her high horse straight away, as she always did when Marjory gave her a soft answer. Mother and daugher had agreed that they were very pleased to have attended the meeting; they even congratulated themselves on having been so daring and so socially aware.

Then later – Marjory could not remember how it happened – the two women had begun discussing the merits of the Contagious Diseases Act, and the fireworks had begun. Marjory had thought it was perhaps a good idea to have such a law, since something had to be done about this terrible disease. Mary Beth had been incensed: it was an evil law, designed to humiliate women. Anyway, doctors only examined women to satisfy their perverted urges, not to cure disease at all.

Marjory thought this was a terrible slander against a decent group of men, and said so so rather forcefully. For fifteen minutes, she and Mary Beth had quarrelled about the Act. Mary Beth had eventually stormed out of the room, and her attendance at the meeting had not been mentioned again. At least, not by Mary Beth. For several days, Marjory and the countess could speak of little else.

No, Marjory reflected now. She could not tell Mary Beth that Falkner had the pox. Nor could she order her daugher to break off her engagement. *How love of our children makes cowards of us all!* she thought. But that didn't mean that a mother could abandon her innocent daughter. What was needed was a plan of action.

That evening, Bennett was seated in his favourite chair in the library when he heard Marcus being admitted at the front door. He called out to his son.

'Are you still up, Father?' said Marcus, coming into the library. 'It is almost one o'clock.'

'I haven't seen you very much lately, so I thought we might have a brandy together. Will you pour?'

'What a good idea!' Marcus went to the brandy decanter and poured a generous measure into each of the brandy balloons. 'Your health, sir. Have you been looking at Mama's photographs?'

The doctor looked a trifle guilty as he patted the album on his lap. 'Not tonight. I usually do, you know. But not tonight. Lady Manton lent me an album of hers. Most extraordinary pictures. See here, the Mississippi river. It's vast!'

Marcus frowned at the mention of Marjory's name, but he obediently went behind his father's chair and peered over his shoulder at the photograph. 'Very impressive.'

'And this,' said Bennett, 'taken after the battle of Shiloh in the American Civil War.'

'Good Lord! Why would any woman want a photograph of a field of dead men?'

'Because the man here in the foreground was Lady Manton's uncle, her mother's brother. And these men here, here and over here, were his three sons. Lady Manton keeps the picture to remind her of what they sacrificed to save the Union. They were only tobacco growers, not professional soldiers at all. With the exception of a cousin in, I believe she said Oregon, she has no living relatives, except her son and Miss Hanson.'

'Does the album consist of nothing but the photographs of dead men?'

'In a way.' The doctor turned the page. 'Here is a picture of her father's place of business. He was a ships' chandler, you know. This is Lady Manton here, with her parents and the man who was to become her husband. Mr Hanson. I have forgotten his Christian name.'

'To think her fortune was created by that ramshackle shop! How strange they all look. Not a smartly dressed person among them.' Marcus was holding the brandy glass cupped in his hand. With a slight circular motion, he swirled the liquid round the glass and tasted it before going over to straddle the arm of the red leather

152

chesterfield. 'Papa.' Mr Bennett stiffened, mistrusting the tone of voice. 'Remember when you were very friendly with Mrs Carmody about two years after Mama died?'

'Of course I remember.'

'You found her company agreeable, and I have to admit she was – indeed probably still is – a most charming person. She had been a widow for many years, was naturally lonely and understandably anxious to marry again. That is the way with widows.'

'I have not forgotten, Marcus.'

'Well, sir, we agreed then that we – you and I – were very well as we were. Two unmarried men sharing this fine old house, devoted to our work.'

'That is so. You were eloquent on the subject, as I remember.'

'Well, nothing has changed. We still do very well on our own, do we not?'

'Indeed, we do. And we remain devoted to our work.' The doctor looked up at his son and met the younger man's eyes. 'I take my work very seriously and often worry about the fate of my patients.'

'That is natural, I'm sure.'

'There was a young prostitute here a few weeks ago. She was so beautiful and so young! I urged her to find some decent occupation. I wonder whatever became of her.'

Marcus finished his brandy and stood up. 'I expect she found some rich protector and is bleeding him white. You should not concern yourself with these girls, beyond curing them of disease, Father.'

'She wasn't diseased. She was healthy. Don't you remember? I told you so at the time.'

'I cannot recall. I am very tired, sir. I think I will go to bed.' Marcus started towards the door, then turned with the ingratiating smile of one who, having got his own way, now wants to be loved for it. 'You don't regret not having married Mrs Carmody, do you?'

'No, no, I don't regret not having married her, I promise you. She has married someone else, and I believe she is very happy.'

'And we are happy as we are, aren't we?' persisted Marcus.

'Yes. Happy as we are. Good night, Marcus.'

After Marcus had gone, the doctor sat perfectly still for several minutes. His feelings towards his son were so complex that he had long ago decided not to attempt to analyse them. Marcus had been a solitary boy, studious but remote. At school, he had, therefore, surprised his parents by adopting a protective attitude towards Jeremy Grimshaw, preventing other boys from bullying him, even taking a considerable risk on one occasion to hide the consequences of a regrettable lapse in Jeremy's behaviour.

The doctor had been deeply impressed and proud of his son when Jeremy had confessed to his godfather that he had stolen some money from another boy. Marcus had entered the boy's room and returned the money, knowing that if he were found there, his own reputation would be ruined. Bennett had lost no time in sending for Marcus to praise him for his courage and kindness. How surprised he had been when Marcus admitted that he felt no affection for Jeremy at all!

'But in that case, why did you go to so much trouble on his behalf?' the doctor had asked.

And Marcus had said: 'Because *you* love him, Father.' From that day the doctor had stopped trying to understand his son.

He preferred, now, to forget the incident of the young girl. Action, of the sort he had forcefully recommended to Marjory, was not to be thought of where Marcus was concerned. For all he knew, Marcus had acted nobly, just the way he had done all those years ago with Jeremy. Yes, that was it. Marcus' intolerance of impure women showed the highest tone of mind, but in taking the girl to Wainwright, he had thoughtfully saved her from a much worse situation. No need to feel uncomfortable about the business. Marcus knew what he was doing and, anyway, Falkner had probably wickedly misrepresented the situation.

Glad to have sorted out this knotty problem, the doctor looked down at a photograph of Lady Marjory Manton, a studio portrait, this one, taken when Mary Beth was about four years old and Samuel was three. Marjory's dress and that of the children looked much like British clothing. In fact, the photograph might have been taken in Europe.

'And yet so different,' he murmured. Marjory's dark hair had no hint then, of the white streak which added drama to her appearance now. But the large eyes were the same: bright, intelligent and perhaps a little sad.

14

It was Thursday afternoon again. Marjorie had long since ceased to look forward to her At Homes. They were, after all, just like the tea parties back in St Louis, the little gatherings for women only that she had always been so anxious to avoid. Momma had held one every week or so and enjoyed them hugely. Mrs Schwartz would come into the parlour and open the conversation by praising Momma's new cutains, or whatever, or saying: 'I declare, you are good at needlework, Bertha.'

Then Momma would say: 'Have you heard from Clyde?' (Mrs Schwartz's son who was in Alabama). 'How is he?'

Mrs Schwartz would say: 'Oh fine,' and the two of them would be off and running.

Every person within miles, whom they both knew, would be enquired about. They would take turns in bringing up a name, and in answering: 'Oh, fine,' or – Momma's favourite expression – 'not so pretty good,' as the case might be. If some other lady arrived for tea or coffee or lemonade, according to the season, the whole business would have to be gone through again.

And afterwards, Momma would always say how nice it had been to 'set a piece' with her friends and hear all the news. Marjorie always wondered how anybody could enjoy wasting so much time.

At first, it hadn't occurred to her that English At Homes were exactly the same. But really, only the accents and the actual names were different. She and Maud Pringle had seen so much of each other at recent At Homes that they could no longer go through the

156

standard catechism. They both knew all too well who was 'fine' and who was 'not so pretty good.'

Bored, she leaned back in her chair and fiddled with the finely pleated ruffle of her left sleeve. The first inkling she had that this might be a rather different At Home from the usual, was when Mary Beth came into the drawing-room looking quite stunning in a yellow and white striped gown with yellow bows planted in a row all down the back. Marjory had just started to ask why on earth Mary Beth had got herself so dressed up, when Brogan opened the door to announce Frederick Bennett.

Marjorie leapt to her feet. She had a distinct, apprehensive tingling of the scalp, as she held out her hand. 'Good afternoon, Frederick. How nice it is to see you here. Have you – '

'Mr and Mrs John Quinn. Mrs Wilson Grimshaw. Miss Susannah Quinn. Mr Jeremy Grimshaw,' intoned Brogan.

Bennett, who had been holding Marjory's hand rather tightly, scowled furiously as he murmured: 'Damn it!' under his breath.

Marjory was completely thrown by the doctor's swearing. So unlike him. She found Mr and Mrs Quinn the most terrible bores, and Mrs Grimshaw was either a fool or a very nasty lady; Marjory could not decide how to take the widow's murmured asides. But that didn't explain Bennett's mood, surely. She greeted her guests, muddling their names, and almost tripping over the hem of her tea gown as she kept glancing at the doctor's thunderous expression.

'Oh, Mr Bennett!' exclaimed Mrs Grimshaw, waddling up to him. 'How fortunate that you are here. I have been suffering of late from palpitations of the heart. What do you recommend?'

Marjory was aware of the doctor's intense annoyance

157

which seemed to settle like fog on the room. 'Consult a physician,' was his brusque reply.

'Oh, but Dr Toomly has been no help to me at all.'

'A strong purge,' said Mrs Quinn, positively. 'That will cure your palpitations, Mrs Grimshaw. I have treated Mr Quinn most successfully on several occasions by that method. Black draught followed by castor oil.'

'But, Mr Bennett,' urged Mrs Grimshaw, determined to have her free medical advice. 'Can you not, as an old and valued friend, advise me?'

'Don't lace yourself so tightly,' said Bennett. 'Vanity is the prime cause of palpitations, in my experience.'

Ugly red blotches leaked on to Mrs Grimshaw's neck and cheeks. Jeremy looked to be on the point of saying something strong in defence of his mother. He opened his mouth and lifted an admonitory finger, but then appeared to change his mind.

'Really, Mr Bennett,' said Mary Beth. 'You do our sex an injustice. Confess now. You would not like to see us in ill-fitting clothes without the benefit of our corsets. What we wear is not due solely to our vanity.'

'On the contrary, I would be very happy if corsets were banished from the wardrobe. They are pernicious devices. It is ridiculous to say that your clothes would be ill-fitting without them. Your mother looks quite charming today, and she is not – ' He stopped in some confusion.

Marjory was, in fact, wearing a loose tea gown which, as everyone knew, didn't require the discomfort of whalebone.

'Yes, Doctor? You were saying?' enquired Marjorie sweetly, knowing perfectly well that he would not be so indelicate as to finish his sentence. He was clearly disconcerted, but was saved from further embarrassment by the arrival of Lucius Falkner. There was a certain amount of confusion, because the painter came

158

into the room almost at the same moment as two nervous servants carrying the tea trays.

Mary Beth brought Falkner to her side with a jerk of the head, much as a dog-owner brings his pet to heel. Marjory sat down and began to pour the tea. Mrs Grimshaw fanned herself feverishly, still pouting because of the doctor's rebuff, while Bennett, a law unto himself on these occasions, sat upright on a chair which he had placed slightly out of the circle of guests. He churlishly refused all offers of food; Mrs Grimshaw, on the other hand, was never angry enough to refuse seed cake.

Then it began – the naming of names. How is so and so? Where is x? Have you heard that – ? But all the answers, from whatever quarter were flat, lacking in that spark of greedy interest that could keep people happily talking about those not present. Eventually, silence fell, and to save her life, Marjory could not think how to get things going again.

Shortly afterwards, Mary Beth took control and elec-trified the small gathering. The girl set down her cup with a rattle and a flourish. 'I have an announcement to make.' She looked fondly at Falkner who seemed at first mystified, then downright alarmed. Marjory, less mystified than Falkner, had the feeling she was falling into a bottomless pit, with no way to save herself. 'Lucius – that is – Mr Falkner and I are betrothed,' said Mary Beth.

Falkner, resigning himself to a stronger will than his own, took Mary Beth's hand somewhat defiantly, as he looked first at Marjory and then Bennett.

'Well, this is a surprise,' said Marjory coolly. 'It seems very sudden, but I guess you know your own hearts. You don't plan to marry very soon, do you?'

'Oh, no, ma'am,' said Falkner so anxiously that under other circumstances Marjory would have laughed out loud.

'Well, I think it's charming,' said Mrs Grimshaw. She turned to Marjory. 'Although I dare say you were hoping – '

'Allow me to congratulate you, Mr Falkner,' boomed the doctor. Falkner flinched.

The Quinn family said all that was appropriate to the occasion, but they spoke with such faint enthusiasm and wore such appalled expressions that Marjory might have felt sorry for Falkner if she didn't hate him so much.

'And,' said Mary Beth triumphantly, 'Lucius has been very successful of late. Important people have praised his work. He receives a great many commissions and charges large fees, and he has taken a fine house in Doughty Street, where we will live if we don't move to something grander.'

Now the praise was more genuine. A successful artist could be instantly forgiven for painting a disgusting nude, which miraculously became a work of art as his fees went up. Pretty soon Marjory reckoned, they would be saying it was not such a terrible thing to have the pox. She lifted her cup to take a long drink of tea, but her hand shook so violently that she quickly set it down again.

The doctor was the first to indicate that he intended to leave. Marjory walked to the front door with him.

'I have nothing further to say,' said Bennett in response to her silence.

'Just as well. I'm not in the mood for one of your lectures.'

He drew himself to his full height, apologized stiffly for any irritation he might have caused her in the past, and left.

Marjory stood in the hall for several minutes. Bennett unnerved her. He made her feel young, and that should have been a good thing. But her youth had been an unhappy time, a period in her life when

160

everyone was bent on telling her what to do and what to think. She was forty years old now and thought she had earned the right to think for herself. Obviously, the doctor didn't share that view. He was a large man and loomed over her, both physically and metaphorically. She had the uncomfortable feeling that he could see right into her head, and didn't like what he saw. He was, in short, a man who brought out the worst in her, and she ought never to have seen him after that first occasion. She was an honest woman, however. No denying that it was more fun to be mad at the doctor than on good terms with anyone else. Except Mary Beth.

She returned to the drawing-room with a heavy heart, knowing she was going to have to tread warily over this business of the engagement. Mary Beth had looked very aggressive when making the announcement. The truth was, Marjory was afraid of her daughter, of what she might say, what she might do. She knew the ways of men and had always thought that Samuel would leave home one day, but she couldn't bear to be separated from Mary Beth. Daughters were supposed to be a comfort to their mothers.

The guests seemed much more relaxed and talkative now that the doctor had left. Jeremy Grimshaw assured Marjory that he was delighted with the match. Miss Hanson would make a lovely bride, and Falkner was the best of good fellows.

Miss Susannah Quinn said in her breathless manner that she did so envy dear Mary Beth, who would be choosing a trousseau and furnishings for a new home. Every girl hoped to be similarly occupied at some time in her life, said Miss Quinn, looking directly at Jeremy Grimshaw. Marjory smiled to see the lawyer so embarrassed, and thought the young woman would do better to find herself a more enthusiastic lover.

Later, Mr Quinn managed to manoeuvre Marjory

161

into a quiet corner where he told her solemnly that the situation *could* be a great deal worse, and perhaps it wouldn't come to anything in the end. This well-meant statement did nothing to raise Marjory's spirits.

The guests seemed reluctant to leave. There was nothing to do but serve them more tea and smile, smile, smile. Marjory had run out of conversation and confined herself to a bright listening attitude, aware that Mary Beth's eyes were almost always upon her.

By the time they were alone, each had thought of a few things to say to the other.

'I don't want to discuss it, Momma. It was my decision. I'm old enough to make up my own mind.'

'And Lucius Falkner's too. The poor man didn't know what was going on. Did you have to rope and tie him? Couldn't you just have waited to be *asked*? What's the matter with you, girl?'

'Lucius is an artist, and they tend to be rather dreamy and impractical people. He needed a nudge, but he wasn't unhappy about the announcement.'

'You think you can do what you please with Lucius Falkner, but you just wait.'

'I can handle him.'

'Yeah,' said Marjory. 'You can handle everybody, the way you trampled on my feelings, suddenly announcing your coming marriage when you hadn't even told me first. You're real smart, Mary Beth Hanson, the smartest fool I ever met.'

'I value your opinion, Momma.' Mary Beth walked briskly out of the room, and Marjory put a hand over her eyes.

'No,' she said to herself, '*I'm* the smartest fool who ever lived, and I wish I was dead.'

It was Mary Beth who sent the announcement to the newspaper; Mary Beth who sent for the dressmaker; Mary Beth who consulted her diary, searching for the perfect wedding date. Both Falkner and Marjory refused to take any interest at all in these activities.

Mary Beth would never forgive her mother for her lack of support. But what of Lucius? Not to forgive *him* would be to admit that Momma was right about the man. Mary Beth felt she had no choice but to pursue her fiancé and force him to show some enthusiasm for their future life together.

Accordingly, she travelled to the house on Doughty Street where she made enemies of the staff by insisting on inspecting the premises from attic to cellar, enquiring after the linen, and making copious notes about what was needed. Falkner was not so much angry in the face of her interference as supine. He would not quarrel. He had a great deal on his mind, he said. He wasn't feeling too well these days. He had some very important work to do.

Mary Beth listened to his whining excuses with disgust. Then she heard her own voice in response. It was the voice of a stranger – screeching, vindictive, totally out of control. She went away wondering what on earth was the matter with her. She must leave Falkner alone for a while. He would soon see how much he missed her. He would soon come round to Cavendish Place.

In the meantime, she would throw herself in to business, because there could be no question of sitting round amicably with her mother these days, gossiping and arguing as they used to do.

She invested some money in a piece of decaying property and sent in the builders to turn it into bachelor apartments. She bought a small haberdashery business, immediately opened two more and three days later sold the lot for a handsome profit.

During this time, Falkner sent no communication. No one had seen him, Grimshaw told her. He must be very busy. Like a sore that could not be allowed to heal, Mary Beth began to pick at Falkner by means of letters – sometimes as many as four a day. When they brought no response, she paid another call on Doughty Street.

Falkner was in his studio, and greeted her with a very heavy sigh. How different this studio was from the humble room in Wych Street! The white marble fireplace was flanked by two gaslights on handsome wrought-iron brackets, shaded by milky glass globes. The brown walls had not been disfigured by sketches tacked to them. Instead, a faded tapestry nearly covered one wall. Everywhere were easels with half-finished portraits resting on them. Falkner seemed to be working on four or five paintings at once.

However, when Mary Beth entered the room, he was working on none of these. He was sketching with a stick of charcoal that continually fragmented, sending pieces of charcoal flying in all directions. Josie Smith was seated on a two-tiered dais, turned sideways to Falkner. Her knees were bent, her feet apart. She was completely naked.

Mary Beth drew in her breath so sharply she almost choked. For a moment all three occupants froze as if posing in a *tableau vivante*. Then Mary Beth marched across the richly patterned parquet floor, snatched up a robe which had been left on a nearby chair and flung it at Josie.

'Get yourself dressed and out of this house,' she said. 'Mr Falkner and I are to be married. You are not to come here again.'

Josie flinched as if expecting to be struck, then pulled the robe around her and darted behind a screen.

'Stop making a fool of yourself, Mary Beth,' drawled Falkner. He had his hands in his trouser pockets and was now leaning against a large oak chest, but the narrowness of his eyes and the set of his mouth betrayed his anger. He raised his voice.'Josie! You will come

164

here again tomorrow at ten o' clock. I have not finished the painting. I, and I alone, will decide when your services are no longer needed.'

He wore a blue velvet jacket without either a cravat or tie. Some conceit had prompted him to grow his whiskers longer at the sides, which changed the apparent shape of his face. Mary Beth thought he looked like a stranger. With a casual gesture, he indicated two leather chairs set before the empty fireplace, and without waiting for Mary Beth to be seated, sprawled in one of them, his pose a studied insult.

She would have preferred to maintain a position of supremacy by standing, but her legs felt so weak she was afraid she might collapse right there on the floor. Seating herself primly on the edge of the chair, she squeezed the inner corners of her eyes until the thumb and forefinger of her glove were wet with tears.

Falkner watched her for several seconds, then snorted in disgust. 'You really are an ignorant young woman, Mary Beth. You know nothing about artists. Your lack of imagination and compassion makes it impossible for you to understand a way of life different from your own. How dared you speak to that poor girl in such an insulting way? Every artist employs models. It is a respectable means of earning money for beautiful young women who might otherwise starve. I will tolerate a good deal of managing from you, but you must not interfere in my work.'

'You don't want to marry me.'

'I never said so. You can't claim that I ever said so. I think it is too soon to be choosing wedding dates, however.'

Josie Smith emerged from behind the screen, looked shyly in Mary Beth's direction, then left the studio, shutting the door quietly behind her. Mary Beth and Falkner gave no sign of having noticed her departure.

'Come, my dear,' said Falkner in a softer tone.

'Admit that you have been a trifle stupid today. No harm has been done, however. Josie will continue to sit for me and the painting will be a success. You'll see.'

Mary Beth didn't trust herself to answer. She stood up, straightened her hat, tugged the jacket of her travelling suit into place and left the room without so much as saying goodbye. Her mother's brougham was waiting at the kerb, but before she stepped into it, the coachman spoke in a voice heavy with disapproval.

'Miss Hanson, a young person just came out of that house and says to me she must speak with you. Said she'll be waiting round the corner. We can take a different direction if you prefer not to see her.'

'No, no. We will take her up and drive her to her destination.' Mary Beth sat down in the carriage and made a determined effort to compose her face before Josie joined her.

Josie Smith climbed nimbly into the coach when invited to do so. Her features were so delicate, her eyes so large and luminous, that Mary Beth couldn't help feeling envious. Josie still wore the simple shift and black skirt gathered to her waist by means of a drawstring that she had been wearing when the two women first met. On her feet, were ugly black boots.

'What is it you wish to say to me, Josie? I haven't much time, I'm afraid.'

'No, ma'am,' said Josie, studying her clasped hands as if she had never seen them before. 'Now, I'm here, I don't know if I ought to speak. But I *got* to tell you.'

'Oh, do get on with it, girl.' Mary Beth's voice was harsh, but a premonition of disaster was squeezing the breath from her lungs.

'Well, then ... you mustn't marry Mr Falkner because he's got a disease. There, now I've said it.'

'My God! I don't believe you. You're lying. How could you possibly know such a thing?'

166

Josie looked up at Mary Beth with sudden defiance. 'You don't know nothing what goes on. You fancy women with your velvet and furs. He wanted me, see. I saw the sores. Now, I'll probably get it, too, though he says he caught it off me.'

'It can't be true. We are engaged. He wouldn't be so disloyal.'

Josie smiled now, sadly but with a certain warmth towards Mary Beth. 'Men don't know about loyalty, Miss Hanson. They're different from us. And sometimes they think if they can go with a pure woman, you know, a fresh girl, it will cure the disease. Maybe that's true. I don't know. But I thought you ought to have the chance to decide if you want to risk it.'

Mary Beth sagged against the cushions and closed her eyes. 'I suppose the coachman has heard every word.' It was a stupid remark; she didn't even care if the coachman had heard their conversation. She simply couldn't think of anything else to say.

'I'm sorry if you're upset, ma'am. I'll get out now.'

The coach was stationary, the coachman having no intention of driving the likes of Josie Smith anywhere if he could help it. As the girl reached for the door handle, Mary Beth held out a guinea which Josie ignored. 'I suppose you think I should be grateful for this . . . this information. Take the money, I say! Take it!'

Josie stuffed the coin into the pocket of her skirt. 'I had to tell you, ma'am. You should be grateful.' She climbed down from the carriage, closed the door and turned to look at Mary Beth directly in the eye. 'I beg of you, Miss Hanson, don't let him know what I said to you. It may not seem so to you, but things is ever so much better for me since I took up with Luc . . . Mr Falkner.'

Mary Beth sat back in the coach and closed her eyes. 'I won't mention it, I promise you. You must do

167

whatever you think best. By all means, continue to pose for him if that is what you want to do. As Mr Falkner has said, it is none of my business.'

It took twenty-five minutes to reach Cavendish Place, and during that time, Mary Beth sat in the open carriage, staring about at the passing scene dry-eyed. She felt a certain numbness for some time, but that gave way to the unbearable pain of rejection and the knowledge that she had been deceived. Vague thoughts, stupid thoughts of extravagant revenge, flooded her mind, but by the time she reached her own front door, she was limp with defeat. She wanted to see her mother, to find the comfort in Marjory's presence that she had enjoyed when she was a child.

Marjory was basking in the damp heat of the freshly watered conservatory.

'I have been visiting Lucius, Momma. We had a lovely chat.'

'Sit down a minute and talk to me,' said Marjory. 'I hardly ever see you these days. How is he? Is he keeping well?'

Mary Beth was having difficulty pulling off her gloves.'Oh, just splendid. The dear man has grown sideburns. So distinguished. He has several commissions. Really, he is rushed off his feet.'

Marjory frowned. 'Have you fixed a date for your wedding?'

'Oh, Momma, you're always trying to rush me into marriage.'

'*I'm what?*'

'There's no hurry. Lucius is so busy and, really, I'm only twenty-one. I want to have some fun. I think an engagement of six months would be about right, don't you? I want to do the correct thing.'

Marjory blinked. In her experience, Mary Beth was

inclined to discover the correct thing merely in order to do the opposite.

'Will you excuse me, Momma? It is a hot day and I'm rather tired.' Mary Beth gave her mother a bright smile before walking briskly out of the room.

It seemed to Mary Beth that she couldn't trust anyone these days. And she certainly couldn't trust her own judgement. She went to her bedchamber and allowed her maid to undress her. Then, with the blinds drawn, she did what she had always despised in other girls. She lay down on the bed in the middle of a perfectly beautiful afternoon.

But what else could she do? Her confidence had so deserted her that she couldn't bear the sight of another person. Particularly not the other person who resided in her mirror.

Since she had turned sixteen, her friends had been pairing off, finding beaux, getting married, having children. The boys (later the men) she knew had always steered clear of Mary Beth Hanson, a long meg who was taller than half the male population and smarter than three-quarters of it. She was not yet twenty-two, but spinsterhood stared her in the face. The spectre of the lonely years ahead had kept her chasing Falkner, had made her shrill.

But she had decided long ago that a useless husband was better than no husband at all. She had abandoned all hope of a love match. Other girls might adore their husbands, hang upon their every word, blush at the smallest compliment. Not Mary Beth. She would wait until Lucius had recovered from his illness and then she would marry him. Nothing could stop her, not the reluctance of Lucius himself nor her mother's displeasure.

Once they were married, things would be very different. Lucius would come to heel. He would do as he was told. She would manage his home efficiently, guide his career and bear his children. Above all, he would behave himself or she would make him wish he had never been born.

15

Marjory lay awake at nights worrying about Mary Beth. The girl was behaving in a very strange way. So energetic, so bright and happy until some slight irritation set her off in an unseemly display of temper. Even Perks was losing patience with the girl. Marjory was afraid to speak to her, but had to keep trying to divert Mary Beth's thoughts. She suggested that they return to America, and when that idea met with a firm no, she proposed moving to St John's Wood. Maybe the two women should open a store to rival Swan and Edgar's, or give a charity ball. Mary Beth's replies were sometimes angry, but at other times she would give a hearty laugh which bordered on hysteria. Really, she would say, Momma could be so amusing! Didn't she know that Mary Beth was busy ordering her trousseau?

When Marjory reached the point where she thought she could stand it no more, her thoughts turned to Guy Dundalk, who seemed to be a remarkably resourceful young man. She had to see him.

Whereas once she had found it amusing to sneak away and meet the young man in some out of the way place where nobody would see them, this time the need for secrecy just irritated her. She settled on the Midland Grand Hotel at St Pancras station. It was new and very luxurious. She had been there once, but didn't think any of her acquaintances would be likely to visit it at three o' clock on a summer's afternoon. She briefly considered hiring a room and meeting Dundalk there, so that they could talk in complete privacy. The young man would be sure to misunderstand, however, so she abandoned the idea.Instead, she told him to meet her in an alcove on the first floor landing. There was a very pretty painting on the wall of the alcove. She thought he couldn't miss it. On the other hand, he was not to expect to recognize her, because she would be heavily veiled.

Dundalk arrived promptly at the appointed time. 'Well, Lady Marjory, this is a surprise. What are we to make of this meeting? You look very fetching in your disguise, by the way. How may I help you?'

'It's hard for me to say this, Mr Dundalk. I don't like being disloyal and I don't like interfering in my daughter's affairs. But, well, I've got to stop her from marrying the man she is engaged to.'

Dundalk had taken a seat beside Marjory, now he jumped to his feet. 'No, ma'am, I don't want anything to do with affairs of the heart. I'm not interested, not able to help you, no matter what you've got in mind.'

'Sit down. I can't talk to you if you're going to be jumping all over the place. I won't mince words. Mary Beth's fiancé has a disease.'

Dundalk smiled. 'That's common enough, ma'am. Few men escape it. He'll get over it, you know. Especially if he has proper treatment.'

'Well, that's a fine attitude to take. I'll not enquire about *your* health, young man, because it doesn't concern me. I'll just say that the fact he caught it at all at this time means that he hasn't exactly been faithful to her. But that's neither here not there. I'm going to do something. You must help me, or I might shoot him.'

'Lady Marjory, you are right to say it is none of your business how I conduct my affairs, but I'll just remind you that I'm not one of your swell friends. I take good care of my health. Apart from that, I don't see what I can do about your daughter.'

'Don't get mad. I didn't mean to insult you. I've

been crude and heavy-handed. Can't you see I'm upset? Let's start again. Let's pretend we've just met. How do you do, Mr Dundalk? I've come to ask you to do me a favour. I want you to strike up an acquaintance with my daughter. Find a way so she won't think I had anything to do with it. I want you to flirt with her a little. Nothing serious, of course, just make her feel good. Make her forget about Lucius Falkner.'

'I'm a busy man,' he said coldly. 'I have a living to earn, Lady Marjory.'

'I know that.' She frowned as she studied his expressive face from beneath her veiling. 'I'd appreciate it if you would do this for me. I'd give you twenty pounds for expenses.'

Dundalk smiled, but his eyes stayed hard. 'London is an expensive city, ma'am. You have no idea.'

She might have known. He drove a hard bargain, but he could be forgiven on the grounds that he had his way to make, and undoubtedly saw her as rich and foolish. 'How much, Mr Dundalk? Just give me your price.'

The entrance to Hyde Park at Marble Arch had, in recent years, become an open forum for those who wished to test the establishment's interpretation of free speech. Anyone could speak, provided he didn't incite to riot or say anything blasphemous or obscene. Much was made of this new privilege at first, but serious agitators for reform quickly found better places to express their views.

On the other hand, religious zealots and misfits of every persuasion found what became known as Speaker's Corner to be their only platform. Along with rather pathetic performers came the barrackers, those wits who attempted to raise a laugh at the expense of the speaker. There was always a good crowd these days to watch the show, and many young men came expressly to bait those who were foolhardy enough to mount a box.

As Guy Dundalk approached the Corner on this very hot summer day, he saw that there were at least fifty people in the crowd, all well dressed, all evidently enjoying themselves while a ragged, white-haired man attempted to threaten them with damnation. Dundalk had no sympathy for the speaker whom he happened to know was a sinner named Rummy Rob. The man hadn't a bed to call his own, but earned a crust by begging.

Despairingly, Dundalk looked in the direction of the park and sighed heavily, not wishing to have to search three hundred acres or more of parkland for two women he had never seen and one gentleman who was so small that he could easily be overlooked.

Fortunately, a careful search of those watching Rummy Rob showed him Jeremy Grimshaw with a young lady on each arm. Dundalk nervously straightened his tie before flicking the ends of his moustache into place. There was a certain sinking feeling in the pit of his stomach. What a fool he was! He was about to take a considerable risk, and fifty pounds was hardly a suitable recompense.

'Make up to my daughter,' Lady Marjory had said. 'Turn her head.'

He should have said no. Jeremy had warned him about the daughter, had told him how shrewd she was. Dundalk knew he ought to avoid her, but the desire to test his wits against hers had proved too great. Naturally, Lady Marjory had expected him to do it for nothing. A favour, she had called it. But Guy didn't do anything for nothing. Driving hard bargains was his forte, and by the time he had finished talking, the lady had been positively eager to pay him fifty pounds as 'expenses'. Only then did he think he should not have got involved at any price.

Now that the moment had arrived, now that he was about to approach one of the women (and he didn't know which one) he wondered if he were about to make the mistake of a lifetime.

Steady, Dundalk, he said to himself. *You've taken the money. Now do your damnedest.*

Grimshaw saw him approaching and shook his head to warn him away. When Dundalk kept coming, the lawyer looked as if he might turn tail and run.

Dundalk smiled broadly, very glad not to have taken the timid little man into his confidence. Now the ladies were looking his way: an exceptionally pretty little woman with a meek but friendly expression, and a dragon of a girl, bold, tall and not the least bit encouraging. *Let it be the tall one*, he thought. It would be a pity to mislead the gentle little lady, and probably more difficult, too, because she must have had her share of admirers, men who had paid her every conceivable compliment. Whereas the tall one . . .

'Grimshaw, old fellow! What a surprise to meet you here!'

'Yes,' said Grimshaw, glowering. He had mentioned to Dundalk only the day before that he intended to bring Miss Hanson to see Speakers' Corner this afternoon. 'Ladies, allow me to indroduce Mr Guy Dundalk. Miss Quinn and Miss Hanson.'

Miss Quinn murmured 'How do you do?' but her voice was all but drowned by Miss Hanson's hearty greeting as she thrust her hand out to him.

So it was the tall one! Dundalk, aware of a quickening pulse, welcomed the challenge. He easily convinced himself that she always reacted with ill-conceived hostility whenever she was introduced to a gentleman. Here was a woman accustomed to rejection.

For his part, he thought he detected a quick mind and a sense of her own intellectual and financial worth. He already knew about her sharp tongue. Grimshaw had regaled him on many occassions with tales of the lady's ill-natured remarks.

'Miss Hanson?' he said now, appearing to be uncertain of her identity. 'I am acquainted with Lady Marjory Manton. Might you be the Miss Hanson who is her daughter?'

'I am, but don't look for a family resemblance. The Thorpes are all small. We Hansons are . . .' she looked away and finished lamely, 'are not.'

'Such statuesque beauty as yours ma'am could only have been bred in the United States of America, I believe.'

He accompanied his awkward compliment with a graceful bow and saw that Grimshaw was furious and Miss Hanson looking deeply suspicious. Smoothly, he turned his attention to Miss Quinn who responded to his raillery with such a profusion of blushes and stammered replies that Dundalk's confidence was soon restored. He suggested that they all walk in the park, and made as if to take Miss Quinn's arm. Grimshaw pulled his lady to his side, then watched, fuming, as Dundalk took Mary Beth's hand and tucked it into the crook of his arm.

Mary Beth matched her stride to Dundalk's and they moved several yards ahead of the other couple.

'I hope you enjoyed Speakers' Corner, ma'am. Anyone may speak there, you know.'

'I do know,' said Mary Beth, 'so long as they don't say anything that anybody cares about. And they have only had this remarkable privilege for the past three years, a freedom that was too long in coming and doesn't amount to much, anyway.'

'Ah, the voice of the New World! We have our strict rules of conduct, I admit, but then, we are not a nation of savages.' He glanced at the girl, caught her out in the hint of a smile, and laughed softly. Once again, he blessed himself that he had not been set the task of charming the little mouse who was at this moment clinging to Grimshaw's arm. Dundalk *did* prefer the contestants of any battle to be well-matched.

'When did you meet my mother?' said Mary Beth.

'I called upon her one morning to beg for a worthy cause. Your mother is a most remarkable woman. She has told me how she arranged for a pregnant maid to marry a coachman employed by Grimshaw's mother.'

Mary Beth laughed delightedly. 'Momma thinks marriage solves all problems. Perhaps in the case of the maid she took to Greenwich, marriage was the only answer. But Momma knows that I won't dance to her tune.'

'No, indeed,' said Dundalk. 'I'm sure it would never occur to your mother to order you about.'

Although he was with her for only an hour, Guy managed to make Mary Beth laugh out loud on several occasions, and to win her confidence so completely that she agreed to meet him in Hyde Park on the following afternoon at five o' clock.

However, the next day when he arrived at the appointed place, he discovered that she had armed herself against a damaged reputation by bringing a friend, Lady Fenella, daughter of the Earl of Dumfries, and a chaperone in the form of a thirtyish widow named Mrs Booker.

Mentally, Dundalk acknowledged Mary Beth's shrewdness and his repect for her rose. He regarded the friend as a hindrance. Lady Fenella was not the first daughter of a nobleman he had ever met. He was tolerably well-acquainted with the species, and swells made him uncomfortable. He thought of them as a rackety lot, full of high-jinks and 'aren't the middle-classes boring?' Then all of a sudden they would turn nasty, stick their noses in the air and put you in your place.

On the other hand, Mrs Booker gave him great hopes

for the future. He knew her type well; the indulgent widow who was always prepared to turn her back, or failing that, close her eyes, so to speak, when the young people in her charge wished to ignore the rules of correct behaviour. Foolish mothers trusted the likes of Mrs Booker, but their daughters knew better. The question in Dundalk's mind was: did Miss Mary Beth Hanson invite the widow along out of ignorance or because she wished to be a little free and easy? He decided it must be the latter. She had Lady Fenella to advise her, after all.

His predictions were borne out a moment or two later when they were joined by another gentleman. Lady Fenella's cheeks were glowing, her round eyes more prominent than ever, as she introduced Lord Hemsby to the party.

Hemsby was tall and thin, wearing a well-tailored frockcoat and striped trousers and with a languid air of indifference towards the world. He was barely civil to Dundalk, looked Mary Beth up and down in such a rude way that Dundalk wanted to strike him, and gave the sketchiest bow to the widow whom he appeared to know. Mrs Booker immediately put a gloved hand to her forehead and complained rather unconvincingly of a sudden headache. She would just sit quietly on this bench, she said, if the young people would be so good as not to wander out of her sight.

'Sorry to hear of your indisposition, Mrs Booker,' said Hemsby. 'Come on Lady Fenella, I fancy a short walk to settle my digestion.'

The couple strode off at such a pace that Dundalk gave Mary Beth a quizzical look which made her laugh.

'Another rude lord,' she said, as they walked away from Mrs Booker in the opposite direction from Hemsby and Fenella. 'Sometimes I think it's great fun living in England and knowing all these fancy people, but then again I find all their silly rules very irritating.

My friend, Fenella, wanted to meet you, and she said I would be *ruined* if we met without a chaperone in broad daylight in the park.'

'So it was Lady Fenella's idea to invite Mrs Booker?'

'Yes,' said Mary Beth. 'Don't you like her?'

'Got nothing against her, although your mother might have. Mrs Booker won't be too strict a chaperone.'

Mary Beth laughed. 'That is just what Fenella said.'

'She'll warn you against me,' said Dundalk. 'Lady Fenella, I mean. She'll tell you I'm not as fine as I make out, that I'm not quality. She'll tell you to watch your money and perhaps your jewellery as well.'

'Mr Grimshaw has already performed that task.'

'Has he, by George! That is too bad of him.'

'I make up my own mind about people, however. We Americans don't approve of these snobbish judgements.'

Dundalk's assault on Mary Beth's sensibilities went very well over the next three weeks. He was shrewd enough not to pay her foolish compliments about her delicate beauty. She was no fool and knew she had none. On the other hand, she seemed more attractive every time he met her. Happiness and the confidence that comes from knowing one is admired had turned a forbidding young woman into a laughing Diana. Her taste in dress was, to his mind, impeccable. Her energy was unflagging, and he found her free and easy ways a wonderful change from the simpering, blushing young women he had half-heartedly courted in the past.

One day, she asked him about his source of income. Before he realized what he was doing, he had begun to tell her a large portion of the truth. 'I own some hackney cabs.'

'But how interesting!' said Mary Beth. 'How many cabs do you have?'

'Ten. Five hansoms and five four-wheel clarences.'

'The ones people call "growlers"?'

'That's right,' said Dundalk, calculating the difficulties he would soon be in if this topic of conversation carried on for much longer. He had, in fact, not ten but twelve cabs. The two he hadn't mentioned were driven by pounceys who worked in partnership with one or more whores.

'And how much does each cabman earn for you?'

Dundalk sighed; she could be very persistent in her questioning. 'Twelve shillings a day in the season – May, June and July – and nine shillings the rest of the time. They have to pay me that whether they earn it or not.'

Mary Beth was silent for a moment. 'Let us say, at the lowest estimate, thirty-one pounds a week, for fifty-two weeks. Why, that's about sixteen hundred pounds a year!'

'I've got expenses. Where would you like to go today, Miss Hanson?'

'Of course! How stupid of me. You must buy the cabs and horses, and stable and feed them. I suppose your expenses must be about half the takings.'

'That's right. Shall we go down river? That might be interesting.'

'How much do you pay for a horse? How much for a cab?'

'Three quid for a horse, sometimes more, and I need three for every cab. Cabs cost about forty or fifty pounds, depending on the condition.'

Mary Beth smiled, looking at him through her lashes. 'You're annoyed with me, Mr Dundalk. I'm sorry, but I really am interested in business, you know. Yes, let us take a ride on the river.'

They came ashore at Greenwich, and Mary Beth suddenly worried that Mrs Grimshaw might pop up from behind a nearby bush and see that Mary Beth and Dundalk were unchaperoned. Dundalk assured her that Mrs Grimshaw was most unlikely to be dining at the Trafalgar Tavern. He ushered her inside this riverside establishment where a waiter showed them to a very secluded table.

The couple had been silent most of the time as they steamed down river, each lost in thought. Dundalk was sure Mary Beth had no idea what thoughts were jostling for attention in his bone box. Equally, he was certain that he knew what she was thinking. And he was quite right.

'You know, Mr Dundalk, I think I would like to invest some money in your business. If you had three times as many cabs – '

'Forget it ma'am. I don't need a partner. Now, what are you going to have to eat? I don't suppose people like you eat dinner at midday, but I'm hungry and that's a fact.'

She was offended, as he had expected, but at least his rudeness put an end to her prying. He needed money right enough, but he couldn't have this sharp article looking over his books.

He had been working at odd jobs since he was eleven years old, trying his hand at anything that would turn a penny and hoping all the while that he didn't get caught. By the time he was twenty, he had developed a longing for two things: education and respectability. Why shouldn't he live like the swells did? Only the accident of birth had placed him in the back bedroom of an East End tavern while some other chap popped into the world in a mansion Up West.

He had learned to read as a nipper, was quite quick in that direction. Now he began to read any book he could get his hands on, although the most important part of his education had come from watching the toffs; what they wore, how they spoke, what they talked about. After a few little adventures he didn't care to remember, he had got together enough money to buy a pair of horses and a hansom cab. He became what was known as a long day man: out at eight in the morning and not home again until four a.m. You couldn't do that for long, not even with the help of large quantities of gin to deaden the pain and make you forget how tired you were. And for all his hard work, he'd earn no more than a guinea a day and have to pay out too much of it in expenses of one sort or another. You couldn't be a swell and work those hours.

Finally, he'd taken a chance, gone to a moneylender and agreed to pay extortionate rates on a loan of three hundred pounds. He was in business, but the money didn't come in fast enough to service the loan. Then Grimshaw, who had drawn up a few contracts for him, had happened to mention an American lady, and he had seen his chance. Lady Marjory's three hundred pounds had got him out of *stück* Now all he was left with was a possible charge of fraud. Miss Hanson might calculate that he had an income of eight hundred pounds a year. They both knew a man could rent a fine house and fill it with servants on eight hundred pounds a year. What the lady *didn't* know was that he had yet to benefit greatly from any of the money he received. That time would come, however, if only he could find a way to get his hands on three hundred pounds to open a shelter for fallen women, or pay back Lady Marjory before she hailed a crusher. The thought of it took away his appetite.

On their fifth or sixth assignation, Mary Beth began to talk about paintings, admitting that she knew nothing at all about high art. She felt foolish in her ignorance, she said, but just couldn't take an interest as she ought to do.

'Does that matter?' asked Dundalk. 'You have other

gifts. I've never encountered as shrewd a business mind as yours, ma'am.'

'Oh, making money is easy, don't you think? I can *see* a profit or a business potential the way some people can see the artistic possibilities of a foggy day. They paint a picture of it and you notice things you never saw before. By the way, what do you think of the paintings of Mr Rossetti?'

'Never heard of the chap, I'm afraid. Is he well known?'

'I'll show you,' said Mary Beth with a militant look in her eye, and took him straightaway round to Agnew's Gallery to show him a typical sample of the artist's work.

'Don't fancy that at all,' said Dundalk.

'The point is, do you think I look like the woman in the painting? Do I have the sort of face Mr Rossetti would want to paint?'

Dundalk was patently surprised. 'Why no, of course not. You look nothing like that girl. She's ugly. Don't know why the fellow wished to paint her in the first place. Who told you such a thing?'

'My fiancé.'

Then, of course, he had to pretend not to know that she was betrothed. He was so successful in affecting shock and hurt feelings, that she apologized for having misled him.

The next day, it rained heavily. As Mary Beth had not bothered with Mrs Booker's services since the first occasion, the two of them were alone and in need of a warm dry place in which to talk. All the obvious refuges, like Swan and Edgar's and the British Museum, for instance, were likely to be full of people known to Mary Beth.

'I know! I'll take you on the underground. You won't meet anyone you know there,' he suggested.

For two hours they trundled back and forth on the

trains, sometimes alone in a carriage, sometimes rubbing shoulders with navvies and city clerks.

'Those are my kind of people,' Dundalk said when three filthy working men shuffled into the carriage just before the doors snapped shut. 'I come from Wapping, not the sort of neighbourhood you'd like. I've moved Up West now, but you wouldn't think much of my new home: set of three rooms kept spick and span by the landlady who brings me a good breakfast each morning at half past eight, and all for ten shillings the week. My business has just begun, you see. I'm not a rich man yet.'

'Are your parents still alive?'

'My dad is. Still in Wapping, too. My mam died when I was a nipper. Dad remarried ten years back. I've got two half-brothers and three half-sisters, but I never see any of them. We don't get on. My father runs a public house and does quite well, I can tell you. We never went without the necessaries when I was a boy.'

'You've done very well, Mr Dundalk. You can be proud of your success. My grandfather was a ships' chandler, and my father worked there until he died. Then Momma did all the purchasing until she married Sir Gilbert.'

Dundalk already knew this from Grimshaw, but pretended ignorance, asking several probing questions about Mary Beth's youth. 'Your family may have been shopkeepers,' he said when she had finished, 'but there's no comparison. You are a well brought up young lady. My background is very different. I've lived next to rough folks all my life until about two months ago.'

Mary Beth gave him a tender smile. 'Did you ever know any prostitutes?'

He was taken completely by surprise. 'I've known dozens.' He saw Mary Beth's look of alarm and disgust

184

and added: 'I don't mean . . . I was never a petticoat chaser.'

This was true enough as far as it went. He had deflowered many a willing girl in his adolescence, but had never consorted with prostitutes. As he grew older, his energies turned towards making his way. Chasing women endlessly had led many a man to his ruin, but then so had getting too deeply involved with *one* woman. He'd been careful. Besides, closing a profitable deal was as exciting as anything he had ever experienced with a girl. Taking a girl's virginity had not been too difficult in his neighbourhood, whereas separating a sharp character from his money required skill and cunning.

Then too, he knew the local prostitutes very well, knew the risks they ran. The younger ones he had known as children. A certain fastidiousness prevented him from dealing with them once they had become professionals.

'I'm fascinated by prostitutes,' confessed Mary Beth. 'They know about things that girls like me can never know. What are they like?'

'They are all sorts, just like any other section of society. Some are good and kind, and turned to the life only to keep something in their bellies. Others are mean old sluts – I beg your pardon – whom you wouldn't want to know whatever their line of work.'

'Do you think the Contagious Diseases Act should be repealed?'

'I haven't the faintest notion,' said Dundalk. 'Don't know anything about it, and I don't think you should, either.'

She made a little face at him. 'Now you sound like everybody else I've met in England.' Her light-hearted mood faded. 'I think Mr Falkner would prefer every prostitute in the country to me. He obviously thinks I'm ugly.'

'The man's a blind fool,' said Dundalk with feeling. The words were out before he had thought how they might be interpreted. He chewed his lip as if trying to retrieve them.

'Thank you for that,' said Mary Beth softly. Tears filled her eyes, but she managed to prevent them spilling on to her cheeks. Dundalk reached out to squeeze her hand briefly. The sight of this strong-minded girl being reduced to tears by so slight a compliment moved him deeply. She couldn't meet his eyes. 'You remember I told you my fiancé had compared me to a Rossetti model?'

'I remember. Shocking thing to do.'

'Well, I wrote to him yesterday afternoon, breaking off our engagement. He wrote back so promptly and so warmly, saying he was sure I was doing the right thing, that I know he never wanted to marry me. I think he proposed when he had drunk too much champagne.'

Dundalk thought most men proposed under those conditions, but made a sympathetic reply, assuring her that she had acted wisely.

'I'm so glad you think so,' said Mary Beth, and turned her head to look deeply into his eyes.

Dundalk was startled. He should have expected it, of course. The poor girl had been very badly treated. It was only natural that she should feel grateful and even loving towards the first man to pay her some attention. All the same, the strength of her emotion made him feel very uncomfortable. And what was more, he was very angry with Lady Marjory. How dare the old trout mess about with this dear girl's feelings in such a callous way. Now he was going to have to be very clever to extricate himself from Miss Hanson without breaking her heart all over again.

'Well, old girl,' he said heartily. 'I think we'd better get off this train before it takes us to China.

Mary Beth giggled in quite a girlish way. 'You know, I've never been called an old girl before. You are such fun to be with, Mr Dundalk.

'Yes,' he said dryly. 'Better than a barrel load of monkeys, I am.'

16

During the weeks when Mary Beth was meeting Dundalk secretly on every possible occasion, Marjory was busy on a very exciting social round of her own. The Earl and Countess of Dumfries invited her to a series of soirées, breakfasts and theatre parties that kept Marjory busy five days out of six. The other guests varied, but Marjory could always count on seeing Frederick Bennett among the party. They became the best of friends, addressing each other by their first names when no one else could hear, and discussing every subject under the sun, except Mary Beth's engagement.

Bennett talked obsessively about Mr William Acton, the brilliant surgeon who lived and worked just three doors away from Bennett's own home in Harley Street. Acton's name was so frequently on Bennett's lips, his praises were so regularly sung, that one evening Marjory asked what it was the man did that was so marvellous.

'Among other things, he has written a fine book about prostitution. Very thorough. He writes for the general public. I'm afraid I have not his way with words.'

'And medical textbooks, I suppose,' said Marjory.

'No, as a matter of fact, he has not written any textbooks.'

'I'm sure this man Acton is no better a doctor than you are, Frederick. He has the advantage of you, because he can puff himself off with his writing.'

'But that's just it, my dear Marjory. He expresses

what all of us would like to say, if only we could find the words to do so.'

'He's not perfect,' she said quietly.

'How do you know, my dear? You haven't met him.'

Marjory laughed. 'I've never met a man yet who came anywhere near being perfect, and I don't expect to. Now tell me about this play we're going to see tonight. What's it called? *The Cousins Across the Water?*'

It turned out to be a comedy about Americans in England. Marjory found the actors' American accents deplorable. The so-called humour was entirely at the expense of the American characters, but the play wasn't funny, anyway.

The countess had gathered a party of ten together for this evening, and Marjory was the only American. From the corner of her eye she could see who was laughing and who was trying valiantly not to laugh. Frederick Bennett, she noticed with gratitude, was confining himself to the occasional chuckle, which she thought was a dignified response. After all, he had to pretend to be enjoying himself so as not to offend his hostess.

But when the second act was reaching its climax and the rich American bumpkin was being particularly stupid as he tried to marry his daughter to a lord, Bennett so far forgot himself as to laugh out loud. Pretending restlessness, Marjory pushed his arm roughly off the armrest that divided them, and Bennett turned to her in some surprise.

'I'm terribly sorry, Frederick. Did I jog your arm?'

He was not deceived. 'Forgive me, my dear. I shouldn't have laughed so rudely, but you must admit it is a very funny play.'

'Must I? To see Americans made fun of? What's funny about being an American? Tell me that. Caroline had no right to put me in such an awkward situation. If I laugh, I'm disloyal to my countrymen. If I don't laugh, I've no sense of humour. She shouldn't have done it.'

'Oh, you know what Caroline is.'

'Yes, a countess,' said Marjory.

'She never thinks of that.'

'Of course she does! Do you ever forget you're a doctor? I never forget I'm an American, I can tell you that. Caroline is someone special, and she knows that whatever she does is all right.'

'You must not take this so personally,' he said as the second act curtain closed to tumultuous applause. 'Caroline thinks very highly of you. She has invited you to her country home in August, hasn't she? That, I assure you, is a rare privilege.'

'Yes, I admit I'm looking forward to that. You'll be there, too, won't you?'

'I will. It will be the first time in ten years.'

'Good heavens! What sort of people does she normally invite? If *you're* not good enough for her . . . what sort of people will be there? Will I like them?'

Bennett leaned over to lay a gentle hand on Marjory's arm. 'I can't say if you will like them, my dear. They will adore you, of that I'm sure.'

Marjory's cheeks coloured slightly, and she looked away, unable to meet his warm gaze. 'I'm sure glad you're going to be there. I'm kind of nervous about the whole thing.'

The countess, happening to glance down the row of seats at that moment, raised her eyebrows in surprise. It would be very interesting, she thought, to have her cousin and Marjory Manton as guests at Feldlands. There was not a great deal to do in the country except watch one's guests and hope they behaved entertainingly. Marjory was always amusing, of course. One never knew what she would say or do next. But until these last weeks, Caroline had found her cousin Bennett rather a dull dog.

These summer days were very stimulating for Marjory. The weather had been exceptionally good, with very little rain, yet it had never once been so hot that she felt disinclined to go out. July and August could be the very devil in St Louis; day after day of scorching sunshine, with temperatures hovering around one hundred, and the air so damp you could hardly catch your breath. It could be so miserable you didn't want to do anything but sit on the front porch with a pitcher of lemonade by your side and a strong fan in your hand.

So the English weather, for all its evil reputation, suited Marjory very well. On the other hand, her intimacy with the countess had provided her with a rapid course in the subtleties of English manners. Understanding the English and how their minds functioned meant sensing that she was invited to parties mostly because she was odd, an outsider, someone whose very manner of speech caused amusement.

'English people have got more ways of being rude than Americans ever dreamed of,' she said to Bennett on one occasion. 'They can lift an eyebrow, turn a shoulder, pretend they're not in when you call, and a whole lot of other tricks Americans wouldn't sink to. If a person comes to your door and you're at home, you let them in. That's only common decency. You don't get your servant to say you're not at home.'

'And in America if you don't like what they say to you, you shoot them.'

'Right between the eyes!' said Marjory, laughing. 'But not when they're guests in your home, Frederick. That wouldn't be polite.'

The stimulation came not only from studying native Britons, but from the many outings she made with Bennett, whose practice was suffering as a result of the time he spent on Marjory's education. He had wanted to take her to the opera, but Marjory said she only

191

liked music that made her smile, and opera didn't qualify. So he twice took her to the Gaiety theatre for the 'morning' performances which actually began at two o' clock in the afternoon and ended at five. That meant they at once had to hurry to their homes to change in order to attend a different theatre in the evening with the earl and countess. Evening performances began at seven, which scarcely left time for a cup of tea and a biscuit in between. As a rule, they dined after the performance at half-past eleven or even midnight, by which time Marjory was ravenous.

She loved farces, so Bennett took her several times to the Adelphi which had 'screaming' farces that made her laugh as loudly as the rest of the audience, but left the doctor wearing a pained smile. He drew the line, he said, at music hall entertainment, but she persuaded him to take her there, too. They went to Gatti's Palace of Varieties and, to Bennett's surprise, enjoyed themselves hugely.

On other days, Bennett conducted Marjory round the Egyptian Hall, the British Museum, the Gallery of Illustration and Madame Tussauds. Then she insisted on taking him for a ride on the underground. He had never travelled on the infernal train and, afterwards, said he never would again. He asked Marjory under what circumstances she had ridden on these dangerously speeding cars. The question strained her imaginative powers, because she had no intention of telling him the truth about her visit with Guy Dundalk.

Marjory chose a quiet moment while they were strolling through the Crystal Palace on a hot cloudless day to tell Bennett that Mary Beth's engagement had been broken off. The doctor (who did not seem surprised at all) solemnly congratulated her on having finally exerted her parental authority. After a moment's reflection, he congratulated himself for having had the wisdom and sense of responsibility to advise Marjory.

'For I don't normally interfere in the business of others, you know. I keep silent even when I see impending danger. I could not remain silent about your daughter's circumstances, however. You are new to our ways. I would not have forgiven myself if I hadn't dropped a slight hint.'

'You are a discreet man, Frederick.'

Since Marjory's secret scheme involving Dundalk had gone well, she was happy to allow her friend his tiny self-deception. Yet, she marvelled that he didn't know of his reputation for interfering in the affairs of others on every conceivable occasion. Young Mr Grimshaw spent half his time complaining about his godfather. Marjory could well understand that a grown man might find even benevolent meddling a trifle irksome.

Dundalk and Marjory met once more at the hotel at St Pancras. She didn't need to be told that Mary Beth was looking much happier these days. And, like Dundalk, she had also detected a mood of recklessness in the girl. It was as if nothing mattered to her any more, except having a good time.

'She's in a dangerous frame of mind, ma'am,' said Dundalk. 'She needs my steadying influence. She needs . . . ma'am, can you arrange to have me invited to Feldlands? Miss Hanson is not as happy as she pretends to be.'

'I guess I could get the countess to send you an invitation if you give me your address. But I want you to be honest with me, young man. You want to come to Feldlands for your own reasons, don't you?'

Dundalk was suddenly very earnest. 'Lady Marjory, I won't deny this would be a very great opportunity for me. I promise you, I will escort your daughter everywhere. I will take good care of her and keep up her spirits. I will conduct my own affairs discreetly,

193

and at times that will not inconvenience Miss Hanson. It would be nice for her, wouldn't it, to have an admirer in attendance so that everyone could see that she is an attractive and desirable woman. Her broken engagement is common knowledge now. I know her friend, Lady Fenella, thinks she made a serious mistake. She needs me at this time, ma'am.'

Marjory gave one long sigh, which signalled the end of her resistance to the scheme and the beginning of a new realism. 'You'll need some money, I suppose.'

'Well . . .' He grinned at her.

'See you get the proper clothes, young man. Here's fifty pounds and that's the end of it.'

Mary Beth had developed a strange craving for dangerous situations that she couldn't explain or justify even to herself. She wanted to be thrilled, and that meant taking chances. Dundalk was genuinely worried about her, and how to go about controlling her. In so far as was possible, he gave in to her requests, merely doing everything in his power to minimize the damage to her person and, more especially to her reputation.

That was why, two nights after the meeting with Marjory, when one of Dundalk's cabs drew up to the entrance to the Cremorne Gardens, Dundalk leapt out and looked sharply in every direction before handing Mary Beth out into the road. It was late, half-past eleven, and the grounds were lit up like a fairy grotto. The paths were dry, the trees and shrubs lushly clothed, and the various shoddy structures, brilliant in the artificial light, had lost their daytime tawdriness. Together the couple walked through the gates. Dundalk paid a shilling for each of them, then Mary Beth strode off alone. Dundalk allowed her to get ten yards ahead of him, then he, too, began to walk.

Mary Beth was wearing an extravagant gown of purple silk, and Dundalk could see quite clearly that she was swaying her hips to make her low bustle swish provocatively. Therefore, it was not surprising that within about three minutes a well-dressed gentleman stepped in front of her and lifted his hat so that she was forced to stop.

Dundalk couldn't hear what was being said, but he didn't hurry to Mary Beth's aid. This evening's sport had not been *his* idea. Let her discover for herself just how insulting a stranger's attentions could be. But no, to his surprise, it was the gentleman who appeared to be insulted. The man soon walked away.

'Good evening, sir,' Mary Beth said when Dundalk approached her. She fluttered her eyelashes and put her hands on her hips. 'A nice night is it not?'

'Very pleasant, ma'am,' he said solemnly, tipping his hat. 'As you seem to be alone, do you mind if I accompany you? A lady on her own is in danger of being insulted in this place.'

Mary Beth laughed, quite out of character. 'Yes, and so are impertinent men if they are not careful. I told him he didn't look rich enough to suit me.'

'You are a dangerous woman,' said Dundalk sternly, 'and you are playing a dangerous game.'

'I don't care. It's so exciting. Tell me – what should I say to you now?'

'I haven't the faintest. I've never done business here, as I told you. I expect you set a price.'

'And how much should I ask?'

'In your case, not less than ten pounds.'

'Not enough,' decided Mary Beth. 'I think I'm worth a thousand.'

'Ladies who are worth a thousand pounds don't walk about Cremorne Gardens after dark. Ten pounds is quite steep enough.'

'Very well. Agreed. I shall be simply the most expensive soiled dove to ply her trade in Cremorne

Gardens. Now will you buy me some supper? Shall we dance? Will you give me champagne?'

'All of those things, and I pray to God we don't meet anyone you know.'

They strolled off arm in arm, drawn inexorably towards the sound of music where they joined a large crowd circling the dancing area.

Being just two or three inches shorter than Dundalk, Mary Beth could look directly into his eyes as they danced. 'Aren't you glad you came, Mr Dundalk? Aren't you having fun?'

'I am very glad I came, miss, for I wouldn't have you walking about this place in the dark without me.' He smiled at her as he whirled her round in the waltz. 'What's more, you dance a treat. Now don't talk any more, if you please. I want to concentrate on my work.

They danced until Mary Beth said she was too dizzy to stand. Supper, served in their private box, was excellent and the champagne no more intoxicating than the heavy scents of the warm night.

Dundalk poured the last drop from the bottle into Mary Beth's glass. 'You'll be tipsy.'

'No, I won't. We Americans have strong heads, although I have to admit we didn't drink much champagne back in St Louis. Oh, doesn't it taste so much better out of doors under the stars than it ever does at a stuffy party?'

'I expect so. You know, I've only had half this bottle, but I'm dizzy, even if you're not. Come on, my girl, let's get out of this wooden box and walk a bit. I want to clear my head.'

She took his arm and they strolled silently down a broad, well-lit avenue until they reached a narrower path leading off to the right.

'Where are we going?'

'I told you,' he said. 'We're going for a walk to clear my head.'

The path was dark and deserted; not so the shrubbery. They could hear the buzz of whispered conversations, full of erotic innuendo and smothered laughter.

'There are people in – ' she began, but he told her to hush.

She was silent for a few more paces, then leaned close to whisper: 'I'm so happy here. I never want to go home. Never.'

'Neither do I.' His voice was hoarse, his senses reeling as he looked at her gaudy, low-cut dress and met her startlingly abandoned gaze. She seemed to have discovered some new dimensions to her nature, a sense of freedom, a capacity to give something precious of her inner self. Did she realize how seductive she was being as she swayed into him, squeezed his arm, brought her face close to his, laughing intimately? Impulsively, he pulled her into the shrubbery, pushed her back against a tall oak and held her close, pinning her hands behind her.

'What are you doing?' she asked, then, acting again: 'Oh, sir, you are frightening me.'

He lifted one of her hands to his lips and kissed the palm, prepared to play the game. 'Ten pounds I've paid you, wench, and I intend to get my money's worth.'

'Oh, help me, save me!' she said very softly, for fear of being overheard and actually saved by some helpful stranger.

'No! I mean to have my way with you, trollop!'

Mary Beth giggled. 'This has gone far enough,' she said in her own voice. 'You may let me go, Mr Dundalk. It must be nearly one o' clock. I had difficulty in arranging this evening without Momma knowing I'm out at all. It would never do to arrive home with the dawn.'

'But I don't want to let you go. Mary Beth Hanson,

197

you are the most wonderful, exciting woman I've ever met. Besides . . .' He held both her wrists firmly behind her again. 'You are in my power, my little love, and cannot break free.'

'I am? But no, no man is stronger than I. Have you not noticed how well constructed I am? I have it on good authority from a young man in St Louis that I am a perfect workhorse. See?' She struggled energetically against his grip which only tightened on her wrists. 'Oh, Guy, my dear, I do believe I really am in your power. What are you going to do to me?'

'I'm going to kiss you, of course. How could any man be so close to you and resist the temptation? Lift your head, my darling, there is nothing you can do to stop me.'

She had no intention of stopping him. After a moment, he released her wrists and put his arms around her waist. She immediately put her freed hands to his face. Now it was her turn to hold him close, to imprison him with her fevered kisses on brow, cheek and chin. Finally, with her lips parted, she pressed her mouth to his until he groaned with pleasure.

'Is this the way a prostitute kisses, Guy? Is it? No wonder they do it. Imagine being paid to feel like this. Oh, Guy, I can't get close enough to you. Again! Kiss me like that again.'

'Gorblimey,' murmured Dundalk against her mouth, and wondered where it would all end.

After a while, he pushed her away, trying to laugh but not managing to sound very sensible. 'No more, Mary Beth. I can't stand any more. I must take you home. What would your mother think of me?'

'I sincerely hope you aren't going to tell her about tonight, Guy.'

She, too, knew that it was time to go home. She straightened her gown, smoothed her hair and primly stepped out on to the pathway. Her whole life had been turned upside down in the last few moments. She needed time to think, to adjust to the emotions that were making her half swoon. Of one thing she was certain, she would ask Momma if an invitation to Feldlands could be procured for Guy. She couldn't bear the thought of being separated from him for a whole month.

17

Bennett was in his consulting room when Jeremy Grimshaw was ushered in.

'It is good to see you, my boy. How are you? Haven't seen you in some time, not to speak to, that is. No, don't sit down. We will go into the library. No point in staying here in my examining room. I was searching for a book which I have mislaid, but I can look for it later. Marcus is always chiding me for my untidiness.'

Jeremy stood up and looked about him in some bewilderment. There were books on every surface. The chair opposite Bennett's desk was the only one on which there were no books. 'What was the title of the book? Perhaps if I help you to find it . . .'

'It's an American book. Gross is the author. Professor at Jefferson Medical College in Philadelphia. *A Practical Treatise on the Diseases, Injuries and Malformations of the Urinary Bladder, the Prostrate Gland and the Urethra.* Medical books always have long titles, you know. A colleague lent it to me. I must give it back tomorrow as he has asked for it; wants my opinion. The devil of it is, I have not so much as glanced at it. I've been rather busy lately, what with one thing and another.'

Jeremy joined in the search and soon found the book with a pile of others with equally daunting titles on the floor behind the sofa. He could not resist flipping through the pages before handing over the book, and since it was copiously illustrated, rather wished he hadn't been the one to discover it.

'You have it! Splendid. I'll just put it in the bookcase.'

'Why not put it on your blotter, Uncle Frederick? Then you won't mislay it again. And can take it with you to the hospital.'

'Done!' said Bennett, beaming. 'You have brought a little order out of the chaos. Come on, we'll go into the library.'

'Well . . .' Jeremy sat down in the chair where Bennett's patients normally sat.

Bennett looked keenly at him. 'You're not unwell, are you?'

'Oh, no, sir. Never in the way you mean, I do assure you. It is just that I am seeking a little medical advice, a little clarification, shall we say, and it seems more appropriate to speak to you about it here.'

Bennett returned to the worn leather chair behind the desk. He was due to leave for Feldlands the next day. He and Marjory had agreed not to meet until the following morning at the train station, so the rest of the day was free to fill as he chose.

'How may I help you? Have you asked Miss Quinn for her hand? Are your affairs progressing?'

'Not yet, sir. I have been worried by . . . oh dear, it is very difficult to explain. I am worried, to put it bluntly, about my duties as a husband. I am not a passionate man, Uncle Frederick. It wouldn't be fair to dear Miss Quinn if she is hoping . . . well, you know, I have no idea how often I will be expected to – '

'Say no more, Jeremy. You are not the only young man to be concerned on this point. No indeed, not by a long way.'

Bennett stood up and walked to his bookshelves, surprised to find himself a little embarrassed, and rather disappointed by his godson's lack of vigour. But he hid his feelings in hearty chitchat until he could lay his hands on the book he wanted, before returning to his chair with an encouraging smile.

'Let me see . . .' He put on his gold-wire spectacles

and thumbed through the pages rapidly. 'You have heard me speak of Mr Acton, the great surgeon? Well, Mr Acton has written a most excellent book and I propose to quote from it.

'Acton writes: "I should say that the majority of women (happily for them) are not very troubled with sexual feeling of any kind. As a general rule, a modest woman seldom desires any sexual gratification for herself. She submits to her husband, but only to please him; and, but for the desire for maternity, would far rather be relieved from his attentions. No nervous or feeble young man need, therefore, be deterred from marriage by any exaggerated notion of the duties required of him. The married woman has no wish to be treated on the footing of a *mistress*." '

Bennett looked up from the page. 'There you are. Hasn't that put your mind at rest? You could ask for no greater authority than Mr Acton.'

'No,' replied Grimshaw gloomily. 'I suppose there is no further impediment to . . . naturally, I am very pleased to have the matter so conclusively settled.'

'You should be married, Jeremy. You need a wife.'

'I suppose so.' Grimshaw rose from his chair. 'I must be going, sir. I have an appointment. I had thought that perhaps marriage is not a good idea in my case. But if you say . . .'

'Trust me. Trust Acton! Marriage is the ideal condition. I believe you can have no idea how happy you will be when you have a home of your own. I am only sorry that you cannot afford to marry in the near future. Too bad your visit has been so short. Had you more time, I'm sure I could put you in the proper frame of mind to propose to Miss Quinn. When I return from Feldlands, you must come for dinner. We have not enjoyed your company here for some consider-able time.'

'But I am dining here tonight! Peregrine Manton

has come to town, and Marcus invited us both to dine with himself and you. I am surprised you didn't know of it.'

'No matter. I know of it now.'

Bennett gave no outward sign, but he was deeply disappointed. He was planning to be away at Feldlands for a month, after all. Unfortunately, he would be separated from Marcus during that time, because his son had refused Caroline's very kind invitation, pleading the pressure of work. Bennett had very much wanted to be alone with Marcus this evening. Instead, his last night in London was, he now discovered, to be spent in the company of Jeremy and a young man he had always despised.

'However,' said the doctor briskly, 'since I will have no time for tiresome chores this evening, you must excuse me now. I have a dozen matters to set in order before I leave tomorrow. Until tonight, then. And, Jeremy, don't worry further about this business we discussed. I assure you there is no need.'

Sir Peregrine Manton, a heavily muscled, pug-faced man, was reasonably well behaved when sober, but totally obnoxious when in his cups. Like any other weak-headed man, he was unaware of the fact that he couldn't hold his drink. Half a bottle of claret taken with a meal was enough to slur his speech. A full bottle (his normal tipple) left him with a very uncertain temper. Later, after the port had circulated a couple of times, he would need to be helped from the table, and might well endear himself to his host by being sick on the dining-room carpet.

Marcus, an abstemious man, had always disliked Manton. When the three boys had been at school together, Manton's temperament had led him to plague Jeremy at every opportunity. In consequence, Marcus had bloodied Manton's nose or blacked his eye almost every week.

Why then, wondered the doctor, had these three ill-assorted men gathered tonight? The answer, he was certain, was Lady Marjory Manton. Sir Peregrine wanted to talk about her; Jeremy wanted to hear about her, and Marcus, unforgivably, wanted his *father* to hear whatever damning tales Manton chose to tell. Bennett was as close as he ever came to being angry with Marcus as he entered the drawing-room that evening.

The others had arrived a few minutes earlier, and the atmosphere was already tense. Bennett hated to see his godson in so nervous a state, but then Jeremy had never overcome his fear of Manton. Marcus was cool, but during dinner was an over-attentive host, plying his guest with wine, urging him to drink rapidly and deeply.

Manton sprawled in his chair as he boasted of fences he had cleared, scoundrels he had outsmarted and improvements he had made to his estate. He mentioned his wife once in passing, but did not speak of Marjory until the servants had set the port on its way and left the dining-room.

Marcus inhaled his cigar deeply and allowed the smoke to drift from his mouth as he smiled coldly at Manton. 'Grimshaw here finds your step-mama very charming, Manton, and your step-sister positively overpowering.'

'I wouldn't exactly say that,' said Jeremy. 'I just feel – '

'Damned fool, that's what you are, Grimshaw,' said Manton rather indistinctly. 'The woman was a scheming title-hunter. Besmirched the family name.'

'A name to which *you* have added such lustre,' said the doctor.

'Don't have to add lustre. Don't have to do a damned

thing. I'm a Manton. My father must have been mad to have married her. Well, I know he was, but there was no point in having him committed after the deed was done. A damned shopkeeper's daughter! Wouldn't have been so bad, but she made a point of telling everyone what she came from.'

'A wealthy woman, however,' murmured Marcus.

As he spoke, Marcus looked hopefully towards the port which had come to rest before Bennett. The doctor narrowed his eyes and shook his head at his son. He had no intention of sending the decanter on another round. Manton had drunk more than enough.

'Well, rich, yes,' admitted Manton. 'But you have to be a damned sight richer than she was to make up for shopkeeper's blood. I don't know how she did it, but she managed to hold on to most of her fortune after Father died. It should have come to me. Fair's fair. She got the title; I should have had the money.'

'Your father was a difficult man,' said Bennett, harshly. 'Perhaps his widow felt she had earned the right to keep her own money.'

Marcus looked swiftly at his father, frowning slightly. Jeremy, aware that he was witnessing some sort of battle between father and son, began to fidget nervously in his chair.

'Do you know, sir?' said Manton. 'My father was so ill from the disease that killed him, that his signature was all but unreadable on the will. We had it drawn up just a month before he died, making sure she got no more than necessary. I was afraid the woman would contest it, but she didn't.'

Bennett quickly raised his glass and finished off the contents, aware that Marcus was watching him closely. 'What was the cause of your father's death?'

'Well, Mr Bennett, that is more in your line than mine. The death certificate says heart failure, of course. Hope I don't go the same way myself. It was pitiful to see. That woman must have known his mind was affected.'

'I take it you are referring to the tertiary stage of syphilis, Manton. What do respectable women know of such things? Lady Manton probably does not know to this day that her husband was suffering from the final stage of syphilis.'

'No *respectable* lady, I grant you, but that woman probably knows all about these things. American women have no delicacy. No, she must have known. He had distressing lapses of memory, and letter writing became impossible for him. He ceased to be able to spell at all. His writing was incomprehensible.'

'Well, Lady Manton might have put such things down to his age. He was in his sixties, I believe.'

'And his behaviour in company,' said Manton. 'One evening – thank God my wife was not present – my father suddenly stood up from his chair and straight away relieved himself on the carpet. I said to my step-mother: "Can you not see that my father is deranged? You took advantage of him. You tricked him into marriage." Do you know what she said to me?'

'I can't imagine,' said Bennett sadly. He glanced at the others. Marcus had turned his head away so that Bennett could not see his expression; Jeremy was obsessively pleating his table napkin.

'She said she was the one who had been tricked, and then she walked out of the room with that daughter of hers, leaving me to deal with my father.'

Bennett remembered Marjory's copy of *Gunn's Domestic Medicine* and wondered if Marjory *had* known of the nature of her husband's illness, but quickly dismissed the idea. He and Marjory had spent too many hours together for her to be able to deceive him on such an important matter. If she had so much as suspected such a thing, he would have soon discovered it.

'Fortunately, the tertiary stage is not infectious,' he murmured to Marcus, then, more loudly: 'The final stage of syphilis is indeed a dreadful sight, Manton, but it is the wife who often has to bear the terrible burden of her husband's irrational, even brutal behaviour. Can you honestly say that your father always treated your step-mother as he ought?'

'No blame can be attached to him, Mr Bennett,' said Manton, barely coherent in his anger. 'In fact, it was the other way round. Why, one day she broke a bone in the back of his hand. Stabbed him at breakfast with her fork! What do you think of that?'

'She must have had good reason.'

'Good reason?' bellowed Manton. 'Why, he only made some half-joking remark about Mary Beth Hanson being a clumsy great elephant of a girl, and his lady wife stabbed him! Right there at the table while the family was gathered for breakfast. My wife and I were not yet married. She wondered what sort of family she would be joining, I can tell you. Father was very brave about it. Wouldn't let me say a word to the old besom. Told the local sawbones he'd fallen awkwardly on his hand.'

'Perhaps the tale was one he didn't wish to repeat,' said Marcus, quietly. 'It certainly showed him in a poor light.'

'Lady Marjory *is* an original,' said Grimshaw. But he made sure he spoke too softly for Manton to hear.

'I had my revenge after my father died.' Manton rested both elbows on the table and propped his head in his hands as if it were too heavy for his neck to support. 'Ran that snivelling little son of hers clean out of England. Bought him a ticket to America, drove him to Liverpool and saw him on to the boat. Oh, how she did cry when she found out he was gone!'

'So you were responsible for that! How ... er ... clever of you.' Bennett stood up from the table. 'You must excuse me, gentlemen. It's getting late, and I've a dozen things to do before I leave London tomorrow. Marcus, we may not see each other in the morning, so I will say goodbye to you now.'

Marcus jumped to his feet. 'Father, I – '

Bennett glared at his son, daring him to say anything more, nodded curtly to Manton and left the dining-room.

He was halfway up the stairs before he remembered that he had not said goodnight to Jeremy.

18

The next day Marjory and Mary Beth arrived at the train station in good time, accompanied by several trunks, three hatboxes and a large picnic lunch in a wicker basket.

Early as they were, Frederick Bennett was even earlier. He helped to settle them comfortably in a first-class carriage. Marjory talked animatedly to Bennett, partly to disguise her own nervousness and partly to draw his attention away from Mary Beth, who was unusually quiet. It pained Marjory that the doctor and her daughter didn't like each other. She couldn't complain; she disliked Marcus, whom she thought of as a pompous snob, too handsome for his own good.

After a while, even her talent for high-spirited chatter deserted her. She lapsed into silence, and almost immediately the doctor's eyes closed. The odd snuffle told her he was asleep.

Mary Beth, seated by the window, was staring determinedly out at the racing houses and trees. Marjory, whose seat was next to the corridor, had to look over the girl's shoulder, as it were, at the passing scene. The train ran on a narrower guage than the American ones, but gave a smooth ride. She couldn't compare this train's comfort with American trains, however, because she had never ridden on a train in Missouri. *Never been anywhere*, she thought, *always too busy working, bringing up the children, trying to be a good mother, wife and daughter. No time just to be Marjory.*

Well, now was her chance to be herself, to live for her own enjoyment and edification. This was the moment for quiet reflection, as the train chugged its way between miniature hedge-trimmed farms and around toy villages. How different England was from the untouched flatlands through which the Mississippi cut an erratic path on its majestic way to New Orleans.

She wished she had agreed to visit New York, after all, so that she could have seen for herself what sophistication (and decadence?) the United States had to offer. New Orleans was a beautiful old town, but it was not the sort of place you could mention in a conversation to impress the English. And something told her that in the next few weeks she was going to need all the self-confidence, all the little weapons of social contact, that she could find.

Back home you were poor trash, hard up, fair-to-middling or rich. Her family had been rich. Over here they had different rules. She had discovered she was middle class and Caroline was upper class, and it didn't have one thing to do with how much money you had.

The doctor woke and consulted his pocket watch to cover his embarrassment. Mary Beth said she was hungry. Like children, they found they couldn't wait to open their picnic hamper, and had consumed every sandwich, cake crumb and drop of wine long before noon.

The distance from Paddington station to Bath was just over a hundred miles, but seemed to take no time at all. Even the sooty smuts that flew in through the open window and settled on her clothes couldn't distract Marjory from what she had begun to regard as the coming ordeal.

A carriage from Feldlands awaited them at bath. In fact, there were two carriages: one for the luggage. What little Marjory saw of the town on their way out of it intrigued her: golden stone, winding roads and steep hills that would make life pretty hard for the horses. It seemed the English never looked for a flat piece of ground before laying out a town with a set square, the way they did back home. English towns grew all over the place, up hill, down dale, without a First, Second or Third street to help you get your bearings. The houses were all higgledy-piggledy and of all periods of time. Marjory had gotten lost in every town she'd visited so far.

'Over there!' said Bennett after about twenty minutes. He pointed to a distant hillside where a sprawling stone building covered several acres in haphazard fashion.

Marjory's jaw gaped. 'It looks like the Tower of London with all those towers and turrets and funny tops to the walls.'

'Crenellation.'

'And I can see the spire of a cathedral,' said Mary Beth.

'No, that's just the chapel on the estate, my dear.'

Marjory turned to Bennett. 'You mean they've got their own church attached to the house? Is that place a castle?'

'Good heavens, no. Feldlands was built about sixty years ago by the Wyatts.'

'It's about the size of Buckingham Palace. How much of that great pile is actually Caroline's home?'

'All of it, I'm afraid.'

'Oh, Lord,' said Mary Beth. 'A person could live in that place for a week and never meet all the other guests.'

The doctor found the reaction of the women quite amusing. He had long since had his fill of tales of America's vast expanses. It was pleasant, for once, to see Mary Beth and Marjory awed by sheer size.

'No need to worry, Miss Hanson. Feldlands has about fifty servants who will always be delighted to direct you. The guests assemble in the drawing-room before dinner. You will soon get to know them all.'

Marjory and Mary Beth had little to say during the

211

remaining ten minutes until the carriage stopped at the front entrance. Marjory had met London Society head on with great success, simply by refusing to admit that Caroline and her fancy friends were any different from herself. Feldlands could not be ignored, however. It intimidated her by its magnificence in a way that mere mortals had failed to do.

The entrance hall was large and gloomy, and so was the pompous individual who introduced himself as the under-butler. He led them up the main staircase and along silent corridors until they reached the door of a room which the under-butler said would be Miss Hanson's. Marjory and Bennett carried on to the next door which was opened by Perks who had travelled up on an earlier train. Marjory nodded goodbye to the doctor and Perks closed the door behind her.

The room was small and should have been easy to furnish, yet managed to look bare and unwelcoming. The narrow bed sagged and the single chair was upholstered in green brocade, now mostly bleached to beige. There was no fireplace.

'Not even a gasolier,' said Marjory. 'Must I make do with candles?'

'Yes, my lady, I'm afraid so. This room must be very cold in winter. It strikes a chill even on a hot day like this.'

'That's because the sun never comes through that dirty window. Where's the bathroom?'

Perks nodded her head towards a folding screen, and Marjory went over to look behind it.

'A chamberpot! You mean there's no bathroom? But where's the water closet?'

'The nearest one is three doors away. There are three on this floor and two bathrooms. Otherwise, there's piped water only to the chambermaid's closet, so they'll have to bring hot water in cans.'

Marjory stripped off her gloves and flung them on the bed, then began pulling the pins out of her hat.

'I know it's not what you're used to, ma'am. Nor am I. I have a dingy bedroom in the attic which I have to share with another maid. The trouble is, there are thirty guest rooms, the house is almost full and just about everybody outranks you.'

'How nice,' said Marjory. 'Never mind. You must show me where everything is a little later. Right now, I want my tea. It's nearly five o'clock and I'm parched. And I must, at least, say hello to Lady Dumfries.'

'Well, there's the difficulty. I've been told most firmly that you would prefer to take your tea this afternoon in your room, because you will be tired from travelling.'

'Drink my tea in this chicken coop? And all alone? What's Lady Dumfries thinking of?'

'She is probably rather busy, ma'am. You see, the Duke and Duchess of Poltraine are here.'

'Do tell! I'll bet they aren't staying in a room like this.'

'No, they will be in the principal guest suite. This room really isn't so bad. It's the single gentlemen who get the worst rooms.'

'Poor Mr Bennett. Very well. Show me round, then I'll sit down and wait for my tea. You had better get along to the kitchen to see if anyone will give you a cup. Be sure to come back in plenty of time to help me dress.'

When the tea tray had not arrived by half-past five, Marjory went next door to see if Mary Beth had been more fortunate. She knocked several times, then opened the door and peered in. Nether Mary Beth nor her maid was inside.

At six, Marjory rang the bell with such force she almost pulled it from the wall. When, after fifteen minutes, no one had answered, she wondered if she had actually damaged the mechanism.

Perks returned at half-past six to find Marjory fuming. No, said the maid, she had not heard the bell. And no, she didn't know Marjory had gone without her tea. And no, she did not know where Miss Mary Beth was.

Perks left in search of water so that Marjory could wash, but returned ten minutes later empty-handed. She had finally found the chambermaid's closet, she said, but there was nothing to carry the water in and she couldn't find a chambermaid, either. Marjory silently handed her the jug which was sitting on the washstand, and pointed to the door. This time Perks took only five minutes, but the water she brought was cold.

At half-past seven, with Perks' guidance, Marjory found her way to the drawing-room, which was already crowded. At last, she saw the countess looking very elegant but unusually flustered.

'You must let me present you to the Duchess of Poltraine,' said Caroline. Then, lowering her voice, she whispered in Marjory's ear: 'One addresses dukes and duchesses as Your Grace. Don't forget.'

The duchess was a very deaf old lady who wore a king's ransom in jewels and a black dress that smelled of mothballs. Her white hair was so thin at the front that Marjory could see the pink scalp. Her cap had some very pretty lace on it, but her maid had been too generous with the powder and rouge.

'Who are you?' demanded the duchess, tapping her cane on the floor.

'An American, your grace!' shouted Caroline.

'Americans? Don't like 'em,' said the duchess.

Caroline gave Majory a helpless shrug, and Marjory moved away. *I didn't want to meet her anyway*, she thought, and looked round for Frederick Bennett. Instead, she found Guy Dundalk.

'Are you enjoying yourself, Mr Dundalk?'

'I'm in prime twig, ma'am.' Noticing her eyes on his shirt studs, he said: 'They're paste. I'm very grateful to you for getting me this invitation. Miss Hanson thinks she is responsible, and I have not told her the truth.'

'You don't look like you're having fun. More like the chicken just before they put it in the pot. Did they give you a nice room?'

'I've slept in smaller ones.'

She smiled at him; he looked very fine in his evening clothes. 'I hope this visit benefits your business interests.'

'I'm sure it will. In fact, I'm counting on it.'

She moved a little closer. 'Did you know you have to call dukes and duchesses your grace?'

'Yes, I did know, but it is of no importance to me. I have not been presented to their graces, nor am I likely to be.'

'Don't let these people patronise you,' she advised. 'Where's my daughter?'

'Dressing, I believe. We all went for a walk, and I'm afraid we returned rather late.'

Frederick Bennett joined them, and Marjory made the introductions. The doctor was so cool to Dundalk that the young man left them as soon as he saw Mary Beth enter the drawing-room.

'Who is that young man and how did he insinuate himself into this house?' asked the doctor.

'Don't go getting uppity with me, Frederick Bennett. He's a friend of mine. I paid him a little something to woo Mary Beth away from Lucius Falkner. It worked a treat, too. I asked for an invitation for him so that Mary Beth would have an admirer here. Nobody's going to lord it over her at this broken-down castle.

They'll see how much she's appreciated by a handsome man.'

'My God, what an incredibly foolish woman you are! I wouldn't have believed it possible. You *paid* him? Only a cad would take money for such a service. Only a cad would *perform* such a service.'

'You told me to see to it that Mary Beth didn't marry the painter. Well, I saw to it. You're never satisfied, that's your trouble. It was a brilliant plan.'

'And what will happen now? You can't let her marry *him*! He's worse than Falkner.'

'He's healthy. Besides, it's not going any further. They are just friends. He's only here to give her a bit of confidence. And maybe do himself some good.'

'We must all watch out wallets. With that young upstart following her about, she is unlikely to meet a more desirable *parti*.'

'Frederick, sometimes you aggravate me so – '

Dinner was announced. Before Marjory knew what was happening, Bennett had left her and gone to some fat woman with two double chins. While she was still trying to figure out why he had deserted her, a complete stranger of about her own age approached, introduced himself as Sir Richard le Feyne, and said he had been asked to take her in to dinner.

He was slim and puffy-eyed. What hair he had clung to his scalp like brown paint, but he balanced the picture, so to speak, by wearing an enormous moustache and a beard which he parted in the middle. Marjory thought he looked like a wet rat. She put her hand on his outstretched elbow and counted the couples who outranked her, as she and her partner fell into line for the shuffle to the dining-room. There were twenty people ahead of her, and there would have been a lot more but for Gilbert's title. Frederick Bennett, having no title, was apparently not valued by his cousin, and was some way behind her.

Back home, she had always been one of the first to go in to dine, partly due to her daddy's money, but also because of his standing in the community. She had never seriously considered this business of rank before, probably because in America deference to it happened naturally. There were no rules, just a general feeling of respect for the powerful or those who had done something special, which caused some people to hang back slightly, allowing the chosen few to move ahead.

And there you had, in a nutshell, the difference between Americans and the English. The English had rules for everything. If you knew the rules, you were 'in'. If you didn't, you were 'not one of us'. And, what was more, there were no prizes for originality. She had learned that lesson when she had tried to have herself called Lady Marjory. They just wouldn't do it. No use fighting it; she had lost that battle. Only Mr Grimshaw and dear Mr Dundalk called her Lady Marjory these days.

The dining-room matched the drawing-room in size and shape and was reached by way of a splendidly furnished anteroom. Marjory was surprised to see that instead of one large table placed down the length of the room, there were five tables, each set with ten places, which gave the impression of a restaurant rather than the dining-room of a family home.

Her partner guided her to a table close to the window. Caroline and Lord Dumfries were hovering at the table directly beneath the crystal chandelier, fawning on the duke and duchess. Bennett had guided his partner to a table by the door, and the young people had been placed all together at a separate table out of Marjory's line of vision. There appeared to be one footman for every diner, which led not to better service, Marjory was pleased to notice, but to immense confusion. No one came near her wine glass until Sir Richard summoned a youthful footman and murmured that he was a dunderhead who had better mend his ways. After that, her glass was never allowed to become empty.

It soon became obvious to her that Sir Richard enjoyed irritating his fellow guests. He was the sort of man who had perfected the technique of offending with a smile, making it difficult for his victims to retaliate. Marjory was fully prepared for an attack when at last he turned to talk to her.

'So! Lady Marjory, the lady from St Louie who likes to be addressed as Lady Marjory.'

'It's pronounced Saint Lewis, and I only like to be called Lady Marjory by my friends. *You* may call me Lady Manton.'

She should have known better than to suppose he would leave her alone after that. He imbedded a few barbs in the tender flesh of others at the table, then, when the pudding had been served, turned to her again with a smile.

'Do you enjoy country sports, ma'am?'

'I prefer the city.'

'Oh, but you ride, I'm sure. And I daresay you are a crack shot. Fighting off Indians. That sort of thing.'

'No.'

'But surely, these estimable skills are *de rigueur* for ladies of the wild west.'

'Whatever you might think, Sir Richard, St Louis is a civilised city. It's got its own university and its own philosophical society, and it is *not* in the wild west.'

'I do hope the philosophers don't spit on the floor as, I believe, is the custom in your country. But, I was forgetting. Is not the mighty Mississippi river some- where close by?'

'St Louis is situated on the banks of the Mississippi.'

'The river on which Mr Mark Twain was a captain.'

'Pilot.'

'Mr Twain lectured in London recently. Did you see

218

him?' asked Sir Richard. 'Amusing fellow, I'm told. I didn't attend any of his performances. Afraid I might find his accent too trying for any great length of time. Do you know him?'

'No.'

Sir Richard turned from her to torment the lady seated on his other side. Marjory put down her cutlery and folded her shaking hands in her lap for a moment. *If they want war*, she thought, *they'll get it. But I'm not going to be buffaloed by a pack of stuffed shirts. They haven't got the manners that God gave a goose, and if that Sir Richard makes one more remark about Americans to me, I'll stab him like I did Gilbert. That would give Caroline's friends something to gossip about.*

A sudden burst of laughter from the young people's table cut through her like a knife. At least Mary Beth and Dundalk seemed to be enjoying themselves. *These fancy people better not tangle with that pair*, thought Marjory with satisfaction. *Mary Beth would give them a dressing down they'd never forget, and Dundalk would charm the shirts off their backs.* The thought cheered her up so much that she turned to le Feyne with a sweet smile.

'I was very disappointed in the duchess, Sir Richard. I thought she was rather underbred.'

Le Feyne turned purple, and Marjory began to eat again. 'Underbred' was a word she hadn't heard until a few weeks ago. She had made a note of it. *If you want to get along among the natives*, she thought, *you have to know which words cause pain. The polite phrases are the same in any country.*

The first day set the pattern for the rest. Only the men came down to breakfast; the women were served in their rooms. Marjory's breakfast coffee was invariably cold. By the time she was ready to come downstairs each morning, Mary Beth, Dundalk and the other young people had always just gone off on some

219

expedition of their own. And Bennett had already left to hunt or fish or whatever he and the other men did each day. She had been at Feldlands for several days before she found out why no one invited *her* to ride. It was because she was supposed to be in mourning. To Marjory's way of thinking, that was silly. She didn't ride because she didn't know how, especially not side-saddle. As for Caroline, she looked permanently distracted, and never once sat down with Marjory for a chat, as the two of them had been accustomed to do in London.

Marjory had ample time to pace off the dining-room and drawing-room: fifty feet long, each of them. So was the library, but it was narrower than the other two rooms, as was the entrance hall which was just so much wasted space. There was a conservatory *and* an orangery (unfortunately filled with white marble statues of naked men and women), and a billiard room that stank of tobacco and drew the men like a magnet each evening. She wrote a long letter to Samuel, telling him all about it, adding that you could drop Gilbert Manton's house into the servants' quarters and have room left over for a herd of cows.

She spent solitary hours in the library, took solitary walks in the garden, or joined a small party to explore the town of Bath. But on these excursions she might as well have been alone, because it was seldom the other ladies spoke to her. That she did not speak to them, struck her as perfectly natural.

Socially, she was isolated, but it didn't bother her. What rankled was Mary Beth's changed attitude towards her mother. If Marjory happened to see her and commented on the girl's gown, for instance, Mary Beth would say: 'Oh, don't you like it? Guy says it's quite the finest gown he's seen at Feldlands.'

It was 'Guy this' and 'Guy that' and 'I can't stop now. Guy and I are going to the lake', 'the town' or whatever. Guy Dundalk was a nice young man, and Marjory was pleased that he was doing such a good job of making Mary Beth happy. But Marjory had not intended that he should take her own place in Mary Beth's affections, nor that he should be the principal influence on the girl. It was all very strange. Mary Beth seemed to have given up her own opinions entirely in favour of Guy's. But if she thought he was so wonderful, how come she didn't notice that the other guests treated Guy very coldly?

19

Guy Dundalk smiled often in the company of the other guests. The more pointed their insults, the more he smiled. It was a different story with the servants. Their attempts at rudeness met with the sort of language they well understood. And he understood the servants: prompt service earned immediate tips. Vital information paid them even more.

He learned that Hemsby had a large allowance from his father, a weakness for gambling and an amazing inability to judge a horse. Dundalk gave up one whole day to travel to Newmarket with Hemsby and some of the other men. A few bets among themselves had meant forty guineas in winnings for Dundalk.

Sir Richard le Feyne had, it seemed, a small income with which he tried to support an extravagant lifestyle. As a result, le Feyne was always on the lookout for ways of enlarging his bank account, or better still, of avoiding expenditure. When le Feyne had asked if Guy were one of the Edinburgh Dundalks, Guy had said cheerfully enough: 'Well, my grandfather came from there, so I expect I am,' and had added with a wink: 'One way or the other.'

That was before le Feyne had turned up his nose at Mary Beth, which altered his position. *I'll shut his chaffer for him one of these days*, thought Dundalk, but smiled broadly every time they met.

He didn't have to pay for the information that the Earl of Dumfries was a regular Mr Lushington, but Dundalk didn't see how he could turn this to his advantage. The earl was fond of a game of billiards, but by the time he had drunk his fill of port each evening, he was in no condition to play a good game. Dundalk did what he could to improve matters, including trying to keep the port away from Dumfries. But, as he kept telling himself, nurse-maiding the earl didn't pay the rent.

Most of the time, Dundalk was in the company of Mary Beth. And didn't she have him in a spin? She was a goer, a high-spirited girl who interfered with his serious thinking. Within twenty-four hours they had explored the grounds of Feldlands thoroughly while the others were out riding. One day soon after their arrival, they found a folly, overgrown with holly and sycamore saplings. Inside, the paving stones were giving way to seedlings which pushed their way in great numbers through the cracks. Dry leaves were mulching undisturbed in the corners.

They entered the structure, built to look like a ruin, and he straightaway took out his handkerchief to dust the cobwebs off a stone seat. When he straightened up and turned to her, the girl attacked him! She planted kisses on his face, his mouth, his ear, whatever she could reach, until his heart was pounding and all sense was driven from his head.

He responded, of course. She was a splendid girl, and she had been giving him too many sleepless nights. The next thing he knew, he was unbuttoning her dress all the way down the front. With the gown forgotten on the filthy floor, he set to work on the hooks of her corset, urged on by Mary Beth. Even after the corset joined the gown on the floor, Mary Beth was still wearing more clothing than the girls he had known in his youth possessed! His hands were on her breasts, squeezing their warm mass beneath the cambric when they heard the sound of horses and a few distant voices.

'They can't ride up here, can they?' asked Dundalk.

'Oh, how should I know? Help me put my corset on, Guy. Quickly! They mustn't find me like this.'

'Just put on your gown. We can hide the corset.'

Tears stood in Mary Beth's eyes. 'You don't understand. My dress doesn't fit *me*. It fits my *corset*. Without it, I can't get the gown on.'

So they struggled with the corset, silently, feverishly, and ultimately to no purpose, because the riders never came. By that time, Dundalk had recovered his common sense. Much subdued, he took Mary Beth back to the house, vowing never to be so foolish again.

His good intentions lasted until the next day. They rode out in a dog-cart, ostensibly to explore the lanes. It was not long, however, before they had turned into the cool darkness of a beech wood. There he undressed her at a leisurely pace. They spread one of her petticoats on the ground and spent a glorious, hidden, forbidden hour. Dundalk had never been in love before. He had lusted but not loved. Mary Beth's uninhibited response, her trust, her willingness to do whatever he asked made the act of love a supreme experience for him. He wanted it to last for ever and couldn't think beyond this moment.

Afterwards, he lay beside her, sated, contented, unwilling to consider the future. But Mary Beth stood up almost immediately. He watched her through half-closed eyes as she dressed, and lifted himself up on one elbow only when she perched on a fallen branch and wiped the tears from her cheeks.

'Did I hurt you?'

'No, of course not.' She fussed with her hair, trying to tidy it. Then suddenly bent her head and covered her eyes with her hands. 'Oh, dear God, whatever have I done?'

He was on his feet in a moment. 'You wanted to do it. I was eager, God knows I was. But I didn't force you.'

She looked up to give him a slight smile, heavy

with regret and sadness. 'I know you didn't. I'm not accusing you, but . . . will I have a baby?'

'I don't know. I didn't think about that.' He ran his fingers through his hair. '*You* should have thought about it, though. Don't you know what kind of cove I am? Haven't you seen? You're a beautiful and clever woman. Why did you let me treat you like this?'

'Because I love you,' she said simply, looking over to where they had lain together. 'But that doesn't solve the difficulty. I can't take that petticoat back to Feldlands. And my maid is bound to wonder what happened to it.'

'I'll bury it. Don't let on to your maid. Act innocent, swear you didn't wear it today.' Dundalk began to pace about. 'You mustn't say you love me. Use your head, girl. Have some sense. Your sort don't . . .'

She reached out, took his hand and kissed the palm. 'I'm not *my sort*. I am Mary Beth Hanson and I will behave as I think fit. I don't regret what's happened for one minute. I'm not complaining, believe me. You see, because I love you, I have given you all I have to give: my virginity.'

'No! You haven't given me all you have to give. You haven't given me your money. Fly coves like me are always after other people's money.'

'You may have all of mine with pleasure. Kiss me.'

He did as she asked, bending to reach her mouth, finally pulling her to her feet so that their bodies could touch. It was a minute or two before he remembered what he had intended to say.

'Damn it, Mary Beth, I don't want your money. It's your money and my lack of it that's driving me crazy. One of us has got to be strong. One of us has got to think straight. I just wish it didn't have to be me.'

The fifth day might have passed just like the others, except that the servants excelled themselves and did not serve Marjory any breakfast at all. Perks didn't arrive until ten o'clock to help her into her corset and button her dress up the back, and chose this moment to give notice.

'Why, what in tarnation put that idea into your head after all this time?' said Marjory.

'It's the humiliation. Every one of the servants knows you want to be called Lady Marjory and haven't the right to it. They've all turned up their noses at me. They call *me* Lady Marjory and then they laugh.'

'They're crazy.'

'Oh, well, it's the custom in great houses to call servants by their employers' titles. The duke's servants are called Poltraine. I have no standing below stairs. I have suffered every affront.'

'I'm surprised at you, Eliza Perks. A strong-minded Yorkshire woman like you. I'm the one who has suffered every affront, but I'm not running away.'

Perks eventually allowed herself to be talked out of resigning, and Marjory went downstairs in search of a hot breakfast.

Several men, including Frederick Bennett and Sir Richard le Feyne, were seated in the breakfast room. A bellow of masculine laughter stopped abruptly when she appeared, and every man came to his feet.

'Won't you sit beside me, Lady Manton?' said Bennett. 'Allow me to serve you. What would you like to eat?' He was about to leave his place to serve her from the sideboard, but Marjory tugged on his sleeve.

'Let him do it.' She nodded towards the under-butler. 'I'll have a slice of ham and some scrambled eggs. And I want *hot* coffee.'

'I expected you to have breakfast in your room,' murmured Bennett.

'So did I. I can't say I like cold coffee, but I'll drink it if anybody bothers to serve it to me. And you, there,

226

you can tell the housekeeper I want to see her this afternoon.'

The under-butler silently laid a plate of ham and eggs before her, and signalled to a footman to fill her coffee cup.

'Ah . . . I believe you live in London, Lady Manton,' said young Mr Barnes who had been making sheep's eyes at her for several days. 'What do you think of our great metropolis?'

'Stinks of horse dung.' When Bennett choked on his coffee, she added: 'Well, it does! Haven't any of you noticed? I'm told all foreigners comment on it.'

'How strange,' murmured Sir Richard. 'The beautiful American bride of Lord Randolph Churchill says she finds London enchanting. She has not mentioned to me the . . . ah . . . problem you referred to.'

'Never heard of her, but I'll bet she's one of those rich girls from back east.'

'She comes from New York,' replied Sir Richard with an indulgent smile. 'And for your information, New York is *west* of Bath by quite a long way.'

With flushed cheeks and eyebrows drawn angrily together, Marjory finished cutting up her ham, put her knife across the top of her plate and transferred her fork to her right hand in the American way. This seemed to alarm Bennett.

'And did you happen to discuss the Civil War with the beautiful American bride, Sir Richard?' She used her fork to give emphasis to her words, and was startled when Bennett clapped a hand firmly on her wrist.

'Lady Manton,' said Bennett urgently. 'Do let me show you something of the countryside this morning. Don't wait for me, gentlemen. I'll not be fishing today.'

Marjory shook off Bennett's hand and began to eat her breakfast, paying no further attention to the men. The coffee was hot, so she ordered a second cup when the other men had left. She and Bennett didn't speak, however, until they were out of earshot of the servants, walking down a gravel path that led to the shrubbery.

'What has come over you since you arrived at Feldlands?' asked Bennett. 'I never expected to see such a performance from you. I was disgusted.'

'Oh, you were, were you? Well, I tell you, I've had about enough of these fancy people. I've never met with such rudeness in all my life. That Sir Richard has been plaguing me to death. He talked about the Civil War as if it was some little pop-gun affair. Over six hundred thousand dead, Frederick! That's twice the population of St Louis. Cities were burned to the ground. Why, scarcely a man came back from the war with all his arms and legs. Missouri had a bad time, being divided. Fourteen thousand men died on our side, the Unionists. I don't know how many Missourians died on the Confederate side. And there were hundreds of little skirmishes; men killing each other's wives and children, setting fire to things, getting revenge all the time. And afterwards, for years, the spite, the meanness, the violence whenever Johnny Reb met a Yankee.'

'Although the war has been over for ten years, I'm sure the memory of it is very distressing. But you can't expect Englishmen to – '

'I know. Englishmen don't care about American suffering. You're the most powerful nation on earth and you think Americans are pygmies, or maybe a joke. Well, one day the *Republic* will be the most powerful country. You wait and see. Then it will be the turn of the Americans to think all other people have smaller souls and less right to life, libery and the pursuit of happiness.'

'You are overwrought, Marjory.'

'And another thing. Why did you grab my hand at

breakfast? You've been talking to Peregrine, haven't you? He told you I stabbed Gilbert with a fork.'

Bennett sighed. 'I'm sure you had ample cause. He was a detestable man. I thought you might do the same to le Feyne. He richly deserved it, but such an action would not enhance your reputation at Feldlands. I will take you for a ride in one of Caroline's gigs. It will take me a few minutes to arrange things. You are to sit here and take deep breaths. You are not to make a spectacle of yourself any more.'

He took her by the shoulders and pushed her down on to a garden seat. Marjory folded her arms, clamped her jaw shut and tried to get a grip on her temper.

'Dear Lady Manton!' cried young Mr Barnes, trotting up and taking a seat beside her. 'You were magnificent in the breakfast room! How your eyes flashed when you gave le Feyne a dressing down! The man's a cad and deserved ten times worse! Oh, my heart fluttered in my breast! If you ever had cause to speak to me in that tone, I don't think this poor organ – ' (here he pressed a hand to his heart) ' – could sustain the disgrace of it.'

'Go away, Mr Barnes.'

'But, dear lady, I must speak! I was crossed in love last spring. The woman I had worshipped proved to have feet of clay. Naturally, I hadn't dared to hope that my passions would be aroused again, but by God, I do like a woman of fire!'

Marjory saw Bennett coming down the path towards her and stood up. 'You do talk a lot of hogwash, young man. Go away and find some innocent little girl who may be taken in by your high-falutin gabble. I'm busy.'

Bennett said he was going to drive her to Wells cathedral, which was about twenty miles away. It took them very nearly three hours to reach it, because the doctor didn't want to tire the horse. The journey was

229

pleasant enough, and uneventful, but by the time they entered the small town of Wells, Marjory was very hungry. They went directly to the yard of the Somerset Hotel where they left the horse and carriage.

The doctor had been careful to point out every sight of interest along the way, in spite of the fact that Marjory replied only when she felt inclined to do so. To Bennett's way of thinking, this was not playing the game. One made conversation in company whether one wanted to or not.

In the hotel dining-room, he was acutely aware of the other diners, simple people who might find something to criticize in Marjory's sullen silence. He, therefore, tried once again to bring his companion out of her sulks by setting the conversational ball bouncing.

'I was surprised to hear from le Feyne that St Louis has a philosophical society.'

'I suppose you think that's funny, a town full of hicks having a philosophical society.'

'No, I – '

'Or maybe you think I'm lying. Well, it's the truth,' said Marjory. 'And I believe it's got some very intelligent members. But don't ask me anything about it. My family were all too busy to be philosophical. I don't even know what those people talk about.'

'Marjory.' Bennett leaned forward and spoke in a low but menacing voice. 'I have had all I can bear of your American rudeness and your American determination to see a slight when none is intended. Everyone at Feldlands is stunned by your aloofness and bad manners. Just because you weren't given the principal guest suite – '

'I? I never wanted the principal guest suite. But how people like the Dumfries' can give themselves airs, when they can't even be bothered to look after their guests' comfort, is beyond me. When we invite people to our homes, we make a fuss of them, and try to see that they have every comfort. We don't allow our servants to be rude to them, that's for sure!'

The rest of the meal was taken in silence, and the doctor no longer cared what the other guest thought. Within the hour, they were standing before the west front of Wells cathedral. Bennett asked Marjory if she wished to go inside. She said: 'I don't believe I do.' He snorted and hunched his shoulders irritably. They went back to the hotel straight away to get into the gig for the long ride home behind a tired horse.

Marjory ached in every limb by the time she reached her own room, but she sent a message to Dundalk by Perks, requesting his presence. He returned with the maid, and Perks was sent away.

'I bought a little something for you the other day, Guy.' She removed a small blue velvet box from a drawer in the old chest and handed it to him. 'I don't see why you should go around wearing paste when all these fancy men sparkle like candles on a Christmas tree.'

Dundalk opened the box and frowned when he saw the set of shirt-studs and cuff-links. 'Lady Marjory, you shouldn't have!'

'They're only small diamonds. Just chips, really, but real. I'm ever so grateful to you for looking after Mary Beth. Well, don't look so unhappy about it! You've been put to a lot of expense coming here to do me a favour.'

He closed the box and bit his lip, unable to meet her eyes. In spite of his embarrassment, he couldn't resist calculating the value of the studs and wondering how much he could recover on them when he returned to London. 'Ma'am what I've done for Mary . . . Miss Hanson has been exactly what I wanted to do. You owe me nothing, not even so much as a thank you. I . . . don't know what more to say. I'll treasure them. I'll never forget this, believe me.'

'Get along with you then. I want to have a rest before dinner.'

When Dundalk had thanked her several times and gone off to get changed for dinner, she lay down on the bed fully dressed. But not for long.

Lady Dumfries, warned by her servants that Marjory had returned, was soon knocking on the door. 'I hear you are dissatisfied with the way I run my house,' she said as soon as the door was opened.

'Do you even know how your house is run, Caroline? Rude servants, no water, nobody ever to answer the bell, cold coffee on the breakfast tray if there is a tray at all. You've got all these servants eating you out of house and home, and they're making a fool of you.'

'I'm sorry I can't match the standards you are accustomed to.'

'I don't give two hoots about standards, Caroline. If you didn't even want to speak to me occasionally, why did you invite me here?'

'I don't know,' said the countess on her way out of the room.

Perks arrived, but so did Mary Beth. The girl was mortified, she told her mother. Everybody, just everybody, had heard about Marjory's outburst at breakfast. Mary Beth didn't know how she was going to hold her head up this evening. Marjory said she didn't believe she could spare the time for Mary Beth's mortification, and sent the girl away.

The housekeeper didn't present herself to say her piece until Marjory was just on the point of leaving the room to go to dinner. The woman was tall and fat, in her fifties, with apple-dumpling cheeks and wire-brush hair. A houseful of keys clinked menacingly at her waist.

'I understand you now wish to complain about the service, Lady Manton.'

'I now wish to go down to dinner,' said Marjory. 'If

you have no pride in running a house properly, that is your affair. In my house, the guests are treated with every consideration. But I've already said all I have to say on the subject. Stand aside, please.'

Dinner was not the nightmare she was expecting. Sir Richard had been placed at a different table. It was Frederick Bennett who offered her his arm, a much more comfortable arrangement, although they still didn't speak. When she was seated, she found to her very great pleasure, that Guy Dundalk was beside her. She did like him! Such a droll young man, and didn't they have a great deal in common, both of them being outsiders in this great barn of a house? Ignoring Bennett, she devoted herself entirely to the young man, so that certain persons might see she could be lively and charming when she chose to be, and when the company deserved her best manners. Frederick Bennett didn't appear to notice, however. It was poor foolish Mr Barnes who watched, ashen-cheeked, from across the table as she flirted with Guy Dundalk.

That evening the countess had card tables set up, and almost everyone settled down to play whist. Marjory was in a competitive mood, and the stakes were disgracefully high. She won an indecent amount of money but few friends, especially after announcing that she didn't really approve of gambling and would be putting her winnings in the poor box on Sunday morning. She had shown a few people a thing or two, and her nerves were very much better than they had been just a few hours earlier.

One of the last to go up to her room, she changed into her nightgown and dressing-gown and said good-night to Perks. The trouble was, in spite of the late hour, she was still wide awake. So many guests meant that there were constant demands on the two bathtubs.

It occurred to her that late though it was, this might be a very good time to take a bath.

It was when she was coming back from the bathroom that she saw Frederick Bennett being admitted to Mary Beth's room. *She must be sick*, thought Marjory, and hurried down the corridor.

She did knock, but she opened the door at the same time to find Mary Beth and Bennett, both in dressing-gowns and both looking guilty.

'What is it? What's wrong?' asked Marjory.

'Nothing at all,' said Bennett.

But at the same time, Mary Beth said: 'Mr Bennett believes he saw a man enter my room, Momma. As you can see, that's nonsense.'

'No Frederick, I'm sure you're wrong,' said Marjory. 'I know Mr Dundalk quite well. He wouldn't do such a thing. Look, I'll prove it to you.'

'Momma, no – '

'See here? Nobody under the bed. There's no door to another room and that only leaves the wardrobe.'

With a flourish, Marjory opened the door of the wardrobe, and they all saw Guy Dundalk, coatless and with his braces around his hips as he stood bent-kneed in the small space.

'Lady Marjory, do forgive me,' said Dundalk, climbing out of the wardrobe with difficulty. 'You have always been very kind to me and – '

' – And you chose this way of repaying my kindness.'

Bennett was very red in the face. He stepped forward with clenched fists. 'Lady Manton hired you to act as an escort for her daughter. You had a responsibility to – '

'Guy, no!' cried Mary Beth. 'How could you?'

'Frederick,' said Marjory. 'I think you're making matters worse. I do wish you wouldn't say any more.'

'So all you were offering me was the appearance of love in exchange for a few pounds! I hope Momma

234

knows what she got for her money. But surely you should have paid *her*.'

'No, it wasn't exactly like that, I swear it.' Dundalk started towards Mary Beth, arms outstretched.

'Get away from her,' said Bennett sternly. 'This is no way to show respect for a young woman, Dundalk. Miss Hanson, your mother acted in your best interests. It was essential, for certain reasons I can't divulge, that you not marry Falkner.'

Mary Beth's strong face turned deep red. 'Oh Lordy, Lordy! Do you all know about Lucius? Am I to have no privacy? Why couldn't you all leave me alone? I never want to see any of you again.'

'You have been badly treated, my dear,' said Bennett before Marjory could speak. 'I assure you, I was not consulted. Your mother acted from the highest of motives. But she is an innocent woman. She couldn't have known this scalliwag would sneak into your room.'

Dundalk smiled slightly. 'We are not the only people in this house who meet late at night in each other's bedrooms, Mr Bennett.'

Marjory was startled, but Bennett replied promptly. 'No, but I'll wager you are the only couple who have not waited until after marriage.'

'Yes, sir,' drawled Dundalk. 'Adultery is a fine thing among the aristocracy. Mary Beth knows I love her. I believe she loves me, and once she understands how I happened to meet – '

'Never mind that now,' said Marjory. 'Just get out of my daughter's room before anyone discovers you're here. Take a look in the hallway and if it's empty, skedaddle. As for you, young lady, I'll talk to you in the morning.'

Mary Beth removed a small handkerchief from her pocket and blew her nose. 'I have nothing to say to you, Momma. You've done quite enough for your ugly daughter.'

Dundalk pulled up his braces and adjusted them on his shoulders. 'I'm not leaving until I have a chance to speak to Mary Beth alone, Lady Marjory. So if you and the doctor will please go away – '

Bennett was inclined to argue, but Marjory took him by the sleeve. 'Come on, Frederick, we owe them that much.'

'Will you forgive me?' asked Dundalk when they were alone.

Mary Beth was bright, forcing a smile. 'But of course. You did warn me that you are a scoundrel, didn't you? Unfortunately, it was a little late by then. However, you have earned your money. I hope you were very well paid. It must have been a repugnant task. I just can't help feeling Momma didn't intend for you to ruin me, that's all.'

'Mary Beth, I love you and I want you to marry me.'

'No, thank you. I think I'll write to Lucius. I don't care what disease he has.'

'Do you think he'll have you after the way you treated him?'

Mary Beth made no attempt to stem the tears, but let them roll down her cheeks. 'No, of course he won't have me. Why should he? Why should anyone? Get out.'

'I didn't mean . . .' began Dundalk, then shook his head and opened the door. Without bothering to check if anyone was in the hallway, he walked out of the room.

Mary Beth hurried to the door, ready to close it, when she saw Sir Richard le Feyne walking down the corridor. 'How dare you attempt to enter my room, Mr Dundalk?' she said loudly. 'I've never been so insulted in my life!'

Dundalk whirled to confront her and their eyes met

236

for a long moment. Then he smiled broadly as Sir Richard stood transfixed, looking from one to the other.

'Well done, old girl,' said Dundalk softly. 'That pays me out good and proper. Don't worry, Sir Richard, I'll be leaving this house first thing in the morning. Goodbye, Mary Beth. It's been a privilege knowing you.'

With a sob, Mary Beth closed the door and flung herself across the bed to cry until she was too tired to cry any more.

When Marjory and Bennett left Mary Beth's room, they went by common consent to Marjory's room where they could talk without being overheard.

'Oh, Frederick,' she said, rather hysterically when they were alone. 'It's such a tragedy, and all I could think was it was just like that farce we saw. Remember?'

'At the Adelphi? Yes, but the young lover in the play hid under the bed, as I recall. This is a serious business, Marjory. We must think what is the best thing to do.'

'He'll have to marry her. Only, I don't know if she'll have him, now that she knows I put him up to courting her.'

'She's ruined, no matter what. You have done an extremely foolish thing. Must you meddle? You always seem to . . . What is it? You look pale.'

Marjory put a hand to her quivering lips. 'I don't feel so pretty good.'

Bennett reached her in two strides, borne along by a rush of emotion that caught him completely by surprise. He felt her pulse with one hand and placed the other on her brow. 'You're feverish, and a little dizzy, I expect. It's the shock. Hold on to me, I . . .'

Marjory rested a hand on his chest and looked up at him with tear-wet cheeks. Her closeness took his breath away. He put an arm around her small waist and held her firmly, wanting to say so much, unable to speak at all.

'You think I'm a fool, don't you? Oh, Frederick, I know you're always in the right. I just wish you had more respect for me.'

He caressed her cheek with the backs of his fingers. 'Of course I respect you. What a thing to say!' She smelled of some potent perfume that he couldn't identify. 'Occasionally, you do something which I feel is . . .' His head was so close to hers that his lips just naturally brushed her forehead. 'Which I feel is unwise. But I . . . , oh, Marjory!' His arm tightened around her waist. With his free hand, he attempted to lift her chin, but he had gone too far. She pushed him away rather forcefully, turning her head to hide her embarrassment.

'I'm better now. I'll just sit down here on the bed. It won't be so bad, you know. Guy shocks you because you're used to a different sort of man. But he'll fit in to our family easily enough.'

Bennett sighed. The brisk tone of her voice did not encourage him to say anything personal. 'We'll talk about it another time. You need a composer. Have you any laudanum? If not, I can fetch some from my room.'

Marjory hugged herself and shivered slightly. 'On the washstand in that little brown bottle. It's just as well I've got it. Now you won't have to walk the passageway in your dressing-gown. Somebody might see you and misunderstand. I wouldn't want these folks to think *I'm* an aristocrat.'

He moved heavily over to the washstand, prepared a few drops of laudanum in a glass of water and brought it to her in his best impersonal medical manner. The dangerous moment had passed. He didn't know whether to be glad or sorry. His feelings for her ran deep; he couldn't deny that. But he was a cautious man, one who considered every move, and never entertained an inconvenient emotion. Marjory was naturally charming, an original, a good woman. It was her children who disturbed him: a son so weak he allowed himself to be driven from his mother's side when she needed his support, and a daughter who gave free rein to the sort of passions nice women knew nothing about. He would be happy to think the bad blood, which so obviously ran in their veins, was Jonathan Hanson's.

20

Mary Beth, quick off the mark, was pounding on her mother's door the next morning before Marjory had even hooked her skirt into place. Once again, Perks was sent from the room to wander the long corridors.

'I've been very disappointed in you recently, Momma. First of all, it's obvious you knew Lucius had contracted a disease, but you weren't prepared to tell me straight out and let me decide what I wanted to do.'

'If *you* knew he was diseased, you should have broken off the engagement immediately. Didn't it occur to you he must have been up to something nasty? Where's your pride, girl?'

'I planned to wait until he was better, then make a decent husband of him. Then I met Guy. Momma, I *loved* him. Losing Guy is much worse that losing Lucius. How could you have paid him? And how could he have taken your money?'

Marjory lifted her hands in a helpless gesture. She was in the wrong, no matter what she did or said. 'Give me a chance to speak, will you? I didn't know for sure that Lucius wasn't . . . healthy. I just sort of guessed. I didn't know what darn fool thing you would do if I told you. And I was right to worry. You were going to marry him just the same! I'm glad I did what I did, so there.'

'I'm not some unmarried pregnant maid to be disposed of as you choose, Momma.'

'I know that,' said Marjory, crisply. 'You are my only daughter. I want you to be well and I want you to be happy. I apologize for caring, but I can't help it.

I just wanted to divert your mind. I guess I'm a poor judge of men. I thought Guy Dundalk was a decent man with a lot of charm who would make you laugh a little. I asked him to arrange to meet you and entertain you. What happened after that was entirely your doing.'

'You both took pity on me, because I can't get beaux of my own. I'm a great strapping girl whom no man wants to know. You *bought* his company for me.'

'Mary Beth, I must ask this. Did you and he – '

'Did we what?' asked Mary Beth sharply.

Marjory's courage failed her. 'Did you and he come to an understanding?'

'There was no time. Guy sent a note to me this morning. Apparently Mr Bennett went to Guy's room last night and demanded that he leave Feldlands first thing this morning. Guy refused unless Sir Richard le Feyne was sent away too.'

'Sir Richard? Why, what has he to do with anything?'

'Oh,' said Mary Beth, waving a hand. 'He saw Guy coming out of my room. He may have jumped to the wrong conclusion.'

Marjory gave a massive sigh. 'No one can force Sir Richard to leave Feldlands.'

But in this, Marjory was wrong. Bennett had seen both men on to an early train. His greater height and bulk, together with his knowledge of some unsavoury incidents in le Feyne's past, gave Bennett the leverage he needed. He had also asked Dundalk the very question Marjory had been afraid to ask her daughter. Dundalk's answer caused him considerable concern.

Afterwards, he and Marjory spend the day quietly away from the others, since neither was in the mood for loud company. They walked the paths and later went for a refreshing drive in one of the Dumfries gigs. Just before they returned to Feldlands, Bennett

241

broached the subject that had been uppermost in both their minds all day.

'I'm afraid you have no choice but to insist upon the marriage, Marjory. I suggest you see that they are married quietly as soon as possible. Perhaps you could purchase a small house for them in the country. I believe that would be the best thing.'

Marjory folded her arms across her chest and sighed. 'She'll marry him if she wants to, and I'll be told, not asked, if they require a house. I can tell you one thing: Mary Beth won't retire to the country. She likes the city, and he would be like a fish out of water surrounded by grass and sheep. But I give up on the pair of them. I'm only her mother.'

At dinner, everyone was wondering at length what had happened to Dundalk and le Feyne. Did *both* men have pressing business in London? Was there some scandal? Had they, perhaps, quarrelled violently?

Marjory feigned ignorance. She was not interested in either of them, she said over and over again. When no answers of any sort were forthcoming from any quarter, the curiosity died of starvation, and the guests turned to other subjects.

The evening was damp and hot, but Caroline had thought of a pleasant diversion. After dinner, many of the guests paired off and went walking down several of the broader garden paths which had been illuminated with Japanese lanterns. A small orchestra had set up business in the orangery, and the music drifted romantically out of the orangery doors to charm the couples, and give a few of them unseemly thoughts of seduction.

Bennett intended to take the woman of his choice for a cooling stroll in the gathering darkness, but Caroline, her cheeks rosy with the heat, caught up with him and took his arm firmly in both hands.

Marjory saw them walking close together in earnest

conversation and thought she knew the subject under discussion. Not wanting any part of one of Caroline's interrogations, she ducked down one of the unlit paths. She had been avoiding Caroline all day, so it was bad luck that she ran into Caroline's husband in the dark. The earl was extremely drunk. He was also very curious.

'Been tryin' t'get you 'lone all day, m'love. Where the devil's le Feyne? That man never passes up a free meal. D'you send him packing?'

'I know nothing about it, Dumfries. You're tiddled.'

'No'm not,' said the earl. 'I'm drunk. Dundalk's gone, too, dammit. Used to help keep me off the daffy. He'd say I've tipped the whole nine tonight. Disgraceful fellow. Rough type. Talks cant. Shouldn't have had him in the house, but I liked him. D'you send *him* away? Sniffing round Mary Beth, was he?'

'Dumfries,' said Marjory, loosening his fingers from round her upper arm, 'I'm getting aggravated with you. Let me go. Why don't you stick your head in a bucket of water? That ought to do the trick.'

Laughing, Dumfries lurched forward. He was very unsteady on his legs, but he knew exactly what he wanted. Arms outstretched, he fell upon Marjory. His weight buckled her knees and sent her crashing back against a small tree, as the earl's arms encompassed her as well as the tree.

'Dumfries, old chap!' said Bennett, smiling broadly as he approached the grappling couple at a leisurely pace. 'I want a word with you.'

Dumfries looked round in surprise. Seizing her opportunity, Marjory threw off his arms and regained the path. She looked directly at Bennett, although it was far too dark to read his expression. 'Men!' she said in disgust. 'I've had enough of them for one day. I'm going to bed.'

She went to her room, half-expecting Bennett to tap

on her door as soon as he could get away from Dumfries. He did not call, however. Exhausted by too many emotions, she fell asleep early and slept soundly all night.

It seemed she was not destined to be allowed to dress in peace. The next morning it was the turn of Caroline to visit her before she was ready to be seen by the polite world.

'Let me start at the beginning,' said Caroline, lounging on the unmade bed. 'Richard le Feyne was rude to you and Mary Beth, and he knew too much. I was happy to let Benny send him away. As for Dundalk, I already knew he was an admirer of Mary Beth's; Fenella does occasionally confide in her mother. I admit I was curious to see him. Marjory, he is charming. A very dangerous sort of person. Fenella says he and Mary Beth are devoted to one another, and, well, hot blood, you know.'

'I wouldn't have said Mary Beth was hot-blooded.'

'Nor I,' laughed Caroline. 'Aren't people strange? Benny can't understand how the girl could have permitted it, but you and I know Guy Dundalk is irresistible, don't we?'

'Oh, Lord, I suppose we do.'

'Anyway, Benny insists that the marriage must take place, but, on the other hand, it's too soon. After all, not so long ago Mary Beth was engaged to Mr Falkner. It's a pity about that. Lucius Falkner is the talk of the town, they say. A new talent. Everyone who matters says he is a genius. Poor Mary Beth would have done better to stay with him. I think she would have enjoyed being married to a man who is going to be rich and famous.'

'She wouldn't have enjoyed walking in his shadow. Besides, he seems to have done very well without her.'

Caroline stood up and looked round the modest room. 'I have a bone to pick with you, my dear friend.

I invited you to Feldlands at this particular time, because I thought you would enjoy meeting the people I planned to entertain. Duty visitors, not friends, but all of them from the finest families. The duke and duchess are old, spoiled and cantankerous. They make terrible demands on one, just as all old people do. They are also connections of Dumfries. The duke is the head of the family, and I must be polite to them both. I knew I wouldn't have much time to spend with you, but I thought you would understand.'

'Caroline – '

'Let me finish. They will be leaving in three days' time, and with them will go over half my guests. I can then move you to a better room. I do hope you are not thinking of going back to London immediately. The atmosphere at Feldlands will be so much more relaxed. We could have such good times together.'

'I have behaved badly and must apologize,' said Marjory. 'Of course I appreciated getting close to a real duchess. You know, I'm afraid I've been guilty of thinking of the English, especially the fancy people, as not being quite real. I mean, not flesh and blood. That was wrong of me. We are all alike under the skin. In fact, I knew an old lady in St Louis who looked a lot like her grace. She was a mean old so-and-so, just like the duchess.'

'I wonder what the duchess would say to that! My dear, you must not apologize for anything. I had no idea until I spoke to Benny just how many worries you had on your mind. And as for Richard le Feyne, I shall never forgive him for the way he has spoken to you. He's a bore.' The countess was fond of under-statement; she would have described an axe murderer as a bore.

'He did more than bore me. What a fool you must have thought me. Wanting to get into society, I mean. Why, there's nothing to it, no pleasure in it, at any rate. Society is like a column of smoke. You can only see it at a distance. Once you're in it, you can't see a darned thing. I haven't met anyone I'd care to meet again. I prefer Mrs Pringle and, heaven help me, Mrs Grimshaw.'

'Yes,' said Caroline. 'Social climbing is nonsensical. You know, these people are not some special breed to me. They're just family and friends. I've known many of them all my life. Of course, there are certain customs and rules of conduct in our set, but I believe that applies everywhere. We know what our friends and relations will and will not tolerate.'

'There's a lot of bouncing on bedsprings around here. That wouldn't do where I come from,' Marjory said laughing, then blinked at her friend in surprise. 'Why, Caroline! Whatever is the matter? What have I said?'

The countess took out a handkerchief and blew her nose. 'I've always been rather amused by the pairings-off, the summer affairs that fade away with the autumn. Until last evening, that is, when I happened to see Dumfries in the shrubbery kissing some woman. One of *my* guests, Marjory! I couldn't see who she was. Benny was closer; he knows her name.'

Marjory smiled. 'I expect he told you there was nothing to it.'

'No, indeed! Benny was very angry, but he refused to tell me who she is. He said Dumfries was intoxicated as usual, and the woman was entirely responsible for what happened.'

'*What?*'

'I begged to be told her name, but he said he would never divulge it because I would be terribly hurt. I suppose it is to avoid my questions that he left Feldlands this morning.'

'Gone?' asked Marjory faintly. 'Frederick's gone without a word? Did he leave a letter for me?'

'Why, how should I know? If you haven't received

one, then he obviously didn't write one. He's visiting a cousin of ours in Yorkshire.'

'Is he, by golly? Caroline, I'd like his address in Yorkshire. There's a few things I must tell him.'

It seemed as if Frederick's departure was directly responsible for the worsening weather. It rained so hard that day, none of the women went out of doors at all. The men, of course, would not be prevented from pursuing their sports. They wrapped themselves up warmly and tramped out of doors, talking loudly. They returned in time for tea in the same loud good humour.

The women, having spent an idle, boring day in close proximity, responded to all this bonhomie with coldness. During the hours of needlework and gossip, Caroline had succumbed to the strain and been betrayed into an unseemly outburst of temper when one of the servants tripped and dropped a tea tray.

Since Mary Beth, Fenella and some of the other young girls had closeted themselves in Fenella's boudoir, Marjory was left to face the claws of the other women without an ally. And they used the whole feminine arsenal against her, from the direct snub to damning with faint praise. Marjory had to admit she deserved this Turkish treatment. She had made a point over these past days of being boorish, openly critical of English customs, towns, houses and servants. She had even, on one occasion, criticized English trees. She blushed to think of it, couldn't even remember now what she had found to dislike in the trees. She had let herself down that day, and must hope others had forgotten it. *I'm underbred*, she thought with a wry smile.

After dinner, card tables were set up, and they all settled down to play whist. Marjory's attention was certainly not on the game. She laid down several cards mechanically, and was brought sharply back to the present when Lady Dortford, seated next to her, questioned one of her discards. For some reason, everyone stopped talking at that moment. Lady Dortford's words hung on the air for several seconds.

Marjory had no idea what cards she had played or whether she had been following the rules. She was just about to explain that she hadn't been concentrating when the duchess, at the next table, spoke the thought that was in several minds.

'Has the American been cheating?'

There were one or two gasps, a murmur of 'no such thing', and Caroline was suddenly on her feet. Even Dumfries looked both sober and concerned.

Marjory stood up from the table and put her hands on her hips. 'No, *your gracious duchess*, I have not been cheating. I've just been bored. If you will excuse me, Caroline, I think I'll go to bed. I don't want to embarrass you further.'

She started out of the room, head high, back straight. Then her evil genius made her whirl round and glare at the faces turned towards her. 'What I meant is, I wouldn't want to em-bare-ASS you.'

She waited, but there was no horrified reaction, no one gasped or reached for the smelling salts, just blank faces blinking at her. She sighed heavily. She had ignored her strict upbringing to use a very crude word, and nobody had been the least bit shocked. Then she remembered. In England 'ass' was not a vulgar word. The English equivalent was 'arse'. Her grand, defiant, departing gesture had gained her nothing at all except a few puzzled expressions.

So be it, thought Marjory. *I tried*. Just as she was about to leave the room, her eyes happened to fall on the one person who was both profoundly shocked and ashamed: Mary Beth. Now more deeply depressed than ever, Marjory went into the hall, but Caroline was hard on her heels and soon caught up with her, begging her to come back for another game.

'Caroline, I'm just exhausted from having such a good time at Feldlands. Mary Beth and I will be going home tomorrow.'

'Please don't do that. The visit hasn't worked out as I had hoped, but I value your friendship and must apologize for my other guests. It was disgraceful of that cat, Eliza Dortford, to question your cards. The duchess is senile; there's nothing I can do about her, except to say I'm sorry.'

Marjory grinned wickedly. 'You know, I meant to say I didn't want to em-bare-ARSE you. It loses something in the translation, but at least it would have offended them. I'd have like that.'

Caroline shook her head. 'You don't understand us at all, do you? That word would only have made everyone laugh. But don't despair. You shocked them when you addressed the duchess as "your gracious duchess". My guests have been snobbish about you, I know, but you could have won them over with your charm if you had tried. On the other hand, upper-class Americans would not have been so willing to be amused by you. That's why I didn't invite any.'

'Do you think I don't know that? Forget it. Let's just forget the whole thing. I'm what my mother used to call "tuckered out". I want to go back to London and think what I'm going to do for the rest of my days. I'm used to working for a living. I'm no good at being lazy. The devil has found work for this idle tongue of mine. I've let you down, Caroline. And that's too bad, because I've never had such a close friend as you. When we're alone, we get along just fine. I look forward to seeing you back in London.'

In a rush of genuine affection, Caroline bent forward to press her cheek against Marjory's. 'You and Benny have had a misunderstanding, haven't you?'

'I guess so. We'll get it straightened out once we're both back in London. Mary Beth is giving me no peace.

I don't know what is to become of her. I'll say goodbye here and now, my dear. I can't say it hasn't been interesting.'

21

At the beginning of August, Marcus sent a short letter to Florence, informing her that Mr Wainwright was going to Wales to his country home during the parliamentary recess, and that Marcus would be looking after her during the coming weeks and would be visiting her the following day.

When he arrived at the small apartment at the appointed hour, he found the girl wearing a very fine carriage gown, eager to go out with him. He thought she had lost a little of the youthful plumpness in her cheeks. She was not precisely gaunt, but her eyes appeared to be more deep-set, and she had laced herself to achieve a handspan waist without apparent loss of breath. He guessed she was about ten pounds lighter than when he had last seen her.

'You will take me for a ride, won't you, Mr Bennett? Please say yes. The old man buys me any clothes I ask for, but he won't give me so much as a farthing for myself. The only person what I ever speak to is the landlady when she brings my meals. And the maid, but she's simple. I can't even go out for a walk and buy a dish of ice cream for myself.'

Marcus frowned. 'I hope you have not decided to supplement your income by . . . er . . . other means.'

'What? Entertain other men, do you mean? No indeed! It's bad enough having to . . . to entertain Mr Wainwright without putting up with anybody else. I have no money, sir, and that is the truth. Did you come in your own carriage? Shall we go out? Wait, I want to show you the painting that the old man bought.

251

There, on the wall above the bed. I keep a scarf over it when he's away.'

Florence took Marcus by the arm to lead him into the bedroom, then lifted her skirts and walked across the bed in her kid boots to pull the scarf away so that he could view the *Slave Maiden* for the second time. He didn't fail to notice the alterations the artist had made since the painting had been hung at the Summer Exhibition.

'Cover it up,' he said, already turning to leave the bedroom. 'If you wish to go for a ride, you must hurry. I am engaged to dine out this evening. I haven't much time.'

She followed him into the sitting-room, her eyes round and tear-filled. 'Ain't you going to take me to supper? I been stuck in this place for days. He don't come here much. Not that I'm complaining, but – '

'Shame on you, you ungrateful girl! Where would you be without Mr Wainwright? He troubles you very little, and you seem to receive quite a lot in return. That gown looks very expensive to me.'

Florence pouted, every inch the sulky child. 'I hate him. He's smelly and old, and he says dirty things to me.'

Lacking a suitable reply to these comments, Marcus changed the subject. 'What do you do when you are alone?'

He looked round the room curiously. It was far tidier than he had expected, but lacked all personal touches. Whatever money Wainwright spent on his love nest, none had been laid out on ornaments, pictures, antimacassars, or decorative cushions. There was not a book or a magazine in sight. He couldn't see a needlework basket, although that didn't mean there wasn't one somewhere.

'I sit and think,' said Florence. 'I plan how one day

I'll have saved enough money to give up this life and live decent. Maybe get married and have children.'

'There is nothing to stop you from giving up prostitution now. However, it is too late to think of decency and children. You should have considered those things before embarking on this life.'

Florence didn't answer, but treated him to a cynical look that sat oddly on the thin young face.

He took her for a drive round Paddington where he thought he was unlikely to meet anyone he knew. Later, they stopped so that he could purchase several magazines for her and some sweets. They finally drove to a subscription library. Having no illusions about her literacy, he helped her to choose several books of light fiction that would not test her reading skills too highly, while not corrupting her morals, either. It did occur to him that he was shutting the stable door after the horse had bolted.

By this time, it was getting late. He returned the girl to her rooms, advised her to improve herself by reading every moment she could spare, and then, on being begged so pitifully, promised to come again the next day.

'Oh, you are kind!' said Florence. 'Thank you, sir.' Impulsively, she stood up on tiptoe and planted a swift kiss on his cheek.

She caught him completely by surprise, arousing him with the softness of her lips, the delicacy of her perfume. His reaction, beyond his control, nevertheless disgusted him. He rubbed his face with the back of one hand. 'Don't ever do that again. Do you understand me? I will not come here again if you persist in this improper behaviour. You belong to Mr Wainwright.'

'I'm not his slave.'

'No, you may leave him at any time. But you will not kiss other men when he is away if you wish to continue to be supported in comfort. I warn you.'

'I don't know what you're getting so bothered about, I don't really. It was just a friendly kiss, but I won't do it again. Please come tomorrow. I'm going crazy here on my own.'

With his father away and parliament in recess, Marcus was at a loose end. What better way to spend his time (he told himself) than in schooling Florence, educating her, correcting her speech and improving the tone of her mind?

The next day, he gave her ten pounds as her very own spending money, and immediately told her that he would fine her threepence every time she made a grammatical error in her speech. As a result, he had the greatest difficulty in getting her to speak at all when he drove her to Kensington, so frightened was she of making a mistake.

In spite of it all, the day was a long and happy one. They dined in a modest hotel where Marcus was sure he was unknown, and then Florence begged to be taken to Cremorne Gardens. The old man had taken her there, she said, and she had enjoyed it ever so much. Wouldn't Marcus please take her?

Marcus would not, although he didn't tell her why. It was precisely because men of Wainwright's standing frequented Cremorne Gardens that he refused to risk going there. He dreaded being recognized while in Florence's company. He rebuked her for addressing him as Marcus, then had to assure her she would not be fined for her impertinence before he could explain that he would take her, instead, to the gardens at North Woolwich.

These gardens catered to a much lower order than Cremorne. The lights were not so plentiful, the prostitutes not so well-behaved, the orchestra not in tune at all. Florence loved it.

They danced as best they could on the crowded

platform until they were too hot and tired to continue. Then they drank cheap warm wine to refresh themselves for more dancing.

By the time they reached Florence's home in Paddington, Marcus had a severe headache. All evening long he had glanced sideways or over his shoulder for fear he was being observed by someone he knew. As if fear of discovery were not enough of a strain, he had also to resist the girl's devilish attractions: her apparent sweetness, the perfection of her features, the trusting way she looked at him. She was the devil's instrument and Wainwright's property. He had to be careful.

For her part, Florence had relaxed and enjoyed herself so much that she had forgotten to guard her tongue. Consequently, she owed Marcus five shillings. Being the man he was, he never considered indulging her by waiving the fines. She would quickly learn, he told her, because failing to do so would rob her of her precious independence.

The days passed agreeably. There were many trips to the subscription library and several evenings spent quietly in Paddington with Florence reading aloud, or answering questions about the books she had read. On these occasions, she was always very nervous. She kept her voice low and wiped her hands with a handkerchief continually. Nevertheless, she seemed to enjoy the challenge and never wanted the teaching sessions to end.

During the first two weeks, she lost a whole pound of the ten, for a variety of mistakes. Then she got a grip on the English language and didn't lose another threepence. Whenever Marcus ended a session with some carefully chosen words of faint praise, she was so relieved that she laughed and cried at the same time, and on one occasion looked as if she might rush forward to hug him. Alert for signs of excessive gratitude, he quickly lifted a book before his face and moved to put the table between them.

About four weeks after he had started escorting her round the town, Marcus told her he would take her dancing the following evening as a reward for all her hard work. He was secretly tired of rough company, having had his fill in recent days, and decided to risk meeting someone he knew by taking her to a famous casino, the Argyll Rooms.

The premises were elegant, if notorious. Heavy mirrors lined the walls, bouncing the glow of hundreds of gas lights from one side of the room to the other. Marcus thought Florence was easily the best-dressed woman in the casino, the only one who was not over-painted and the only one to display the anticipation of a harmless treat with complete innocence. In fact, nine-tenths of Florence's charm lay in her unassailable innocence. It was this quality, Marcus told himself, which caused him to persist in educating her.

As instructed, the waiter led them to a banquette set in the furthermost corner of the main room. Florence sat facing the dancing area, while Marcus positioned himself opposite her with his back to the crowd. He saw almost immediately that this would be no great help to him, since the wall facing him was covered by a gigantic gilt-framed mirror. In any case, complete anonymity was not possible in so brightly lit a room. Within the first few minutes, he spotted three gentlemen he knew slightly. Thankfully, they didn't notice him.

Their champagne and glasses had just arrived when a glance upwards at the mirror showed Marcus that an old school acquaintance was heading their way. Arthur Blandings had been a year ahead of him in school, an idle, fun-loving boy, for ever in trouble with the school authorities. Since then, Blandings had lost a good deal of his hair and gained fifteen or twenty

256

pounds, but otherwise appeared to be the same cheerful gadfly he had always been.

Arthur Blandings had his arm around the waist of a woman in her late twenties. Her light brown hair was elaborately dressed and her cosmetics applied heavily but with considerable skill. She was not quite as beautiful as Florence, and innocence was a quality she knew nothing about. Her dress was cut so low, Florence felt ashamed for her.

When it became obvious that the couple were coming directly towards Marcus, Florence looked up and pressed her lips together with disapproval.

'Bennett, old chap!' said Blandings, clapping him on the shoulder.

'My dear fellow.' Marcus stood up and bowed to the young woman.

'This is Prunella,' said Blandings, giving his lady a playful squeeze that made her squeal.

Marcus turned to Florence. 'May I present Miss Drew?'

Blandings guffawed. 'You always were a stickler for the niceties, Bennett.'

Pulling Prunella along with him, Blandings sat down on the banquette beside Florence. 'What's your name, my dear? I can't call you Miss Drew all evening, now can I?'

'My name is Florence, sir. Pleased to meet you both.'

Marcus sat down and signalled to the waiter to bring two more glasses and another bottle of champagne. He was in a quandary. There was no way he could protect Florence from casual insults. While every male occupant of the Argyll Rooms was undeniably a gentleman, every female was just as undeniably a prostitute. He could not pass Florence off as a respectable woman, because no man of sense would bring a respectable woman to this casino. He couldn't announce that she was Wainwright's mistress without raising more questions than he cared to answer. Marcus disliked having Blandings suppose that Florence was his own mistress, but his reputation from school days as a prig still rankled. The only thing to do was to say nothing on the subject. After a moment, he asked formally after each member of Blandings' family by name and forced himself to show considerable interest in the answers.

When the waiter had served some champagne to Blandings and Prunella, Marcus looked over at Florence and smiled. 'They're playing waltzes. Would you care to dance?'

Florence eagerly agreed, and they were on the floor in a minute or two, whirling in unison with all the other couples as they circled the dancing area.

'How did he know?' asked Florence. 'How did Mr Blandings know what I am?'

'All the woman here are – '

'Oh, I see.' She lowered her eyes to the level of his bow tie. 'You wouldn't take me to a proper place, would you? You're ashamed of me.'

'You chose your profession, I didn't. This is where women like yourself congregate. It is not my fault. Blandings is an oaf, but he was entitled to draw the conclusion he did. You must grow accustomed to such insults.'

'I'll never grow accustomed to insults. Why should I? Marcus, do *you* want me to leave the old man?'

'Of course.'

Florence looked up hopefully. 'Where should I go? How should I manage?'

'Obviously, you must find respectable employment in a well-run home. I think I could manage to obtain a letter of reference for you. I might even write it myself. Quite wrong, of course, but it is a deception I am prepared to perpetrate, because you have been trying so very hard to improve yourself lately. And, furthermore, I am convinced you have truly repented.'

Florence looked into his face, seeing the strong, square chin, the peaked eyebrows, the full, censorious mouth. 'No, I haven't repented, Marcus, me old love. Nor will I ever. I shall find a richer, younger protector one of these days and live like a fine lady in a grand house overlooking the park. And I won't ever be common like that Prunella with her dress cut down to her navel. Now, what do you think of that?'

'That you are beyond saving, of course. Let me hear no more of these childish outbursts. I'm sorry Blandings and his . . . friend have joined us. We will not stay here long.'

'They've spoiled it all.'

'There will be other nights, I suppose.'

'*Will* there be? *Will* there, Marcus? The old man will be coming home soon.'

The Argyll Rooms were open each evening except Sunday for dancing from half past eight to midnight. Florence and Marcus had arrived at nine, and despite his promise to leave shortly after Blandings joined them, they were among those dancers who had to be urged to leave the rooms at five minutes past midnight. By that time, Blandings was very drunk, and the two women had struck up one of those sudden intense friendships that are conceived in champagne and born out of shared calamities. Throughout the evening Marcus had been very quiet.

The next day, when he came to call for her, he found Florence dressed in a very simple gown and old boots. She had some calls to make, some debts were owed, she said. She had a friend who must be living on air pie. Marcus must take her to see Lil Crane without delay. They drove to the neighbourhood of Florence's former lodging house and walked down back streets, peeping into filthy courtyards until Florence found a familiar face. She asked the whereabouts of Lil and was told she had died the day before.

Following directions, they found Lil's former home, a basement that smelt so strongly of excrement, Marcus had difficulty breathing. Eight or nine women and children were sitting or lying down in the room which had no furniture whatsoever. Several of the children had cranial deformities or the wizened look of old men and women. Marcus was no doctor, but he was much in his father's company and had been the unwilling eaves-dropper on many a medical discussion. These children, Marcus knew, carried the taint of syphilis and were doomed to short, pain-filled lives.

He felt suddenly fearful for Florence, foreseeing the horrible end and the suffering that would inevitably be hers if she carried on in her present ways. He hustled her from the basement before she heard answers to her questions about Lil, and the pauper's grave which would be the old whore's final resting place.

Florence protested, but was too borne down by grief and shock to resist. Marcus drove them in his carriage out into the country where the air was clean and women like Lil Crane seemed no more than a bad dream.

Later, they dined well at a country inn and returned early to Paddington so that Florence could be taken through her lessons at length. She concentrated hard on the questions asked her, and was furious with herself whenever she gave a wrong answer.

After two hours, Marcus closed the books, folded his hands on the plush tablecloth and looked sternly at the girl. 'Surely the terrible scene you witnessed today has convinced you that your way of life will lead you to the same end. Florence, I beg you to save yourself.'

'Not all whores end in the gutter, Marcus, but nearly all seamstresses do. You are a fool if you think the good is always rewarded and the bad punished. And yes, I do know I made a mistake: the good *are* always rewarded, I should have said. But I'm not paying you any more fines because I need the money. I intend to make sure I never end up the way poor Lil did.'

She stood up and went over to her new needlework box, a present from Marcus. 'You said you can't meet me tomorrow, because your father is coming home and you must speak to him. Well, this is as good a time as any to give you these.' She turned round, holding a pair of embroidered bedroom slippers in her hands.

'Florence – '

'This is to say thank you for teaching me so much. I'm going to need all the educating I can get. They're also to show you that I do appreciate the needlework box. I don't always read, you see, when I am alone. I can sew if I need to. Here, take them.'

Marcus turned the slippers over and over, studying the bright colours on the upper side: a blue background with the letters M and B picked out in yellow. They were the sort of slippers that have no heel.

Anger made his hands unsteady and coarsened his voice as he thanked her. Anger at the waste, the throwing away of a life. He could not think of Florence lying unclothed by Wainwright's side without feeling hideously sick. He wanted to strike her for her stupidity, or take her in his arms and protect her for ever, to shout or cry, to destroy with his bare hands the room in which they stood. But most of all, he wanted to go back to the moment when he had first seen her in his father's house. Had he known what was to come, he would have picked her up and taken her far away. Now it was too late. She could not return to her pure state; he could not forgive.

'As I have told you,' he said roughly, 'I must speak with my father tomorrow. However, I will call upon you the day after tomorrow at the usual time.'

'I wish you didn't hate me,' she whispered.

Marcus turned away quickly, before he forgot himself and told her some small part of what he actually felt.

22

A letter arrived for Marjory two days after she returned to Cavendish Place. It had been posted in Yorkshire and forwarded from Feldlands.

'*Madam,*' it began. '*I find myself unable to decipher your recent letter. I do not know what a four flusher is. I have no idea why you should castigate me as a snake in the grass. Can it be that you think I told Caroline you were the Jezebel who made advances to her drunken husband? I assure you it is not so. I was never in any doubt about how you happened to be pinned to a tree that night. The woman in question is of a distinguished lineage who has long since been disowned by her unfortunate husband.*

'*You have many faults: intemperate speech, a tendency to jump to ludicrous conclusions and faulty grammer are three that come readily to mind. I cannot conceive of your throwing yourself at any man, however, least of all the husband of your dearest friend.*

'*When I return to London, I shall call upon you to receive your abject and unreserved apology. Until then, I remain*

'*Your humble servant,*
Frederick Bennett.'

Marjory clasped the letter to her bosom, wanting to laugh and cry at the same time. All was well. Frederick was a comfortable man to quarrel with, but certain subjects were not joking matters. It was important to know that he could not think she had an interest in any other man. She counted the days until his return.

In truth, she had very little else to do. Mary Beth never left the house, but on the other hand, refused to speak to her mother. When Marjory had endured enough of this treatment, she sent for her daughter and demanded that Mary Beth pull herself together. In response, she received such a torrent of tears, recriminations, regrets and expressions of self-loathing that she wished she had never spoken at all.

This outburst did seem to mark a turning point, however. Mother and daughter managed a visit to the shops in Regent Street the very next day. Unfortunately, every single shop, according to Mary Beth, stocked only shoddy, tasteless articles that no woman of sense would purchase. Following this outing, Mary Beth announced that she would be taking a daily constitutional walk, accompanied only by her maid. Marjory began to look forward to the two hours each day when she was alone in the house. She thought she had never been so completely demoralized in her whole life, and took to lecturing the hapless Perks on the evils of a household composed entirely of women.

Frederick Bennett had been away for so long he had forgotten about his disagreement with Marcus. The two men shook hands warmly when Bennett walked into the library of his Harley Street home shortly before five o'clock in the afternoon.

'Father, how good to have you home again! There must be two dozen messages for you lying on your desk, but I hope you will not look at them just yet. The tea has arrived.'

'Yes, just what I want. Always pleasant to return to one's home and sleep in one's own bed.' Bennett sat down on the chesterfield with a happy sigh. 'And I am looking forward to a good dinner prepared by Mrs Davis,' he added to the butler as the silver tea service was set before him.

'A pair of grouse and cabinet pudding, sir,' answered Davis with a smile. 'We have missed you, Mr Bennett.'

Marcus poured the tea, putting the milk in last as

his father preferred. There were watercress sandwiches and three kinds of cake.

'I suppose it is inevitable that you were a great deal in the company of Lady Manton, Father.'

Bennett bristled. 'She is a fine lady with a lively mind. I enjoy her company, as does the countess. Why aren't you eating? Are you ill?'

'No, sir. I am perfectly well.' Marcus took a sandwich on to his plate. 'I am a little surprised to see how thoroughly you have overcome your prejudice against Americans.'

'I never had any such thing, and you know it. I do not entertain prejudices.'

Marcus smiled slightly. 'Sir, I know, or think I know, that Lady Manton's happiness is of some importance to you. Please, sir – ' He raised a hand for silence. 'Let me finish what I intend to say. Disturbing rumours have come to my ears about Miss Mary Beth Hanson and a certain young man named Dundalk.'

'The devil you say! Who told you? How widely have these rumours spread?'

'In truth, Jeremy seems to be the author of them. I told him quite firmly that he was to speak to no one but me on the subject.'

'Quite right. You did well to say that, Marcus. I am indebted to you. The young man would hardly be my choice, but he is an engaging person and preferable, I think, to Lucius Falkner.'

Marcus poured himself another cup of tea. 'I wonder if you will be of the same opinion when you have heard what I have to say. First of all, Falkner's reputation has been growing by leaps and bounds. Some allegorical painting of his has just fetched a thousand guineas at Agnew's gallery. It is my opinion that Miss Hanson was very foolish to throw him over. Perhaps, if his heart were truly engaged, it is not too late – '

'Out of the question. He was never keen. It is my

belief he was attracted to her money, which he no longer needs. Let it be, Marcus. It is not our business whom Miss Hanson marries.'

'I can't let it rest there, sir. I must tell you that Dundalk insinuated himself into the home of Lady Manton some months ago and proposed building, with her money, the Lady Marjory Refuge for Fallen Women. He has had three hundred pounds from her, but there is no refuge nor ever will be.'

Bennett closed his eyes and massaged his forehead for some time. Marcus waited, not even breaking the silence by lifting his cup.

'How did he insinuate himself into lady Manton's home?'

'Jeremy gave him a letter of introduction.'

'This is a calamity. Jeremy could have done himself irreparable harm. Tell me. Did he . . . ?'

'I'm sure Jeremy knew nothing about Dundalk's plans, sir.'

'I had a suspicion Dundalk was a scoundrel all along. I should have said something. You say Jeremy has no part in the deception? I must believe you. I *must*.' Bennett stood up wearily. 'I will have to see Lady Manton at once.'

'Perhaps tomorrow, Father'

'No, now. But I will dine here with you, of course.' The doctor turned at the doorway. 'And precisely how did Jeremy meet this trickster?'

Marcus looked away. 'I don't know. I presume he concocted some tale and fooled Jeremy, just as he did Lady Manton.'

Bennett chose to be satisfied with that answer. Pausing only to pick up his hat and gloves, he walked the short distance to Marjory's home and pulled the bell half a dozen times before Brogan could reach the door. The butler showed Bennett into the drawing-room, where Marjory very soon joined him.

'Frederick, how nice to see you! I missed you. I'm ready to make that apology now. Shall I get down on my knees?'

There was no answering smile. Bennett's face was grave as he took both her hands in his. 'A silly misunderstanding. You have had so much to try you lately, my dear. And my visit today is as a bearer of sad tidings. You must brace yourself.'

'What is it? Is Mary Beth . . . but no, it can't be her. She's upstairs, safe and sound. It's Samuel.'

'No, no. Nothing like that. Dundalk is a scoundrel, a rogue. He has tricked you out of hundreds of pounds for some damned fool refuge. How could you, Marjory? Why didn't you tell me about it? I never thought you would keep such a secret from me.'

'Just a minute,' she said. 'You say he tricked me? There isn't going to be a Lady Marjory Refuge? But I've seen a photograph of the building!'

'Have you visited it?'

'No. It's on Seven Dials street. I could have – '

'There is no such thing as Seven Dials *Street*. Seven streets converge at a place called Seven Dials. There used to be a monument, but it's long since been pulled down. If Dundalk had really opened a refuge in that area, he would have named the exact street. Did it never occur to you that this man was lying to you?'

'Well, yes, I did wonder. But I put it to the back of my mind, because I didn't want it to be true. Haven't you ever put something to the back of your mind?'

'Of course not. I'm afraid that is a very feminine attitude. I meet each awkward problem the instant it arises. That is why I am here. You must confront this man as soon as possible and demand the return of your money.'

'You must be mistaken. He's due here at any moment. He requested an interview and I told him to come about five o'clock. Mary Beth goes for a long walk at this time every day so that she won't be at home in case I have any callers, not that anyone does call. All my friends are in the country, it seems.'

'I'll wait until he arrives. This is too great a burden for you to face on your own. I have the deepest sympathy for you, Marjory. If Marcus caused me one tenth the heartache your daughter causes you, I should be quite worn down.'

'I am quite worn down. But, Frederick, I do understand why Mary Beth is so unhappy. She has been most deeply hurt. Can you not sympathize with her terrible loss of confidence? She loves Guy, I'm sure of it, but she won't allow his name to be mentioned.'

'She cannot marry a scoundrel who has cheated her own mother.' He stroked his beard thoughtfully. 'On the other hand, she must marry her seducer.'

The doorbell rang. Marjory and Bennett heard footsteps on the stairs: the door opened, Brogan announced Dundalk and the young man strode in, looking very grim.

'Good afternoon, Mr Bennett. Lady Marjory, I must speak to you privately.'

'If it is about the three hundred pounds you have induced Lady Manton to give you, I know all about it,' said Bennett. Dundalk's face was suddenly very pale.

'I'm told that you have cheated me out of the three hundred pounds I gave you in order to establish a refuge for fallen women,' said Marjory softly.

'Yes, ma'am.' Dundalk turned to Bennett. 'I took the money and speculated on the exchange with it.'

'And lost it all, I suppose,' said the doctor.

'No, Mr Bennett. I have made a profit. I am returning your three hundred pounds, Lady Marjory.' He held a wad of notes out to her.

'Aha,' said Bennett. 'But you would not have given

her the money if she had not found out about your deception.'

'That's not true – ' began Dundalk hotly, but he got no further.

The drawing-room door opened and Mary Beth walked in, still wearing her hat and gloves. 'Why, what a guilty-looking trio,' she said sarcastically. 'What destruction are you all plotting for me now?' She advanced into the room, her heavy brows drawn toge- ther, her mouth set in an ugly slash. Only happiness gave Mary Beth the illusion of beauty. At this moment, she looked haggard and mannish.

'Mary Beth,' said Dundalk. 'I came to return three hundred pounds I tricked your mother into giving me to set up a refuge for fallen women. I am ashamed of what I have done. I apologize to you both. I love you, Mary Beth, and I still want to marry you.'

'Well, that's just – ' began Marjory.

'A likely story,' said Bennett gruffly. 'If Marcus had not told me of the deception, this rogue might never have – '

He got no further. 'Marcus told you? Must I now have my life directed by your son?' said Marjory.

'How did Marcus find out?' cried Mary Beth. 'How many more people are going to take a hand in my personal affairs?'

'The informant must have been Jeremy Grimshaw.' Dundalk wore the sad smile that told Marjory he had been profoundly hurt by his friend's betrayal.

'My godson felt honour-bound to inform Marcus once he knew the two of you were . . . involved.'

Marjory began pacing the floor. 'Hey, I just thought of something. I would never have let Guy through the door that day if he hadn't had a letter of introduction from Mr Grimshaw. He must have known what you planned, Guy.'

Dundalk smiled more broadly, but said nothing. The

doctor would not have it. Jeremy could not have known, would not have been a party to such a deceitful act. Jeremy was a gentleman by training, inclination and breeding.

'Undeniably so,' said Dundalk.

'Never mind that now.' Marjory came to a halt by the others. 'The important thing is, only I have been deceived. And I don't mind a bit. I forgive you, Guy. Let's say no more about it.'

'He's a rogue!' expostulated Bennett.

'How could I marry a man who cheated my own mother?' said Mary Beth. 'I never want to see him again, Momma. Tell him not to urge me to marry him.'

'The offer is no longer open,' said Dundalk. 'Excuse me, I must be going. I have other people to cheat.'

The doctor hooked his thumbs in his waistcoat pockets. 'Good riddance, I think.'

'Oh, yes, Mr Bennett,' said Mary Beth nastily. 'I must not consider marrying until your son gives his approval.'

Guy was on his way down the stairs towards the front door. Mary Beth now left the drawing-room and Marjory and Bennett could hear her running up to her bedroom on the second floor.

'I hope you know this is all your fault, Frederick Bennett.' Marjory put her hands on her hips like a washerwoman. 'You are the most interfering man I have ever met. I didn't need to be told what your son had found out. And I don't need your godson sending me scoundrels. Don't tell me he had nothing to do with this business, because I won't believe it.'

'You are mistaken about Jeremy, and I feel sure you are mistaken about me. However, I will not stay here to be insulted. Goodbye, Marjory. When you come to your senses, send for me.'

Within two minutes, Marjory was entirely alone, standing in the middle of the drawing-room floor and wondering what sort of catastrophe had just struck her. Brogan opened the door.

'Shall I bring you some tea, m'lady?'

'No, thank you.' She sat down on a nearby chair. 'I'd rather have a glass of port.'

'There is no port, m'lady. The doctor drank the last of it and you said not to order any more. I'm sure I can't help it if I have not been given the order to buy more port.'

Marjory took a deep breath. She really mustn't argue with her butler. It would require far more energy than she possessed at the moment. 'Then bring me a glass of madeira, or brandy or whatever you have. I need a restorative, Brogan. Surely you can find something.'

Brogan bowed himself out gloomily. She leaned back in the chair and closed her eyes. 'I actually used to wish I'd had six children,' she said to the walls. 'Now I think I've had two too many.'

Bennett could not stay away. The day he did not see Marjory was incomplete. The following afternoon when he was shown into her drawing-room, he found the blinds drawn against the hot summer day. The windows had been opened to catch any stray gust of breeze, but this only increased the bad-tempered noises of the crowded street below.

Marjory was wearing a lavender tea-gown, loose and diaphanous. Even in this faint light, he could see she was distressed.

'Frederick, I've decided that in view of our happy relationship wth Mr Grimshaw in the past, and my fondness for his mother, we'll say no more about the incident we discussed last night.'

'A wise move,' said Bennett. 'You won't regret it, I'm sure.'

'Yes, well, I've got other matters on my mind right now. The Lady Marjory Refuge.'

270

'Forget about it. You have no business involving yourself with prostitutes. It is unseemly.'

'No, I won't forget. I must do something. Don't try to talk me out of this.'

'If you are feeling in a generous mood, then give the money to the Islington Dispensary. Money is desperately needed to treat our poor patients, but the public does not care. No one wants to think about my speciality. Syphilis is taboo as a subject of discussion, even among men. The result is, we cannot raise sufficient funds from the public. I can never understand why people turn their backs on the unpleasant truths of modern life. This disease causes untold distress to the victims and their families, yet you would think it didn't exist.'

'I will give money to your dispensary, but I've got to do more. I thought if I could gather up a few of the younger clever girls and have them trained to use typewriters – '

'That, my dear, is an absurd idea. How would you find such creatures, anyway? By walking the streets yourself?'

Marjory sighed. 'I see I'm going to have to tell you a few things about my past. Oh, don't look at me like that. It's got nothing to do with ladies of the night. Back when the war began, there was hardly anybody to help the wounded soldiers. So many of them just died right there on the battlefield, maybe hours after the battle was over. And, you know, many of those men could have lived. The armies got better organized, of course. People learn. Well, this St Louis surgeon, Dr Eliot (you see, we call our surgeons "doctor") well, Dr William Eliot founded the Western Sanitary Commission in St Louis to care for the sick and wounded. I thought I ought to go and help like some other women I knew were doing.'

'It would have been most inappropriate.'

'That's what Jonathan said. The war was still going on when he died, however. I thought since I was a widow, it would be a good thing to help out a little. This time it was my daddy who said no. You know me, or you should do by now. I didn't let that stop me. I snuck off and went down there, anyway. Frederick, I tell you, there were men everywhere screaming or groaning or lying there pale as death. One of them actually died while I was in the ward. A sixteen-year-old-boy. I never went back, but it wasn't just because of the suffering I saw. It was the *smell*. Sometimes, when I'm sitting alone in the conservatory here in London, I fancy I can smell that place all over again . . .'

'You shouldn't blame yourself for being unable to face such conditions. Most people can't.'

'But I *do* blame myself. I failed. I fell below the standards I set for myself, and I can't forget it. Why, that's the only reason I let Gilbert talk me into selling the store and travelling to England. It wasn't really for the sake of the children at all. It was to get away from St Louis and the memories of my cowardice. It hasn't worked, of course.'

'My dear, you must put these thoughts from your head. You have brought up two fine children and you obviously made a considerable contribution to the family fortune. That is enough.'

'I don't care what I've done. It's what I *didn't* do that haunts me. For heaven's sake, Frederick! Haven't you ever felt like that?'

He started to say no, but his memory played a cruel trick on him, and he found himself reliving an incident so terrible that he had expunged it from his mind for almost twenty-five years.

December, 1850. Thinking about it now, Bennett could still see the coal fire that glowed in the grate of the master bedroom, still feel its warmth upon his cheeks.

Sophia was in labour, and at first the pains were not severe. The accoucheur had been sent for. Bennett sat beside the bed, holding Sophia's hand and occasionally looking at his watch. Time passed, the pains became more severe and more frequent. Still the accoucheur had not arrived. It was only when the pains were coming at five-minute intervals, that Bennett stood up and removed his coat, slightly breathless in the heat of the room, aware of a nagging anxiety.

He was thirty-one years old and had not assisted at a birth since his apprentice days in hospital. In spite of his lack of confidence in himself, he dared not delay. He would have to examine Sophia to see how far the first stage had progressed. This was her fourth pregnancy, but she was in a highly nervous state, desperate for another child. They had buried two sons within the past three years and had only four-year-old Marcus left to them. Anxious as she was, Sophia did not want her husband to examine her; it was not right. The accoucheur would be with them soon. Frederick must not touch her.

Precious minutes were wasted in arguing, minutes he used to pare his nails and remove his signet ring. As Sophia continued to protest, he looked at his square-fingered hands. He was a good surgeon, but he had not the long, slender *main d'accoucheur* so esteemed by both the profession and patients.

Despite his lack of practice, he was readily able to palpate the partly dilated cervix. He felt, to his horror, within the intact membranes, a pulsating cord below the presenting part of the foetus. Sophia, who knew him so well, read the shock on his face.

'What is it, Frederick? What's wrong?'

He didn't answer, but placed his hands on her abdomen and found that he was dealing with a malpresentation, the foetus lying transversely in the uterus with one shoulder presenting at the cervix. He turned

273

away, gulping air. His tongue was sticking to the roof of his mouth, his pulse pounding so fiercely in his temples that Sophia's repeated cries for enlightenment reached him as if from a distance. Breathing too rapidly and too deeply, he tried to fight off the debilitating panic.

What to do? Slow down the labour, that was the thing. He prepared fifteen minims of tincture of opium and bullied her into drinking it, still refusing to explain what was wrong. Unable, really, to trust his voice. What else could he do to slow the progress of labour? Gravity: he decided to relieve the pressure of the weight of the foetus on the membranes and cervix, in the hope that the presenting cord would fall back within the uterine cavity. Otherwise, when the second stage began, the presenting part of the foetus would descend and squeeze the cord against the pelvic wall.

Some wooden blocks had been prepared for the legs at the foot of the bed. He put these in place, then heaved poor Sophia on to the knee-elbow position, knowing that she could not possibly maintain it for more than fifteen minutes. He prayed the accoucheur would arrive before it was necessary to return her to her back.

He paced the floor, not really hearing Sophia's distressed cries. When he could stand it no more, he went out into the hall to shout down the stairs. He was told the nurse had taken Marcus for a walk. Not only had the accoucheur not arrived, but the manservant who had been sent to fetch him, had not returned. Bennett swore, wondering if the good-for-nothing fellow had ever reached the home of the accoucheur at all.

He returned to the bedroom and laid Sophia gently on her back, before giving her another dose of opium. Too much, too soon, but he didn't know what else to do, except, of course, to attempt to turn the child.

Now he was in a blind panic, knowing that he must

perform a manoeuvre he had never attempted before. He placed both hands on her abdomen and tried to manipulate the child first into the head-down position, then into the breech position.

Suddenly, the membranes ruptured and the second stage began. It was too late; he knew the child would die. If the accoucheur did not arrive soon, Sophia would die also. His dear wife, with whom he had shared so many joys and sorrows, was beyond his help. As the poor woman lay in agony, now too busy with the contractions to speak at all, he sat down in a chair, put his head in his hands and cried.

A moment or two later, the accoucheur burst into the room, strode across to Sophia, and with soothing words of comfort, examined her.

Bennett was on his feet. 'The baby is – '

'Get out, sir. Go on. I have work to do. I can't have you here,' said the accoucheur over his shoulder.

Although he had been incapable of performing the operation, indeed, did not have the necessary instruments, Bennett knew just what grisly outrage would be perpetrated against his dead child in order to save Sophia's life. He went to the library. While the accoucheur worked frantically, while Sophia fought for her life, Bennett drank to stupefaction.

Sophia survived, but the death of the infant did not unite them in grief. They sorrowed separately: she convinced that had he not interfered, the child would have been born healthy; he convinced that had he interfered to greater purpose, the child might have been saved. Resentment and regret grew between them until they could scarcely find any safe topic of conversation.

Another pregnancy would have undoubtedly proved fatal; she wouldn't even allow him to share her bed. And so Bennett had taken a succession of mistresses over the years. Always obsessed by their health and afraid that they had gone with other men in his absence, he had come to them in shame. Even after Sophia had reached an early menopause and the mechanics of the marriage bed were restored, they never again experienced the loving relationship they had once enjoyed.

All of this he had put from his mind for twenty-four and a half years. They had never discussed the pain they caused each other, never attempted to talk away the anger that separated them. Marjory would not have endured such an arrangement, he thought now. She would have spoken, would have insisted that they clear the air.

Bennett, ever the reserved Englishman, was not so sure of the wisdom of such openness. The benefits of continual self-examination were limited. Better to forget, to put from one's mind all that interfered with the performance of one's work. How could he have continued to practice medicine if he had beat upon his breast and brooded about the day when panic had all but paralysed him? That was not to say he didn't understand Marjory's need at the moment.

Marjory was watching him closely, her hands clasping his own. He didn't remember her reaching out to him, so completely had he returned to the past. Now, he gave her hands an answering pressure.

'Are you all right?' she asked. 'Do you want to tell me what is upsetting you?'

He shook himself free of the old memories, and spoke briskly. 'You wish to make amends, an understandable attitude. Well, my dear, you won't achieve it by purchasing typewriters for young women. I propose that we build a refuge for diseased destitute prostitutes, the ones who have grown ugly and weak in the practice of their profession. No one cares about their suffering, especially as they tend to be an unrepentant lot. Some of them suffer grievously from arthritis, you know. Those women would appreciate whatever money and time you are prepared to spend on them. Their only wish is to live out their days in warmth and peace. We will make it a joint venture, you and I. I shall help to fund it.

Marjory was delighted. They set to work immediately, looking for suitable premises and staff. Bennett even allowed himself to be dragged to a meeting organized by the supporters of Josephine Butler.

'You don't understand the issues at all,' he had told Marjory before the meeting.

'I understand how any woman would feel degraded by the kind of examination these poor women suffer. It's rape. I'd rather die than have it.'

'A woman with syphilis passes the disease on to her new-born infant. Thousands of innocent babies die of syphilis. Wouldn't a simple examination, a little embarrassment, be worthwhile if it prevented such a thing? Respectable people, especially women, refuse to be told the truth about the disease, but we might stamp it out by rigorous attention to prostitutes and – '

'By examining women and leaving the wicked men alone.'

'Who told you that? In garrison towns and ports, soldiers and sailors are examined regularly.'

After the meeting, Bennett changed his mind, and became a firm advocate of reform of the existing law. Marjory, on the other hand, felt that women themselves must change their attitudes. The two agreed to differ, discussed the subject endlessly, and failed to take notice of their children's activities.

Marcus wrote to Mary Beth asking for a secret meeting. They settled on an upper-class rendezvous, Gunter's tea shop in Berkeley Square. The shop sold excellent ice creams and sorbets, but it was not considered proper for a lady to meet a gentleman in places of refreshment. The custom was for ices to be brought out to a lady's carriage where she and a gentleman could eat them in the shade of the trees in the square. At three o'clock, Marcus managed to get himself and two lemon sorbets into Mary Beth's closed carriage, and the coachman was sent off for his own refreshment.

Mary Beth was dressed in one of her finest blue carriage gowns and had taken great care with her elaborate hairstyle. Nevertheless, she looked unkempt. Her skin was sallow, her expression morose. The square was crowded, and every time someone laughed, she winced.

Marcus was also impeccably turned out. He dressed conservatively, and always studied himself carefully in the cheval mirror before leaving his dressing room, anxious lest he display signs of dandyism or slovenliness. He sat well back in the coach, for fear one of his acquaintances would see him in Mary Beth's company and draw an incorrect conclusion. It would have been difficult to persuade him that no one cared in the least whom he might meet.

'I felt strongly that I must apologize to you, Miss Hanson, for interfering in your affairs. Naturally, at the time, I was thinking only of your mother's welfare.'

Mary Beth's lips curled slightly as she set her empty dish on the seat beside her. 'Is that a fact? Momma could have afforded to lose three hundred pounds. Anyway, Guy came that very day to pay her back. It's easy for you to sneer. Guy didn't have your advantages. He has had to make his own way in the world.'

'I presume, nevertheless, that he knows right from wrong.'

'And Mr Grimshaw,' added Mary Beth. 'Does *he* know right from wrong?'

Marcus shook his head. 'No, he doesn't and never has. My father loves him dearly for some reason. I couldn't expose him.'

'More than you?'

'I beg your pardon?'

'Does you father love Mr Grimshaw more than he loves you?'

Marcus shrugged. 'Love can't be quantified. Father feels comfortable with Jeremy, who is more receptive to his advice than I have ever been. However, I did not come here to discuss myself. You must be very relieved to have discovered Dundalk's true nature in time. I advise you not to let your mother force you into marriage with him. Polite society would be closed to you for ever.'

Mary Beth smiled broadly, but it was an ugly smile. 'You don't say? You have never been in love, have you, Mr Bennett?'

'I hope one day – '

'It's a painful business, a glorious sickness. Until I fell in love with Guy, I was only half-alive. I blush to think what a selfish idiot I was.'

'You make it sound most unpleasant.'

Mary Beth leaned back in the carriage and surveyed him mockingly. 'Tell the truth now. Hasn't your heart ever ached for anyone? Haven't you ever found yourself incapable of going about your daily business, because you can't think about anything but kissing a loved one?'

'That's disgusting! I hope I am a decent man who has his animal instincts under control.'

Mary Beth laughed. 'You are blushing, sir. I do believe you have experienced the very emotion I've described.'

'There are many things to be considered. One has responsibilities. A man must think carefully about his future. He must choose his companion of a lifetime with care.' He leaned towards her, now on the attack. 'That's all beside the point. If you really love your scoundrel, why don't you marry him?'

To Marcus's embarrassment, Mary Beth's eyes filled with tears. 'He has withdrawn his proposal.'

'The bounder.'

'Besides he betrayed me. I hate him now and will never forgive him.' She picked up her empty dish and spoon and held them out to him. 'Thank you for the sorbet. I accept your apology. Good day, Mr Bennett.'

Marcus left the carriage more gracefully than he had entered it. As he crossed the road to Gunter's, he thought about Mary Beth Hanson: broad-shouldered, tall, positive in everything she did. A woman who hadn't really listened to a word he said, hadn't recognized his greater worldliness. She had even turned the tables on him and spoken to him as if he were some red-eared schoolboy.

Unbidden, the image of Florence floated before his mind's eye, and he was nearly run down by a bay horse pulling a sporting cart. He pictured Florence and Mary Beth standing side by side, and found the prostitute superior in every way. He shook his head as if to dislodge Florence from his mind as he handed the dishes to a waiter. Glorious sickness, indeed! Miss Hanson was totally abandoned. Florence would not dream of speaking in such a flamboyant manner. Florence was reserved and dignified. And, what was more, Florence listened to everything he said and took his advice when it was offered.

Marcus began walking in the direction of his home. Miss Hanson made him feel very uncomfortable. If Florence had made him feel like that, he would never have taken her away from the introducing house. He sucked in his breath painfully at the very thought. What would have happened to the poor girl if he had not come to her rescue that night?

23

Warren Wainwright was pleased to be returning to London from the country. He and his wife had been forced to spend so much time in the company of one another that the domestic truce of some years' standing had broken down completely. During the final week in Monmouth, they had quarrelled almost continually.

As soon as he returned to the capital, he retreated to his club and would shortly be enjoying the company of fellow politicians at the House of Commons. He was also looking forward to seeing Florence again. She was immature and feather-headed, but that didn't spoil the pleasure he took in her. To his surprise, the knowledge that she disliked making love to him only increased his own desire. But Florence was a pleasure for the hours of darkness. First, in the late afternoon, he paid a visit to the man he thought of as his protégé: Lucius Falkner.

Falkner was in the process of moving to a large detached house in St John's Wood when Wainwright arrived unannounced.

'Wainwright, old fellow!' said Falkner familiarly. He ushered his guest past tea chests and stacks of framed pictures in the entrance hall to the comparative peace and order of his study. The artist looked pale and had lost weight. There were rumours about his health. Wainwright was determined to keep his distance.

'I hear you spoken of everywhere,' said Wainwright, smiling broadly. 'I believe you recently sold a painting to Lord Cramphorn for a thousand pounds.'

'Guineas, not pounds. So much more satisfying, don't you think?' Falkner leaned against a pine chest and took his time lighting a stubby cigarette. 'And do you know? I owe all my success to Mr Bennett, the surgeon.'

'I say, what has he ever done for you? It's not Bennett who has been assiduous in mentioning your name in all the right places.'

'I beg your pardon,' said Falkner. 'You have been a patron and friend in the truest sense of the word. I would not be able to move to my new house if it weren't for you. No, Mr Bennett was, shall we say, the spur. Or perhaps a better analogy would be that he was the grain of sand within my shell that irritated me into creating a pearl. The man disliked me, although we have since become good friends. But he does not understand artists at all and hates my paintings. Nevertheless, remarks of his, uttered almost in anger, caused me to look at my work and subject matter in a totally different way. Strange, but these are the sort of random sparks that set the creative genius in motion.'

Wainwright did not believe in random sparks any more than he believed in Falkner's creative genius, so he changed the subject.

'Picked up a book this morning. Got it from a friend. Here, take a look. It's called *The Romance of Lust*. Great stuff, eh?'

Falkner frowned over the pages for a moment. 'This is filth.'

'Yes. Rather good, what?'

The artist closed the book and looked at Wainwright, who was rummaging through a pile of discarded photographs. Falkner was very angry. Recent successes had given him a new vision of himself: as a gentleman artist. The small erotic (hardly lewd) sketches he had been prepared to draw and sell to Wainwright's friends in the recent past were merely the necessary means to an end. Now that his reputation was established, he would gladly buy back every one of them if he could. He had a secret ambition, a devout hope that he might be called upon to paint one of the royal ladies. Wainwright, it now occurred to him for the first time, was a disgusting old man. Falkner would have to sever the connection as soon as possible. The politician had served his purpose.

'What I mean is, the book has no literary merit. The writer is without talent.' He stared at Wainwright suspiciously. 'I hope you don't think I produce the pictorial equivalent of this rubbish. I am an artist. I paint women in various poses to express certain ideas. If those men who view my work – '

'Don't be offended, old chap. You are a true artist. Nevertheless, a man's imagination can be stimulated by a badly written book as easily as by a good painting, don't you think? What are you planning to do with these photographs?'

'They are to be burned. I suppose you heard what happened to that photographer, Hayler, last year. The police raided his home and took away over a hundred thousand lewd photographs. I cannot risk my reputation by having the pictures you are holding fall into the hands of the police. Not that there is any comparison. I took those pictures as a record, as studies from which to paint.'

Wainwright laughed. 'I believe you, although the authorities might not.'

Wainwright handed Falkner a photograph of a hollow-cheeked girl of about sixteen looking sly as she sat on a water closet. She was wearing a camisole top and drawers that covered her knees, black stockings and shoes. There was nothing really erotic about the clothing or the pose. The photograph derived its impact solely from the fact that the cistern and chain were visible above the girl's head. Falkner had thought it very daring at the time. He opened a drawer in the chest and shoved the photograph well to the back. There were others to be burned, but he would not search for them until after Wainwright had left. The man had shown altogether too much interest in the picture. His leering smile and habit of continually wetting his lips made Falkner feel sick.

The MP stayed for a quarter of an hour, full of good health and enthusiasm for almost anything; a tiring companion. When he was alone at last, Falkner sat down in an armchair and prodded his aching jaw. Bennett had visited him a few hours earlier and confirmed that he was suffering from mild mercurial poisoning. The treatment must be suspended.

'Mild poisoning!' had said Falkner furiously. His breath stank, his teeth were all loose and he could not control his saliva. He felt wretched and had been unable to work at all for the past week. He had told the doctor he would not resume the treatment. He had no guaranteed income as some men had. He must work to live, and mercury poisoning, no matter how mild, made it impossible for him to paint. Unfortunately, he had already made arrangements to move to St John's Wood. He knew he should have been more cautious with his money. He was haunted by the possibility that he might never paint another successful picture.

Bennett had been most understanding. Falkner had not imagined the man could be so kind. The artist had been urged to grit his teeth and complete the treatment. Bennett had warned of the consequences of failing to do so.

Falkner had been adamant. The disease could not be worse than the cure. He would face the threat of madness at some other time. It might not happen to him, after all. For every man he knew who had suffered dreadfully from the disease, he knew of another who was leading a healthy life.

Remembering Bennett's worried expression, his words of sympathy, Falkner now smiled. Who would have thought the stiff-rumped old curmudgeon could be so friendly? Nevertheless, he would not allow the rubber to come to him ever again. Falkner gingerly passed a hand along the angle of his jaw, closed his eyes and tried to rest. He was very tired. He would continue packing later, when he felt a little stronger.

Other business prevented Wainwright from reaching Florence's apartment until well after nine o'clock. He didn't knock, but used his key to let himself in. Florence, in a loose muslin tea gown, and Marcus Bennett, in his shirtsleeves, had apparently jumped to their feet at the sound of his key in the lock, and now stared at him guiltily. Spread out on the table was a pack of cards and a cribbage board.

'Hello, Warren. How nice to see you again', said Florence faintly. The bright red patches on her cheeks, her rigid pose and unsmiling lips made a liar of her.

Her feelings towards him were no surprise to Wainwright. He was far more interested in Marcus Bennett's reaction. He read hatred in those blue eyes, and was amused. Shutting the door quietly, he smiled at them.

'Well, well. How cosy and informal we all are. It is a hot night, Marcus. How right you were to take off your jacket. I'll do the same. You two have become well-acquainted in my absence, I gather.'

'I have not – ' began Marcus.

'No? Oh dear, how unenterprising of you, my dear fellow. I assure you, all that I have is yours. I draw the line at my wife, of course. But on second thoughts, if you really feel the need, perhaps we could even come to an arrangement there.'

'Mr Wainwright, you asked me to look after Florence in your absence and I have attempted to teach her to be – '

Wainwright raised his eyebrows in mock horror. 'Schooled her, eh? What with?'

'I have purchased several books and – '

285

'Oh, I see. I hope you have worked hard and been a good girl, Florence. Otherwise, I might have to school you with something longer and more flexible than a book.' Wainwright glanced at Marcus, and almost laughed out loud as the pale young man ground his teeth, yet kept silent. 'However, I don't wish to be churlish. You must stay with us tonight, Marcus. Three can have more pleasure than two, you know.'

Marcus lifted his coat from the back of a chair and folded it across one arm. 'I will not stay, Mr Wainwright, as I'm sure you knew all along. I have not been disloyal to you, and I'm very sorry that you have chosen to make such coarse remarks to me.'

Marcus nodded briefly to the stricken Florence, and bowed his head formally to Wainwright, before leaving the room to the sound of his patron's laughter.

'You can't stay tonight, Warren,' said Florence as soon as the door had closed. 'I'll get out of here tomorrow. I don't care if I starve. I'm not ever going with you again. I'm not going to be a whore any more.'

Wainwright laughed softly as he approached her. 'Look, my dear, Marcus Bennett is a handsome man. I can understand that you have come under his spell, but be sensible. You know the sort of man he is. He would never do for you what I have done.'

'I wouldn't want him to. I tell you, I'm not going to be a whore any more.'

'What do you think will happen to you? You will starve.'

'I don't care.'

Wainwright came forward, took the girl in a bear hug. 'Not just once more for Poppa? Come on, what difference does it make? One more time. After that, you can take until the weekend to find somewhere else to live. I'm not vindictive. If Bennett wants you, we'll say no more about it. But tonight you're mine. I'm

286

tired and I've no intention of going home to my dear, loving wife.'

Florence struggled in his arms and managed to slip away. Wainwright was becoming annoyed. She could see his point of view, she really could. How would he understand that she had been willing all those other times, but not tonight? His expression was ugly. She moved to the door and opened it, ready to fly. But there in the doorway was Marcus, hand raised as if about to knock.

'Florence!' He opened his arms and she fell into them, burying her face in his chest.

'I don't want to ever again, Marcus. Tell him. I'll leave right this minute with only what I brought with me. I don't have to let him, do I?'

Bennett glared over Florence's head at Wainwright. 'She doesn't want to have anything to do with you. I'm taking her away tonight.'

Wainwright took a deep breath, controlling his rising fury. 'You bloody fool! You've filled this girl's head with nonsense. You don't want to keep her, and she'll be on the streets within a week. Do you know what you've done to her? Given her hope. Are you willing to take the responsibility for a whore, my high-minded prig of an assistant?'

'No more insults, Mr Wainwright. I'll look after Florence properly.'

'Your disloyalty while my back was turned makes you unsuitable as an assistant. You'll never get into Parliament. Do you hear? I'll see that you don't!'

'So be it,' said Marcus. 'Now, if you will excuse us, I'll just pack Florence's things. We will leave you in peace shortly.'

Wainwright shifted his weight from one foot to the other and stroked his beard as he watched Marcus and Florence gathering up her possessions.

'Oh, never mind,' he said finally. 'I will leave. Get

her out of here tomorrow morning, Bennett, and pay off the landlady.'

Marcus had a book in his hand. Florence was holding the needlework box. They watched Wainwright leave, and only when the door had closed behind him and they heard his footsteps on the stairs, did they look at one another.

'What's going to become of me?'

Marcus set the book on the table. 'I will look after you, I promise. We will think about what to do for the best tomorrow. We can pack up then. You must be tired. You will want to get some sleep.'

'Marcus!'

He tried to smile, but a muscle had begun twitching in his cheek. 'My dear – '

'Stay with me tonight.'

'No!' It was almost a yelp, a foolish, boylike sound. He tried for a deeper tone of voice. 'My father would be worried if I were to stay out all night.' That statement sounded even more foolish and more boyish. He couldn't trust himself to say more.

'I just don't want to be alone in that big bed. That's all it is. I'm not trying to lead you on or nothing.'

Her exquisite face was golden in the lamplight. Pinpoints of fire flickered in her eyes. 'Your sentiment does you credit,' he croaked.

'As a matter of fact, I don't really like all that . . . that sort of thing.'

'A proper attitude.' Only three words, but he could do no more than whisper them.

Florence suddenly smiled. 'But I think I could enjoy a little kissing.'

He grinned. Two paces closed the distance between them, and he gathered her into his arms. 'What an extraordinary coincidence. I was just thinking the same thing.'

It was four o'clock of a fine September afternoon when Marjory returned to the house to find Mary Beth in the hallway wearing a travelling costume and looking quite beautiful. The girl was positively radiant. Marjory thought: *She's going to marry Guy, after all.* At Mary Beth's suggestion, they went into the drawing-room where they could speak without being overheard.

'Whatever is the matter?' asked Marjory.

'Something serious, Momma. Hard to explain, but you've got to understand! I have just been with Guy. He is in trouble. He sent for me, Momma. I believe by now there will be a warrant out for his arrest. He's on his way to Liverpool and will be sailing for America.'

Marjory clasped her hands together. 'Oh, Lordy, I should have known that young man wouldn't be able to stay out of mischief.'

'You don't understand him.'

'And you do, I suppose.'

'Yes, Momma. He wanted to make a lot of money, for my sake. He didn't want to live off my money, you see.'

'So he'll just live off other people's.'

'Momma, I'm going to get angry in a minute. I've got a lot of things to tell you, and there isn't much time. Here's four hundred pounds. I'm depending on you to pay it back to the rightful owner so he'll drop the charges.'

'Me? Do I know the person? Not the doctor. Don't say it's the doctor.'

'It's Sir Richard le Feyne. He and Guy travelled to London from Feldlands together. He's a very greedy man, always looking for ways of making money while sneering at people like you and me. Guy did it to punish him for the way he talked to us.'

'Did what, for God's sake?'

'Sold him some American railway stock. Well, it wasn't really American railway stock. The shares were forged. Guy knows this man – a dealer in queer, he called him. Anyway, it served le Feyne right, and I don't blame Guy at all.'

'I knew it!' Marjory threw up her hands. 'You all are out to destroy me. That rascal will be safe in America, while you and I will be social outcasts here.'

'Not exactly. I'm going to get on a train this evening. I'm going to Liverpool and I'm hoping that Guy and I will be able to sail on the same ship. If worse comes to worse, I'll follow him.'

'No, baby! No! Tell me you don't mean it. I can't bear it.'

'I'm sorry. I guess I don't belong in England and never did. But neither do you, Momma. Come with us now. Or as soon as we're settled, we'll send for you. We'll always look after you.'

Marjory reached out for a nearby chair, sat down, but stood up again almost immediately. She had brought this girl into the world, thought she knew the way the child's mind worked. They had always been close, sharing everything. Now here came a total stranger, a man Mary Beth had known only for a matter of weeks, and the girl was willing to go off to the ends of the earth with him.

Marjory looked at Mary Beth, memorizing her face, as if it were necessary to make such an effort. Every expression, every inflecion in her voice would be in Marjory's heart for ever.

'No, Mary Beth. I'm sorry, but I'm not going. I've dreaded this moment, the good Lord knows I have. Ever since Samuel left, I've been afraid that one day you would leave me, too. But I'm not going back to America to live on your coat-tails. I've got my own life to live. I like it here. I've found peace of a sort, and friends. Lots of friends. You will do what you feel you have to do. I won't try to stop you. I'm letting you go, as every mother should, some time. But my life is here.

I'll come for a visit one day. I just wish you two had got a special licence and been married before all this happened. I hate to think of you travelling so far all alone.'

With tears in her eyes, Mary Beth hugged her mother. But Marjory knew the girl's mind was already on the future. Mary Beth believed her mother could manage very well on her own. And why not? Hadn't she always given that impression?

'Sit down, Momma, and let me explain our plans. It's so exciting. Don't you see? I won't *be* alone!'

Bennett was at the Islington Dispensary when he received Marjory's note requesting him to come to her urgently, because Mary Beth had eloped. He left the dispensary at once, but decided to go first to his own home where he could have a wash and brush-up before entering Marjory's drawing-room. After all, what was done was done. Mary Beth's action was not entirely unexpected, and under the circumstances, she had probably chosen the best way to marry her rogue. Bennett had never managed to strike up a friendship with the girl. The marriage would solve an important problem for him, remove an obstacle to happiness. When he stepped from his carriage at his front door, he found Jeremy Grimshaw approaching.

'Uncle Frederick, I have some good news for you. You will be pleased with what I have to tell you.'

'My boy, I've no time now. Call round tomorrow afternoon. I'm in a great hurry, you see. But . . .' Bennett put a kindly hand on Jeremy's arm. 'I'm afraid I gave you some bad advice some weeks ago. Or rather, I quoted some bad advice of Acton's. Don't marry where you can't feel passion, Jeremy. Only when a man feels that deepest and most mysterious of emotions for his own wife, can a marriage prosper. You must be prepared to use that fire to – '

291

'But, Uncle, I've already proposed . . . Susannah has agreed to be – '

' – to enable you both to weather the inevitable storms of marriage. Why, spending a lifetime with one woman is difficult enough even when you and she are deeply moved by each other. Never marry where you can't feel the all-powerful urge. Now, you go on your way, Jeremy, and I'll see you here tomorrow.'

Jeremy drew himself up to his full height. 'Uncle Frederick,' he spluttered. 'Sometimes I wish I hadn't tried so hard to please you. You don't seem to know your own mind, if you don't object to my saying so. I don't believe I will call upon you tomorrow. You would only give me some *different* lecture, some different advice, and it's too late, sir, far too late. Good day.'

Jeremy took off down Harley Street at a cracking pace. The doctor, considerably surprised by his godson's cryptic words, watched the boy for a second or two, but he had his mind on other matters.

Bennett was in great spirits these days, feeling proud of himself and his work almost for the first time. Acton was ill, suffering pains in his chest. But that was not why Bennett had begun to exert himself among his colleagues. It just seemed to be happening. He wanted to go indoors and tell Marcus about his latest little triumph, a monograph to be published in the *British Medical Journal*. The title was long, of course: *Syphilitic Lesions of the Osseous System in Infants and Children*. He was extremely proud of the work. The words had seemed to flow from his pen.

The butler opened the door to him, and Bennett tossed his hat and gloves to the surprised man before taking the stairs two at a time.

'Marcus! Are you home?'

The drawing-room door opened: Florence, in an elegant dress of wine silk, stepped out in the hall.

Bennett stopped in surprise. 'My dear girl! How often have I thought of you! Florence, isn't it? Are you well?'

'Yes, sir. Perfectly well, Mr Bennett. I was just waiting for Marcus. We – '

'*Marcus?* You call him Marcus?'

Without waiting for an answer, he ran up the second staircase to the large suite of rooms Marcus had as his own. Bennett found his son gathering up some books. A trunk and several grips stood on the floor.

'Where are you going? What is that whore doing, waiting for you here?'

'Father! You must not speak that way! Florence is my wife.'

'Your wife? Not your wife! Don't say such a thing. Isn't she the girl you procured for Wainwright? You mustn't marry her. We'll get you an annulment. You'll be ruined. Don't you know that? Your career will be finished. How could you marry that whore? When did you marry her?'

'About a week ago. I didn't know how to tell you.'

'I should have talked to you more often, taken an interest in your affairs. But you were always so reserved. You can't be an MP, you know.'

'A career based on procuring women for a lecherous old man was not a career to be pursued, I think. Papa, I beg of you, try to understand. You, yourself, were very worried about Florence. You spoke of her often in the kindest way. I don't know how you found out about her and Wainwright, but at least now she is safe from him and all men. I don't understand your anger. You have always had the most tolerant attitude towards fallen women.'

'Yes, but it never occurred to me that I might one day have one in the family. Did you have to marry her? Couldn't you just have set her up somewhere? No one would have condemned you for that. Do you know how many men she's had?'

'About the same number as a woman who has been twice widowed.' Impulsively, Marcus started towards his father, but stopped himself. 'I am sorry to cause you even one moment's distress, but I must live my own life as I see fit. I'll be thirty years old next month. It is time I left my father's home. Florence and I are going to America, leaving now for Liverpool. We will be travelling with Mary Beth Hanson and Dundalk. We hadn't planned to leave in such a rush, but, well, these things happen. Especially, it seems, to Dundalk.'

Bennett clutched his forehead, feeling dizzy. 'They're going too? And Lady Manton? What of her?'

'Mary Beth is downstairs with Florence. She says her mother refuses to contemplate the idea of returning to America. I daresay you could convince her of the wisdom of making her home close to her children, but I don't suppose you'll try. Besides, for Samuel's sake, I hope you won't. The lad is better off separated from such a strong mother.'

'I don't understand,' said Bennett. 'Surely, Mary Beth hates you for informing me about Dundalk.'

'You don't know my character very well, Papa. I naturally contacted her and offered my apologies. She has been very kind to Florence. Dundalk is a charming scoundrel, but Mary Beth is a forceful young woman who will keep him on the right track. We are all going to join Samuel in California.'

Bennett shook his head in despair. 'So far? Was it necessary to travel so far? Couldn't you at least have settled in New York?'

'It is a large country, and I have no other contacts. It will be a help to us all to be together, at least in the beginning. Please come downstairs and give your daughter-in-law your blessing.'

'Never! A blessing to the whore who has ruined my son?'

'A blessing to the dear girl who has saved me from

being a pompous ass for the rest of my life. Try to rejoice for me. We want you to visit us in America one day.'

Bennett glared at his son's outstretched hand and turned away, hunching his shoulders. Marcus grimaced at the gesture, so cold and yet so pathetic. Round-shouldered, prejudiced against all that was new or young, slow of movement. Thus would his father be in old age, and Marcus would not be here to see it, to offer a son's comfort and help. But it could not be avoided. He was married to Florence, and America must be their future.

'Goodbye, Papa. Remember that I love you.'

Bennett would not turn round for one last look at his son. 'Write to me when you're settled.'

At last, Marcus smiled. 'Of course. The moment we know our new address. I want to thank you for a lifetime of love. You think me ungrateful now, but I'm not, believe me. Goodbye, Papa. Goodbye.'

Bennett splashed cold water on his face, then, with unsteady hands, trimmed his beard carefully. Finally, he put on a new black frockcoat, took up his top hat and gloves and walked at a dignified pace to Marjory's home, giving himself time to compose his face and tame his grief.

Marjory had also been given time to get her emotions under control. They greeted one another soberly, holding hands, each silently straining for the strength to offer comfort to the other.

'I've learned of your tragedy,' said Bennett finally. 'I believe you have heard of my shame. I've just seen Marcus. I couldn't wish him well, which was very bad of me. But a prostitute, Marjory. A prostitute!'

'I guess she had reasons for doing it. Good reasons.'

'Oh, she did,' said Bennett. 'But what reason did Marcus have for marrying her? I can understand why

295

they feel it necessary to run away to America. But why did Mary Beth and Dundalk decide to leave?'

'Didn't Marcus tell you? Guy cheated Sir Richard le Feyne out of four hundred pounds. I'm to give back the money and hope he will call off the police. That is, if he has admitted to anyone that he has been tricked. Guy was afraid of being arrested. He felt he had to leave the country.'

'Does the man have no sense? Le Feyne has the most vicious tongue in London. He'll not rest until he has dragged your name in the mud. And the young people have very kindly left you to face the scandal alone.'

'I don't mind what le Feyne says. He can't hurt me more than my own children have done.' She gave a shaky laugh. 'You know, America was made by people like Florence and Guy.'

'By prostitutes and tricksters?'

Marjory shook her head. 'By people who want to make a fresh start, want to leave their shameful secrets behind. People who want to be known not for what they've done or who they were, but for what they can do. I could tell you some stories, and maybe I will one day, but I don't think you're in the mood right now. But I'll tell you this: all four of them are going to be real successful in the future.'

Bennett smiled; he had been searching for some crumb of comfort. 'Perhaps Marcus will become an American legislator and be paid for his work.'

'Well,' laughed Marjory. 'America doesn't work quite like that. Marcus will probably be the one who becomes a snake oil salesman. It's Guy who will be the senator for some new state.'

'And you, my dear. You really want to stay here?'

'Yes, sir. I like it here. I'm going to stay put in London. Of course, it's not so nice a city as St Louis. This place has more snobbery and less hope – '

' – more horse dung – '

296

' – and fewer open spaces – '

' – more theatres – '

'Oh yes, Frederick! More theatres, and I do love going to the theatre with you.' She tilted her head, looking up into his eyes. 'You know, I think we ought to get married. Just friendly-like, just to keep the gossips quiet and share the housekeeping bills.'

'No, Marjory!' he said, so vehemently that she sucked in her breath with the pain of it. 'I don't want to be your husband and companion. I want to be your husband and lover.'

Shocked and embarrassed, she tried to pull away. 'We're too old for that nonsense. Why, I didn't think all that much of it when I was married to Jonathan. And I told Gilbert he could just forget about . . . that side of marriage.'

'We're not too old. It's our children who are too young, snatching at their pleasure, thinking only of themselves and their needs.' He reached out to caress her cheek; she didn't move away. 'I think we are just old enough to know how to love, to be able to savour every touch . . .' His arms came around her waist. She allowed herself to be pulled to his chest. '. . . to be connoisseurs of loving. And what is more, we have the sense to love only those for whom we need make no apologies. Standards, Marjory, that's what age gives us. I cannot love where I don't admire. I love you, not in spite of your faults, but because of your strengths. You are a good woman and a brave one. I want all of you, my love, not just your company and your strange way of speaking.'

'I don't know what to say.'

'Don't say anything. Just look at me.'

Obediently, she raised her head, looked into his eyes and smiled. And then he kissed her, not fiercely or overbearingly, not with animal strength that was intended to leave her weak, but with infinite love and

297

tenderness. And, it must be said, with a considerable amount of experience, showing that he knew just how to go about overcoming a lifetime's denial of her own warm nature.

She broke away at last, out of breath and pink to the roots of her hair. Nothing in the past forty years had prepared her for these swooping, heart-stopping sensations that left her craving for more of the same. Laughing shyly, she made a fist and gave him a playful punch on the arm. 'I guess I could get used to it, so long as nobody ever finds out.'